The Waters of Lethe

A Visionary's Tale

The Waters of Lethe

by

Philip W Lawrence

The Real River Lethe photo by Tom Mille

River Lethe is located twelve miles west of Mount Katmai in the Alaska Peninsular; over many years it has cut a canyon through the volcanic ash from many earlier and ongoing eruptions. It was given the name of *Lethe* in 1917 by R F Griggs of the National Geographic who surveyed this uninhabitable active volcanic area with its indigenous name is '*the land of ten thousand smokes*' due to the continuous emission of gas and vapour from the ground. Griggs though this place was like hell on earth and one he wanted to forget; He was influenced when choosing a name by the tales of Hades and the Greek mythological river of forgetfulness Lesmosyne, also called the river Lethe.

'It is only when the dead have had their memories erased by the Lethe that they may be reincarnated'. (Virgil)

A Special Tribute

At the time of writing my first work of fiction I had lost most of the vision in my left eye. I feared the same would soon follow for my right so thought it would probably be my last book. It's title *Looking on Darkness* seemed very appropriate although it had been chosen for a very different reason.

Fortunately for me the eye specialists at the William Harvey Hospital had other ideas.

A very special expression of appreciation is extended to **Mr Wallace Poon** and **Mr David Schultz** two eye surgeons who along with their dedicated team saved me from certain blindness.

None of my books since could have been written without their week on week dedication to the task of saving the sight of not only myself but countless others. From me and all those who have known your magic touch….
Thank you.

This book is dedicated to my family and friends for their comments and the time they gave to read my work. To my daughter Daisy and those who helped with the arduous task of editing.

To my friends at Ashford Art Society who kept me motivated when times were tough.

To Sanjay Gupta who inspired me to write, although I did not realise how much time it took, not just the writing, that came fairly quickly, but in my personal editing and the constant adjustments needed to make everything fit together, which it never really does.

I like spell-checking software; my dyslexic fingers never match my thought's, or it is the other way around?

Especially to my lovely Margaret who allowed me the space and time to write, when time was so precious. Now alone I have time and space indeed, her memory my inspiration in all I ever did and will do.

Finally my thanks to the artist Dawn Stirzaker who created the wonderful painting used for the cover of this book.

Foreword

I spend an hour with a cryptic crossword most days and come across a word or phrase which fits the answer well enough but sometimes I am unsure of its meaning or origin. Mostly I move on accepting my ignorance but occasionally I am curious and investigate further; *The Mandarin Paradox* being one such expression. My search led me down a path to explore and attempt to understand human moral decisions; I soon realised I had little chance of achieving what some of the best minds had never managed. My search opened up another related avenue, in this case I was faced with Virgil's epic poem 'Aeneid' and the Underworld *River Lesmosyne,* better known as *The Lethe.* I put both subjects aside at the time, too much for my old brain to deal with in one go. I was intrigued however so went back to them later, took notes and explored the subjects in greater depth. My fascination with the concepts of moral judgement, the afterlife and the uncertain future of mankind were the stimuli leading me to write this tale.

The story is of a future where we are continuing to evolve, ever closer to become "Homo Verum" (True Man) where nature and nurture merge and man is an integral part of the abundance about him. A time when moral questions should never arise, where finally there will be no paradox. A long time into the future where Earth's upheaval, brought on by man's greed and unending gross misuse of his environment are finally healing; leaving the land and oceans in the hands of nature.

My tale in many ways is set in a world much like the old Earth but with its human inhabitants at one with nature, but others who still have 'Homo Sapiens' *(Thinking Man)* more selfish desires.

I have used the English language where more than likely any evolved language would have become very different. The names of common items I have kept to avoid long winded explanations but the names of people, places and some of Earth's newly evolved creations are an imagined invention. The characters and plot in this narrative are fictional; in the unlikely chance where a similarity to real persons or events is noticed I can assure you it is unintended and purely coincidental.

If anyone reading this has the same special ability as that of my characters please let me know I would love to meet you; just knock on my door or send me a 'mind speak' message but remember I only have an open mind not a telepathic one.

P.W.L.

The souls that throng the flood
Are those to whom, by fate, are other bodies ow'd:
In Lethe's lake they long oblivion taste,
Of future life secure, forgetful of the past.

From Virgil's epic Latin poem, *Aeneid*

Chapter One

For now gone are the winds from the dark side of the sky; Kelena sits close to the house doorway, the new spring rays filter through the leaves warming the air for the first time this season. Her child Sala plays a few feet away with her small brown haired dog. She throws a ball fashioned by her Pa from the fibrous material left over from the crop of maize. Each time the dog eagerly retrieves the ball and mock fights her as she pulls it from its mouth ready to repeat the process. A dozen throws later the ball is in tatters and the dog, now tired of the game, settles beside its young mistress on the soft grass, her bronze arms and legs stretched out soaking up the rays of the dappled early season sun as they pass through the newly forming leaves of the nearby tree. Kelena loosely holds young Bron curled up across her knees, he is sleeping after his feed. Sala has been with them almost five seasons and Bron her brother is nearing his second. Their Pa Esian, Kelena's Bond partner, is at the meeting to divide the land, a traditional gathering to decide the crop each family will cultivate during the coming season; it takes all day; it is not really necessary that it should take so long for each season is very similar; the rotation is a pattern well known and everyone has their turn with the easier to work fields. Kelena and the other women were aware it is the story telling by the elders and drinking of menga that really takes the time. Everyone loved the stories, so by early afternoon when the dividing had been decided the women and children would meander down to the big barn to join the men. The winters hay was almost used so plenty of room inside for many to find a left over bale on which to sit or a soft spot of tumbled dry grass on which to lie down in the commune square out front and listen.

It begins with a song, it always does; this time a thanks for the completed dividing and the promise of a good season ahead. A new song from the mind and voice of the younger of the three old men seated high on the remaining hay bales piled in the centre so everyone could see and hear. He began, humming a single note, low and pure, he held it long enough till a hush as near silent as a soft breeze filled the air. The words were sung with a tune so simple it was known by all here, they had heard it many times before. The words an affirmation of the certainties of their world and their share within the never ending cycle of their lives together.

The rain I know will come again
Come again the rain I know
Our seeds will fatten in the rain
The rain has set the seeds we sow
The seeds will grow to serve our fare
The land so fair will serve our store
Serve from sweat and breath our share
The sun I know will come once more
I deign not look into the sky
Till cloud and rain our fields pass by

The older man Ezekiel, following the end of the song, waited till the whispering, shuffling and coughing had abated. Silence like the gentle breeze once more returned; he began his tale, one not told before. Ears and minds, young and old strained eager, attentive, not wishing to miss a single word.

"The tree in the middle of the three tall trees was not content; when he looked out in front he could see for miles to the sea in the far distance, when he looked behind the view was wide and beautiful to the hills of green that reached up into the sky but when he looked left and right the view was blocked by his brother trees. They both had the same two views he had but each had another he could never know. He thought long and hard and found the only solution would be for there to be no trees on either side but being a tree he could not do anything to change that, his seed grew where it fell as it did for the other trees; besides he loved his brother trees, it would be very lonely without them. The tree to his left could feel something was troubling his brother so asked him what was wrong. When he explained the left tree said I can tell you what is to my left I know it very well, I see a long road that disappears into the valley and out of sight but I much prefer the view of the sea to the front. The middle tree thanked his brother and decided to ask the tree on his right if he would tell him what he could see. The tree to the right agreed and said he too had a view of the road that went in the opposite direction into the distance and disappeared into a dark wood out of sight; he said he much preferred the view of the hills behind. So now the middle tree was content, the two views he could see were certainly the best but realised his brothers had given him his peace of mind but he had done nothing in return, so told each of his brothers about the others obscured view so all three trees had complete knowledge of their surroundings".

    The old man waited a few moments to mark the end of the story, then continued with a brief interpretation, mostly for the benefit of the young and other less astute and quizzical members of the community.

    "Our place in this world is by chance, like the trees we are born into a different family each with its own unique view of life. We don't have the same abilities or skills so by sharing we can all be as one".

The adults had heard fables such as this many times before and understood their significance; the very young children enjoyed listening accepting them as just stories but those a little older always had questions. Sala turned to her mother Kelena.

"Ma do the trees really talk to each other"?

"I don't know Sala; it is not really true but a made up tale to teach us it is good we should join with our neighbours and share".

"But why say the trees can see and talk to each other when they don't have eyes to see or voices to speak and ears to listen"?

"Perhaps they use their leaves to see and do tree speak when they touch together in the wind".

"Maybe"? she replied in a drawn out voice of doubt. "I suppose it must be like when I know Bron is hungry or has wet his clothes".

"How do you mean"?

"He just tells me somehow he doesn't speak; I feel it, I just know. I tell him not to cry that I will fetch you".

"You speak to him and he understands"?

"Yes of course, sometimes I'm not even in the same room, I just think it and he knows; doesn't everybody do that with their brothers and sisters"?

Kelena was aware of the phenomenon; several children had been shown to have a sixth sense when it came to their siblings, she was an only child so had no experience herself however she should not have been shocked by Sala's words but was surprised none the less to have discovered the gift in her own children. She thought carefully before replying.

"Of course Sala it happens often with children but not everyone is able to talk without speaking out loud".

"I suppose you are right; I've tried sometimes but can't do it with you and Pa or anyone else either".

Her question seemingly answered for now, Sala moved away and went to where the other children had gathered near the old men who were singing a song about the coming Spring.

Kelena looked down into the green eyes of her young son wondering if he and his sister would ever see into each other's minds beyond childhood. She walked slowly back to her home rocking her young infant from side to side which always made him laugh, today was no exception. Their home was halfway from the great barn towards the edge of the fields, it lay one street back from the central avenue with a wide frontage adjoining five others in a terrace; all the roads here had similar terraces each six to eight houses long. Some four hundred homes in all each sharing a long front garden. Kelena grew flowers in her small plot and a mature single fruit tree which bore an abundance of menga pods each season.

The large front room was where they sat, cooked and ate, the rear were the partitioned sleeping areas with beds for all four and room for more besides if other children were to be born. Next to this was a room for washing with the toilet, a shared facility with the others in their block, set back at the rear of the terraces. The waste was collected daily by whoever was on duty and taken to the fields for composting with any unwanted vegetation. Water was supplied from the stream which ran behind the commune with a pumping system running with power from the sun. It had always been there; certainly within the memories of those now living; it had never stopped working and if it did no one now would know what to do about it. The same power briefly brought them light into their homes when it became dark, fading as night and the time for sleep approached. The songs of the elders often mentioned the people gone before and their skills with the ancient science. It was they who had brought the water and the light. The songs purported the skills were not lost and would reawaken at some future time when the commune was ready or in need. Everyone believed in the songs as they had proved their worthiness many times.

The population of the commune remained stable, it varied a little somewhere between four and five hundred. Families lived in houses of a similar construction with the parents and children together. The older members usually left the home when too many grandchildren came into the family and the space became too small. They then lived in groups of four or more in houses near to their families where the infirm could be cared for; no one here lived or died alone or was unloved. Those older folk who were of good health, remained working with their families in the fields for many seasons and continued to proffer their skills passing them on to the young. A few lived to a great age, often more than one hundred seasons and once beyond the age of eighty were named as 'elders', they carried the songs of their youth in memory and were tasked with educating the young. They were considered wise and even if they became forgetful they were always respected. They decided the dividing, ensuring fairness of labour over many seasons. Everything was shared, the homes, the food and those with special talents had workshops where they made items like the basic furniture used in the homes, including utensils and pots for cooking. There were a variety of items used by all and were made by those who had the skill as and when they were needed. There was enough of everything, so contentment flourished. The concepts of ownership and wealth did not exist. Nothing much out of the ordinary happened here, each day blended with the next. The life of farming never stopped, the occasional respite like at the dividing, the completion of planting and the end of the harvest where all celebrated in and around the great barn. Each year at the height of the summer the young men and girls who were to be Bonded came to the great barn to make their pledge, another time for celebration.

Many seasons had come and gone; the dividing had been made each time. Esian and his friends had worked their allotted fields and the crops were plentiful. The new grass was green and lush, the animals would do well this Summer. Sala and Bron had both grown from children towards becoming young adults. Sala was soon to be of an age for Bonding, Bron although younger was taller than Sala and very strong. Bonding was a time when young men and girls sought a partner to join with and form a family. Several sons of the community appeared at their home to talk to her from time to time. Kelena asked her daughter if she had any preference.

"No Ma they all seem nice to me, but do I have to choose now, I am not ready to Bond yet"?

"No my child you do not need to choose yet but soon one of these young boys will excite your senses and you will know."

"The ones I have met till now do not excite me in the least maybe there is no one who will".

"Have faith, you are an attractive young woman, I can tell by the number of these boys who come each day to visit you, one of them will be yours to Bond with".

Sala had her doubts. She and Bron had continued to silently communicate as always, she wasn't sure if her Ma and Pa knew they still had this ability so to avoid confusion they both spoke aloud when in their company. If she was going to Bond with someone she would want to be able to mind speak with them. Perhaps that is what her mother meant when she said her senses would be excited. It wasn't what her mother meant at all; Kelena was referring to an animal magnetism she felt at her first meeting with Esian. She had no real concept of Sala's unspoken communication and how it was the telepathic gift which excited her and not physical attraction.

Kelena cast her mind back remembering the day of her Bonding with Esian and how happy her Ma and Pa were. Her Ma had died six seasons before but Papa Regol was still alive and well, not yet an elder but wise in many ways. He needed little attention but she saw him most days as did the children; she took him food and sometimes to the others in his home. His friends at the house were still in fine health and kept him in good spirits; their families shared in the care of all. His grandchildren were near fully grown but the young brother and sister retained childlike traits so loved to visit and listen to the stories told by their Papa Regol and the other old ones. Here there were only few who became sick when young; most died in old age, there were herbs and potions to help with the passing whatever age they may have been. Sad for a while when a loved one had gone but most had led a full and useful life so regrets were few and the sadness faded.

Porta and Star were good friends of Sala and Bron, their family lived nearby so they spent much time together. Porta was almost two seasons younger than Sala and his sister Star a season younger than him. Porta and Star had the ability to mind speak to each other, occasionally they reached out but could not communicate directly with Sala or Bron although they sensed the others presence when nearby.

Most children in the community went daily to the great barn to listen to the stories told by the elders; there being no written language the education for everyone was from these daily gatherings. No age limit was set with no compulsion to attend; there was not enough space for everyone to be inside at once so the elders repeated their teachings regularly. All the young people were accommodated over time; the young adults too continued to attend as often as they could, except when work was required in the fields or the parents were in need of help. Each family learnt the ways of a natural life from their older relatives; the growing of crops, animal care, and much more. Most families had a particular ability like the weaving of cloth or the carving of wood; many useful trades existed whereby exchange of these skills was freely given. Esian and Kelena made articles of clothing from the animal leathers provided by those who were able to preserve the hides; gloves and shoes to protect the hands and feet of the workers were in constant demand. The songs delivered daily by the elders showed the children a pathway to live a good life and parents the practical means to achieve such a life. All knowledge was committed to memory and passed along the generations.

Sala was frustrated by her limited mind communication and wanted to know more. She decided to question the elders after the next story session; two days later the opportunity arose. After the end of the day's meeting one of the elders remained seated outside in the warm sun, not returning home immediately as he would do normally. She came close and spoke to him.

"Old master please may I ask a question even though the time of learning has ended"?

"Of course Sala, learning is not limited to the time in this great barn, tell me what you wish to know".

"How is it I can speak without words to my brother as can my friends with their siblings but not to each other"?

A very direct question as was the way with children. The old man had knowledge of the phenomenon but had never experienced it himself, even as a child. He had no real answer but thought back to a song he learned many seasons before from another long passed elder. He didn't sing out loud but waited a while for the space about them to clear then spoke the rhythmic words to Sala quietly when they were alone.

"A baby born will keep in vain
The memory of his time a coming
When mother spoke to him through womb
Of brother's and a sister's thinking
To crave a future remain as one
Will speak with you till grown you be
But when our time has moved along
To tell you all both he and she
The voices of the young be gone"

Sala listened and understood its meaning, realising that meeting someone other than her brother with the ability to mind speak with her was unlikely. She further questioned the old man.

"Why does it have to be gone"?

"A mystery Sala, it has always been this way. I have no song to answer your question but do not dwell on this, when it fades be glad you have had the experience, many of us never did".

"You never spoke with your mind as a child"?

"No, I had no brother and my sister was born when I was already fifteen seasons, it never happened for me or for most people here either".

"When will it stop for me and Bron"?

"I have no idea there are no rules but never normally much beyond fifteen or sixteen seasons in my knowledge, perhaps when your brother is a little older".

"But I am nearly seventeen seasons and Bron is already fourteen, do you think we might keep talking longer"?

"You have continued longer than most; if that is your destiny you may well do so. Remember you may have no control over this gift of childhood. Perhaps it would not be so good to know another's mind when you are older".

Sala knew she wanted it to continue for ever and her transferred thoughts were instantly reflected by Bron's wish to do the same; how could it not be good? She'd have to ponder over that last statement of the old man. She stood and bowed, thanked him for his time and left.

He followed her exit with a smile on his old lips maybe she is the one, the one from the 'Song of Light' he had learnt many years before but had never sung; now wouldn't that be wonderful. His younger partner wanted to deliver this ancient song during the dividing some seasons before but the other two elders persuaded him to wait till the prophesy it described appeared to be coming true. Soon maybe he would get his wish. He recalled the numerous songs his old masters had sung and during the education of the young under his wing, he often repeated them so they would not be lost however with lapses of memory causing occasional unwitting changes the meanings may have shifted. The 'Song of Light" however remained entrenched in his mind, unchanged word for word, as sung by his old master now long passed. He sang it to himself, a reminder of future predictions.

> *'The day will come when word will shine*
> *All around this land of thine*
> *Upon the children whose minds do speak*
> *With never pause or moment weak*
> *Light up the life for now to stride*
> *With never thought to step aside*
> *From fateful journeys undertaken*
> *Whilst bearing hopes that never weaken*
> *The one True Man will then embrace*
> *Eternal life and light and grace'*

Sala uncomfortable in her mind, even more so after her talk with the elder, called to her brother who was working with their Pa in the field.

"Bron we need to talk".

He did not respond. The shock was immediate and strange, she slapped her ears as if she had suddenly gone deaf as indeed it felt that is what had happened. She could hear alright there was plenty of noise from activities outside but no voice in her head, no thought from Bron. Was this it; no it couldn't be so sudden; perhaps it was too long a range, maybe the distance was too far to where he was in the fields, they had never tested to see if distance made any difference, it had never occurred to them because it had always worked wherever they were. She went outside and moved closer to the fields and tried again. Relief; he answered straight away.

"Hi Sala, what's about, I'm pretty busy at the moment"?
"Why didn't you answer first time"?
"Sorry had my hands full, needed to concentrate".

"I thought we had lost it".
"Lost what"?
"Our mind speak".
"No big sister, we'll always have that. Wait till I get back Pa is constantly telling me what to do here, so I can't listen to both of you at the same time".
"Fine, I was worried when you weren't there. Don't do it again".

The panic Sala felt was over but very fresh in her mind; Bron was growing fast; already he is much bigger than me and Pa will rely on him to work more and more. I hope his move from child to youth and soon to manhood will not destroy our link. The song of the elder seemed to point that way. She was convinced that by constant use and trying new things they would keep the shared gift alive. She could hear her Ma coming so moved to greet her anticipating the Bonding question to be voiced again.

Perhaps young Porta would be a good choice, she liked him well enough but he had not quite reached the age for boys to Bond, maybe she could choose him and delay the proceedings till next season.

All was quiet in the Esian household, Sala moved outside to wash then to her bed space to change her clothes before her Pa and Bron returned from the fields. Ma was not due home yet from her visit with old Papa Regol so she had plenty of time to freshen herself before preparing the evening meal. She stood in front of the reflective glass imagining herself in the dress of Bonding, she looked fine and would look even better when the time came. Her skin was beginning to take on the darker hue, the deep bronze glow of adulthood and her hair too was slowly changing to from a mix of black and streaky grey to the silver of all the people of the commune; the skinny limbs of a child had filled with graceful lines. Her lips were soft and teeth were white as the summer clouds, her boy like breasts had begun to fill, she liked what was happening to her body, a smile of happiness crossed her face. Her burgeoning beauty is what was attracting the fine young men of the commune to come visiting; she enjoyed the attention but her green eyes saw only their outward appearance, her inner sense felt nothing, the essential gift of mind speaking was missing in all who came.

People shouting and an unusual commotion from outside woke Sala and the whole family. She looked out of the window to find out what was going on but could only see a number of people hurrying to the gathering a short way down the hill. Everyone was moving noisily together towards the great barn. She dressed quickly beating her parents but not her brother to the door. She spoke aloud to him.

"What's going on Bron"?

"Don't know but I'm going to find out".

"Wait for me".

"Hurry up then".

They both trotted off leaving their half-dressed parents inside. They ran fast enough to catch the back end of the crowd in a few moments.

"What is it"? Bron asked the first person he saw".

"I haven't seen who, but they say a strange person arrived from across the fields and asked to speak to the elders".

The group compressed edging slowly towards the barn. The two were not tall enough to see over the closely packed heads. Bron spoke to the man again.

"Has this ever happened before"?

"Oh yes, once when I was very young and again several seasons ago, ten or eleven maybe more I don't remember exactly".

"Did you see him"?

"I did; last time it was not a man but a female, she was very tall dressed in a mauve cloth, she had yellow skin and black hair".

"What happened"?

"She spoke with the elders and left, we watched her run back across the fields, she was very fast".

"Did the elders say anything"?

"Not really they did call us to gather by the barn and sang a song I never understood. My Ma and Pa told me they were the Overseers and everything was fine with us".

"Is that all"?

"Yes, I'd forgotten about it till you asked".

Sala and Bron wondered if this visitor was the same woman or someone different. They eased back as there was no point in pushing forward they weren't going to get any closer or see anything at least for now. Their parents arrived a short time later and joined them on the edge of the square. Sala's Pa asked what it was all about. Bron relayed what the man had told them.

"Can we stay and see Pa"? he asked.

"Of course; like the man said I too remember the last time when the yellow woman came, I was much younger you two were just babies. The elders explained with a song, I don't remember the words exactly but it explained the yellow people are 'The Overseers' who were from a land far away who came to make sure we were all well and happy here. They do the same for many people like us who live in their own places with their own fields all under the one sun".

"Why are they yellow"? Bron asked.

"It just the way it is, we have a bronze skin and silver hair they have yellow skin and black hair. I heard once in a song of people who have a pale and almost no colour to their skin with golden hair".

"I hope we will see the yellow Seer Pa; do you think we will"?

"I think so; he or she will pass here when they leave after speaking with the elders. Remember they are called Overseers Bron not Seers. The old man will probably sing a song about their conversation".

Sala was excited and could sense this was a special day she didn't understand why but knew instinctively this visitor was a young woman.

"What did you mean, 'all under one sun' Pa"?

"I think the Overseer was telling us through the elders song that we are all the same, even if we look different and live in separate communities".

"It feels good to have a visit, do you think we too could make a visit. I would like to meet these other people with gold hair Pa".

"I don't know Sala; they live a long way from here; many season before I heard tell of two who had gone from here to seek out the other people's place but neither have ever returned or sent back a message to know of their fate.

Sala voiced her immediate positive thought.

"Maybe they found it was better and decided to stay in the new place".

Her father considered an answer to discourage his children from expanding upon these speculative thoughts.

"More probably they became lost and never found the way there or back here again; their lives spent alone forever searching till they expired".

Bron again responded aloud with his child like instant thought.

"I don't ever want to be alone, anyway our place is much too nice to leave".

Sala felt differently and tried to hide her thought of leaving to follow the yellow Overseer when she went.

Bron caught Sala's intention and glared at her; no words but a passionate plea for her to desist. His thought hit her with a force she had never experienced before it stopped her mid breath, her mind blanking for a second, she succumbed to Bron's unspoken demand at once. The sudden, brief control Bron had over her was a little scary, she had tried to conceal her thoughts but it had been picked up by her brother almost before she had time to form the idea. What the elder had said about mind speak being a problem when you became an adult became clear. She deliberately closed her mind to Bron and thought again about following the yellow woman.

The thinking this time was like a whisper to herself and not intended to be listened to by others. He showed no response, she wondered if she had managed to conceal her thought or had Bron realised she was testing him so he chose to ignore her. Numerous thoughts came and went in everyone's mind all the time, she didn't hear these from Bron and presumed he didn't either. She had to think of Bron specifically when she mind spoke with him. Like anyone wishing to speak to another person you needed to attract their attention to you by some gesture or by calling their name. The same for mind speak, you thought of the person, effectively calling their name and then spoke with your mind when you knew they were listening. Bron ignoring the call was new to her as was his ability to briefly force his will upon her.

A shuffling of the crowd broke into her reverie as it moved back and parted either side of the square, allowing the stranger room to pass. Sala saw her as she left the building followed by the three elders, she was very tall more than even the largest man in their community, her skin was not exactly yellow, unlike the lemon but more like an ochre colour of the clay they used to make their cooking pots. As she came level with Sala she looked directly into Sala's eyes and mind spoke.

"Stay here young Sala, just two seasons more. Make a Bonding of your choice, you and others may then tread the path I now take".

She was so shocked the Overseer's blue eyes penetrated deep within her, she was transfixed and could not reply directly but the Overseer knew what was in Sala's mind well enough to answer her unspoken question.

"Never fear you will learn to mind speak with your Bond and many more besides, we will meet again, stay calm and be true to your friends; farewell".

The Overseer was now moving rapidly towards the fields running at great speed soon out of sight leaving Sala dumbfounded, wondering if anyone else had heard what had passed between them. She looked around especially at Bron, he and the others showed no sign they had picked up on the shared communication. Once the Overseer was gone the people again moved towards the great barn all wanting to know the purpose of the visit. For some this was not the first time but for many others it was and they were curious to hear what the elders would say.

The elder Ezekiel was confounded by his talk with the visitor, she was new to him, a different and younger Overseer. She was formal and polite as they all were, she introduced herself as named Franil; more forthright than the earlier visitor, generating a level of emotion in him never encountered during previous visits. Unlike before, where he had only been asked about the daily life, the farming progress and the general wellbeing of the community, the questions today more pointedly referred to certain named young girls and boys. Information concerning progress during their daily education was asked for. The subject of their private conversations with the elders was discussed. It seemed Franil already knew much about these young people before the questioning, especially as it was the individuals who had the ability to mind speak were the main topic of this discourse.

She said she would return in two seasons for good things were soon to unfold however the community should continue as before and the elders should keep the subject of this day's events to themselves for now. Ezekiel would of course abide by her request as he too had a feeling that changes were soon to unfold.

The 'Song of Light' sprung to mind, it was indeed pertinent but he was reluctant to sing such a song at this time. No other song came to him so he asked his younger fellow elder to provide a suitable recitation to fit the occasion. The crowd closed inwards and as many as could find space entered the great barn. The younger elder hummed a long note waiting for quiet then commenced with words and a tune unheard before.

All have pleasure in our home
Our visitor was pleased to hear
The fields are ready to be sewn
The stock of oxen hale and clear
The children of the earth have grown
The parents never shed a tear
When Bonded they to one unknown
A time of change to be progressed
As life moves forward in its way
Our land and harvest will be blessed

Come fateful revelation day

    The old man had never heard this song before and was unsure how the younger man had learned this piece, it seemed to hint at the Overseer's words to him. When asked, the young elder didn't know why, he said it just came to him. When the song was over even the elders were unsure of its meaning so offered no further explanation; eventually the crowd slowly dispersed, each voicing their opinion of what the song had meant. The overall feeling was that everything was okay for now at least; whatever this 'revelation' in the song might be it wasn't going to be revealed anytime soon.

    Sala said nothing, it was obvious to her that the elder had been influenced by the visitor to generate such a song, her interpretation was very personal so kept it to herself. She would heed the words of the visitor and speak to her Ma for advice when they were at home alone, aware too that she must shield her thoughts of leaving from Bron as it upset him too much; he may change his way of thinking during the next season or two. She knew of no one who had ever left the community except those her Pa spoke of and would not talk of leaving again. When they were alone she would speak to her Ma about Bonding with Porta, she liked him very much and he was very nice to look at; at least he could already mind speak with his sister so with practice maybe they could find another way to open their minds to each other. Of all the boys who came to visit he was the one she liked the best. He had never come to see Sala with Bonding in mind for he was still well below the accepted age; he was more advanced than others so she did not see any reason for it not to be, even if they had to wait for over a season to make the Bonding promise. Ma would know if they could. If it was not allowed then she would reluctantly have to find another boy in order to do what the visitor had told her, whoever he was they would surely be able to mind speak, it is what the Overseer had promised.

"Ma can we speak"?

"Of course Sala what is it"?

"It's about my Bonding there are many boys and it is difficult to select one from another. None of them excite me like you said; of all the boys I know my friend Porta is the one I like a lot and I would be happy to Bond with him".

"Well you know it may not possible he is not of the age".

"I know, but if we waited say just one season and a bit he would be wouldn't he"?

"You would then be past the time best for you to Bond, it would normally happen for you before next season. If you have to delay so long I think the elders would have to give their sanction. In any case you cannot know if Porta will want to Bond with you, he probably hasn't thought about it before".

"I will ask him of course but I want to know if it is allowed before I do".

"I don't believe there are any reasons for the ages of Bonding to be what they are it is just a tradition in this community. I will seek advice from the elders before you do anything".

"Thank you Ma, it would be nice to Bond with someone I like, the same as you did with Pa".

"We were lucky I had a special feeling when he came to visit, none of the others did the same for me so it was an easy choice. Is that how you feel about Porta"?

"I don't know if it is special like you and Pa? maybe not but I really do like being with him; for certain I feel nothing at all for any of the other boys".

"To like someone is a good start I suppose but there should be more if you want to Bond; we'll see what the elder has to say tomorrow".

Kelena was unsure how to approach the elders, the daily gathering was extra busy, probably due to the visit of the Overseer the day before. The visit was not mentioned during the elder's routine delivery, which today was concerned with the need to work especially hard during the planting. She held back as two others had waited to speak with them and wanted to keep her questions private. Only one elder had stayed behind whilst Kelena waited; he'd recognised her intended but hesitant approach so he too waited till the others had left.

"What can I do for you today Kelena, you have a worried expression, no serious problem I hope"?

"Oh no not really, it is about Sala and her Bonding".

"Yes she is coming of age soon, what do you wish to know?

"Well she is having a problem choosing; none of the boys are to her liking except her friend Porta".

He certainly knew of Porta for he was one of those the Overseer had asked of; he did not show his recent familiarity.

"Porta you say, let me think do I know him, ah yes he has a sister Star I believe".

"Yes that's him; our problem is that he is not yet of an age for Bonding".

"I see; well then she must choose another".

"Oh dear; Sala wondered if she could wait one more season for him to be of the age, you see he is the only one she wants".

"I now understand your dilemma. If she does not mind waiting and if Porta is willing, I see no reason she can't Bond later than usual. Porta may be too young now to know his true feelings however the waiting will bring us an answer. The prime age of Bonding has been a tradition accepted to protect the young from entering a relationship before their bodies and minds were ready. All our young people are eager to Bond as soon as they can, no one ever wanted to hold back before, quite the opposite. Her affection for him must be strong for her to ask you to seek our advice; if she is willing to wait and their feelings remain unchanged then I am happy for her to Bond with the boy of her choice. Tell Sala to come and see me soon, I wish to seek her true mind in this, do not worry Kelena we have plenty of time, she will make the right choice".

The elder watched as the mother left, his knowledge of her young daughter and son's abilities, those of Porta and Star too along with the recent questioning from the Overseer weighed on his mind; the Overseer Franil had shown a particular interest in Porta so maybe he should encourage the Bond with Sala. He would speak with Sala after musing on the advice to be given.

Kelena returned home to find the youngsters in the garden sitting in a circle playing what appeared to be some guessing game, in her mind they were all still children and wondered at how quickly they had matured. She looked at Porta with fresh eyes today, he was taller than Sala and even though he was almost two seasons younger he already had the fine body of youth, soon to be a man. He was probably a good choice for Sala and their friendship of childhood could well grow to where they would make a good Bonding. She didn't interrupt their fun with the elders message for Sala but went inside, she'd tell her later as right now Kelena needed to prepare the evening meal, for Esian would soon be home hungry from his day in the fields.

"Now let's all concentrate, Bron and I will use the same word and try to send it to you. I will send to Porta and Bron will send to Star".

They were holding hands and were looking directly into the eyes of their opposite number.

"Ready Now".

Porta called out first "Overseer" he said.

"That's right" said Star.

Sala thought they had achieved success, they had but not in the way she expected.

Star then spoke aloud "I heard it from Bron first, then Porta heard it from me a fraction later".

"You didn't hear it from me then Porta"?

"No Sala, I'm sorry, I heard it from Star, still it is a success in one way, Bron was able to mind speak with Star, so we now know it is possible to do this with someone other than your brother or sister".

"I know it is possible I have done it with someone else already, I just want to do it with Porta".

Bron was shocked and a little upset, why had Sala not told him something so important, he shot a vexed question to his sister.

"You've done it before who with? You never said".

"Never mind Bron let's try again".

Bron ignored Sala's dismissal demanding an answer with a strong mind message like he did the time before. The answer was in her mind she couldn't hide it.

Bron still angry at Sala's silence shouted at her aloud so the others would know.

"You mind spoke with the Overseer and never told me; what did she say"?

Star looked on amazed at what she had just heard and as Porta cast a probing stare into the eyes of Sala it happened, the mind conversation with the visitor was pouring from her to all three, no words spoken but all knew what was in Sala's mind.
"Wow what on earth was that"!
Bron's mild expletive engulfed them all.
"You have done it brother you've opened the way"
"I heard it too"
Star and Porta mind spoke the same words at the same time; all were connected. Although younger than Sala Bron seemed to have the strongest ability and through his emotional outburst their four minds had fused into one. Sala was elated, she knew it was possible but never realised their childhood mind speaking could become so all embracing. The contact lasted only a brief moment but was long enough for the four to have a common desire. A union they would nurture and perfect with practice. The daily routine of listening to the songs of the elders were used as means to perfect their gift, they would take turn to attend the class at the great barn and send mind speak messages relaying what was being sung to the others; it did not take long before they were able to converse with the mind to any individual or all at once as and when they wished.

The Overseer had told her she would do this only a short while ago, but also told her to take the time, another two seasons she had said. She Bron and their friends would wait, they knew by then they would have mastered the art, then Porta and her would be Bonded .

Bron looked sadly towards Sala, his thoughts he sent for her alone.

"It seems my sister the time will come after you are Bonded with Porta, for the Overseer to return, then you both will make the journey she foretold. I know I cannot be included in your *venture and Star may be too young to join the quest. I'll need to stay with Ma and Pa to work the fields and give them comfort for the loss of their daughter and they to me for my loss of a loved sister, for when you are gone I will sorely miss your presence and your mind".*

"Be not so sad my dear brother, even though I may be far from here we can speak each day and I will not be gone for all time and for sure I will be safe in the land of the yellow skinned people. This is for the future of our community I felt the goodness in the Overseer's mind".

"I fear the distance will be too far to speak with our minds but I have no doubt that you must go. You and Porta both must prepare the parents for their loss and not depart in haste. Seek the guidance of the elders for they may have the words to soften their hurt".

"Not now Bron it is too soon to let them know, there is a season and much more to come before that day arrives, we must practice with our friends to perfect the gift for who knows what may have changed when time is done".

"You hint I may later change my mind. I do not know the future but for now in this I am resolved".

They were aware that Ma was observing them through the window so reverted to speaking aloud as she may wonder why they sat so long without talking. Even so it was still the way for all people to speak easily to each other; mind speaking, at the moment, was still limited to the pairs of siblings.

In the past Sala had been in awe of the elders and was always a little afraid to question their teachings but his summons imparted by her Ma excited her. Perhaps he would tell her what the Overseer really wanted wondering if he knew what had passed between them. She stood at the entrance to the great barn after the learning guided today by the younger elder; all who had attended were now gone.

"Come in young Sala".

She entered the barn and stood close by the elder and spoke.

"Ma said you wished to see me and to wait for you after the final song".

"I hear you wish to Bond with Porta".

"I do, he is the one I choose".

"Does he agree"?

"I haven't spoken to him about it directly but I believe he knows my feelings. I wanted to wait and see if it was allowed for me to wait till he was of the age to Bond ".

"The choice to Bond is for those who desire it and not for the elders or anyone to interfere, the age accepted is a tradition of many seasons which has proved to be the best for the community. Although the difference here is unusual it is not without precedent, I believe it has happened once before. I see no reason against waiting for Porta to reach the accepted age he is already strong of body and of good mind, just delay one more season for him to become full grown and if you both still desire it I will agree to the Bonding".

"Thank you I could not have wished for more. A question further if I may".

"Of course please speak freely".

"You remember our talk before concerning mind speak"?

"Indeed, go on".

"The Overseer spoke to me this way".

"I know, she told me you had been selected as was your brother and Porta, and she would make you aware of things to come, this was why I had no surprise at your request to Bond".

"Selected! Selected for what"?

"Let me tell you a story Sala, it is not a song and not for ears other than yours, it may help explain why we live our lives like we do and what is hoped for us by the Overseers and by me also. Come further inside and sit this may take a while".

Sala followed the old man into the barn, some light entered by the door but he moved to the far side into the shadows and sat on one of the straw bales. He invited her to do the same which she did selecting one immediately opposite. He questioned himself, pausing to collect his thoughts, 'Where to begin' knowing what he said next would have a profound effect upon his young charge.

"The Overseers have been coming here for many seasons; they visited my Pa and his Pa before him and back to when we first came here in a time so very long ago I cannot say. The songs we sing and the stories told have been passed from elders to sons during all this time. With each visit the Overseers brought questions of the elders concerning the well being of the commune and the development of its young people. When times were hard they brought comforting words and a promise of better to come. When times were good they were pleased and said we were to prosper. They always asked especially about the mind speaking children and if their ability had remained beyond Bonding. Of course it never does except maybe one time when my Pa was the younger elder".

Sala moved closer to the elder and tried to mind speak with him but nothing happened, she wanted to know the outcome of the story so just waited silently for him to continue, which of course he did.

"One of the boys and his sister were close to Bonding age and still retained that intimate way of speaking. Well soon the boy did Bond with a girl he had long been friends with but at this time his sister was too young by one season. Their gift remained active even after the Bonding for the two siblings were each able to be inside the others mind whilst the newly Bonded girl was excluded. This remained so for a whole season until the sister finally Bonded with the boy of her choosing. No one knows if the gift remained after that but we suspect it did. Two seasons later during the visit of an Overseer my Pa mentioned the apparent unusually extended mind speaking ability of the brother and sister. The Overseer requested to see the two families. They came to the great barn and the four spoke with her alone; nobody knew what was said, but when the Overseer left the next day the brother and sister were nowhere to be found. They had gone each leaving their Bonds and children behind. It was a sad time at first for no one had ever left before but when speaking to the elders some time later, the abandoned Bonded pair revealed the Overseer had instructed the siblings to follow her when she left and explained it would ultimately benefit the community. She also said they would never return and those left behind should wait a short while and if they wished, should seek the blessing of the elders to Bond again. The two never came back and their partners never questioned the Overseers actions or asked to Bond again".

 Sala realised she and Porta were in almost the same position as those two in the story except they had time to consider which the others never did. She knew when the time came she would probably leave too but with Porta and not Bron or Star. She wanted the advice of the elder before making the final decision. She questioned herself what to say next. Should she tell him now of the Overseers words or wait until they had Bonded, after all they may have lost the gift by then but did not think so.

 "I have something to tell you, it is a little more than about my Bonding with Porta".

"I thought it might be; please continue and have no fear what you say here stays with me alone. I will seek to help if I can but keep in mind I am not fully convinced the Overseers have only good intentions towards us, even so any choice you make I will support".

"The Overseer spoke directly to me through my mind, it came as naturally as it does when I use my voice to speak to you. She told me to Bond with a boy and that we would be able to mind speak and with others too. I with Porta, Bron and Porta's sister Star have already experienced a joining of all four minds, so I have no doubt of what the Overseer said".

"This is great change not been seen before, I don't yet know what to say, is there anything more"?

"Yes and this is where your story of long ago had me fearful of the future. She told me when the next Overseer comes I was to follow with the Bond of my choice and bring my brother and Star with us if they were willing".

The old man's long held knowledge had a vision of this moment embedded in his mind, the prophetic songs now showed they voiced the breath of truth, even so he was finding it difficult to respond in a way not biased by established traditions. He reached out and took Salas hand stroked its smooth unblemished skin with his age-worn palm hoping some of her youthful zest would somehow transfer to inspire his answer. She didn't pull her hand away, accepted his gesture and continued in silence absorbing this meditative moment they both could share.

"You do not need to speak old master I understand the position I have put you in with this revelation. I will do what is right by all your teachings of seasons since gone".

She slowly released her hand and stood to depart, as she made to leave he spoke with eyes closed and his palms pressed together under his chin.

"This season will soon pass young Sala, we will talk again, our deliberations will gravitate to what is good for all concerned. You have wisdom beyond your age; I am content".

Sala thanked him and left; she too was content; her future would unfold as it was meant to be.

Chapter Two

Franil ran along the pathways by the fields of commune Five, her light and agile frame, which belied her age, lent itself to the exercise which she relished when away from home; it was not deemed a faculty suited to young Overseers. Of course she could not travel too far at such speed but fast running like this left the commune with an impression that she could do so and probably did. She was close to arriving at her flying machine but stopped to look back at the forest view surrounding commune Five. Tall and lithe, the pale mauve robes of the younger Overseers gently complemented the creamy yellow of her skin; unlike the intensity of her piercing blue eyes now surveying the scene with a little envy. Although she enjoyed the technically advanced comforts of home, the uncomplicated lives of these people gave them a contentment she never felt in the confines of Lethe. The communes had no idea of the technology available to the Overseers which would remain so for the foreseeable future. A short walk beyond the ridge brought her to the aircraft way beyond the area used by the people and well out of sight. She took one last look around then boarded the machine which had taken her from Lethe to seven of the communes inhabitable lands.

Flight was not new to the Letheans the machines had been built many seasons before Franil was born. The science of old used the power of the weak forces to create a reversal of gravity to lift the vehicles from the ground and the earth's rotating momentum to drive them forward. Franil grasped the basic concepts but did not fully understand the physics of inverse gravitation even though she had spent much time learning with the Science Master Peto. Franil was more than adept at controlling the machine with her thoughts through its one simple control which is all that is needed for the task in hand. There was room for up to ten people as well as the controller, in an enclosed bowl shaped cabin with a clear glass roof and sides. It could move as slow as you wished or with a speed sufficient to traverse the globe in two full cycles. Commune Five was the furthest away on this trip, even so the machine had enough stored energy to make all the journeys she needed several times over even at full speed. She settled in her seat relaying her command to return to Lethe; without stopping for a rest she should be back before dark the following day. The machine rose slowly at first and once clear of the surrounding trees turned and accelerated away in the direction of her home.

This visit had proved fruitful and the news she carried was good. Not all of the communes produced useful children, some had failed to survive or had fallen back into primitive ways beyond the control of the Overseers. Commune Three had two possible mind speakers but most significant there was a definite gifted group of four from commune number Five. She had been able to communicate directly with the one called Sala at commune Five; her positive response and the thoughts of those around her showed a need for further development. A little more time was needed before they would make the journey, however Franil was unsure if all four would travel. Those most willing were the least gifted but were certain to come when asked. The male Bron although with the superior ability may yet remain firm and not conform to our request, for at the moment a request it was and not a demand.

Franil was to explain the wonderful opportunities offered by coming to her home and hope the chosen people from the communes would respond but there was no obligation to do so. It must be given freely if it was to be accepted, at least that is what she had been told by the elders of Lethe. Unbeknown to her and the lower ranked Overseers the senior elders and Science Masters had other motivations. She had left it to Sala to soften Bron's determination and persuade him to change his mind.

The journey had taken many days with a stop at each commune for a day or sometimes two; with additional days of rest between the different communes where her flying machine would assimilate new energy from the sun; a precautionary process in case of an unforeseen delay; generally there was enough power to make many journeys but Franil was wary of the living crystals need for replenishment and would not risk being stranded. The families in the communes continued to thrive with improvements in crop yields along with a secure environment ensuring the prosperity of its people. The elders carried forward their traditions within the songs and the teachings to the young ensuring a continued growth in mind speaking young people for Lethe to reap as needed.

The flying machine had enabled her to traverse the great distances required to visit each group with ease. The forest covered land, the sometimes large expanses of water and dangerous forbidden contaminated areas between were formidable obstacles against travelling very far; making it impossible for the different communes to ever meet. It was no secret there were other communities but the people in the developed groups seldom engaged the Overseers with pertinent questions concerning the others and they in turn never volunteered information about them. The songs of the elders included stories and parables of their distant cousins but they were a mysterious entity almost mythical and were allowed to remain so.

On arrival at Lethe Franil would go to the building of the leading elder Science Master Metrin to report on her journey and what she had found. This was always a private meeting, a courtesy from the past but one she feared for Metrin was formidable and raged at any unwanted news. This time she thought the progress of the children from commune Five would find Metrin pleased with her news. Metrin would call a meeting of the elder Overseers to plan for Franil to go back and arrange their transfer to Lethe. Her next stop at Three may provide even more good news, either way what she had discovered at Five was good enough for this trip to be considered a success.

The ordinary people of Lethe lived a controlled existence, technically advanced with the ancient sciences providing them the basic necessities for life with little effort. They were a tall race with predominantly yellow skin and black straight hair, most had pale blue eyes others a darker hue. For a multitude of seasons all Letheans had been of one mind each generation forging their lives for the good of the other. Their history and the reason for their existence as a highly educated group, when all others in the world were much more primitive, was obscure, even how they had acquired the knowledge of the sciences was lost in the past.

Children when first born stayed with their mothers only briefly, the fathers were unknown as pregnancy was achieved by insemination using a random selection process from seed collected and frozen long ago; once initial nurturing had passed children were separated into groups where their personal aptitudes were assessed and channelled accordingly. It wasn't until they were beyond ten or eleven seasons and considered self-reliant before they moved from group living to single room accommodation. A significant difference between Lethe and the communes was written language and a profound knowledge of mathematics; it had worked well for many generations.

Franil had been brought up in this way and had studied language and the different ways of speaking used in the various communes. She had a particular way with spoken words, more expressive than most and with a soft mesmerising tone. This aptitude led to her achieving the position of novice Overseer and one of the liaison officials between Lethe and the communes. For many seasons she had been one of three Overseers who travelled the world keeping the communes under watch and her elders informed of progress with the telepathic children. The other two had recently passed on so she was given the full status of Overseer to the communes.

Mind communication was as natural to Letheans as talking was to the commune people however the regular exercises of the mind during the education of the children revealed a weakening of the ability to communicate in some and to be almost non-existent in others; a growing a worrying trend.

The Overseers were aware of the catastrophic events of the past from songs and stories told by their elders and also from the writings in the old tomes. Of the surviving humans they were the superior beings who from small beginnings had grown in numbers and knowledge leading to an exploration of the lands beyond their own. The development of the flying machines had given them the means to travel afar and in their travels had discovered small pockets of primitive human habitation.

In the minds of the Letheans these peoples were inferior living a poor existence barely feeding themselves almost at the point of extinction. The Overseers came with their skills and knowledge providing the means for them to grow crops, installed a source of power and basic tools enabling them to provide themselves with permanent shelter. They educated the older men, slowly introducing a way of learning through songs, easily deployed and accessible to all. The communes were born.

After more seasons than can be counted they were now successful and thriving. Exclusion of the written word as part of the education process was a deliberate decision to ensure there would be no development of technology or skills beyond those required for the basic requirements of life. There would be no challenge to their authority from the communes

The people of Lethe had remained stable and content for many seasons but now were fearful of losing their telepathic abilities. Conception was always generated by artificial means there being fewer men than females in their midst, a condition which had been so since Franil could remember. The number of males born was less than one in five.

In the past everyone communicated as one being, this was no longer the case; there were some who still had the ability to communicate through their minds as if they were one; they were known as readers in Lethe, similar to the mind speakers of the communes but with a universal merging of thought rather than individual word or single thought exchanges. They remained as individuals when choosing to be so but interlinked as they wished. The readers were the ones who were later trained to become Overseers. Like the males the telepaths were slowly being lost, the new children who all used to have the gift were now becoming fewer with each generation. The Overseers and readers could enter the minds of these children and influence their thoughts but were unable to have them aware of the communication.

Metrin and her elders independent of the remaining readers had a quest to seek from the communes new telepaths both males and females who would provide the genetic variety to perhaps regenerate the gift in new-born children fulfilling their desire for their kind to continue as before.

The physical differences between the peoples of the communes were small, skin, hair and eye colour were among the minor difference. The heavier physique of the males in the communes was more noticeable as the men did most of the work in the fields so their bodies were much more muscular. None of the people were as tall as the Overseers or had a yellow skin. These differences were considered insignificant for breeding between the Letheans and those of the communes. The basic genetical structure was identical so there appeared to be no obstacles that is except one, its significance not understood.

Many seasons before a commune male and female who were siblings were brought to Lethe, they had healthy bodies with signs of positive mind talking skills. The male seed was used to inseminate six Lethean females and the female was likewise inseminated from a Lethean male. Several attempts were made but conception did not materialise. The science of the process was well known as they had been using the method since time forgotten, so they set to work to find out why it had failed.

In the study that followed a serious unrelated problem with their current method was highlighted. Allowing random male selection from a general bank had inadvertently introduced the real possibility of close blood related conception, similar to cousin with cousin or brother with sister; although the latter was unlikely it had probably happened on occasion. If the seed of a male from one of these related conceptions was used in another related insemination the genetic distortions could spread and magnify through each generation This had been the case for so long the effect had become significant, they had inadvertently hit on the reason for the decline in the telepathic gift and a lack of male babies, it was due to accidental familial interbreeding. The current breeding cycle was immediately changed where each male donor was selected and the genetic pattern examined to be as different as possible before insemination. It would take several generations to prove the theory and correct the trend.

The brother and sister brought from the commune had previously cohabited with their Bond partners before they were taken from their commune producing two children. This proved their viability before they came to Lethe; thus pointing to another problem. Maybe the two groups were incompatible. It was considered if there were minor differences in genetic spirals it could pose a problem. A full analysis was conducted as maybe this was the reason for the lack of conception but on examination none were found to cause the current fertility problem.

The Letheans appeared to have no desire to cohabit and conceive naturally, unlike in the communes they never Bonded, interaction between the males and females was through the mind. There was very little empathy and no physical sexual contact. The Bonding in the communes was generally guided by a physical attraction and usually a loving one but always with emotion. Emotional attachment was hidden away so deep in the psyche of the people of Lethe it never showed in their thoughts or actions; perhaps this is where the difference lay.

It was concluded it may be necessary for the commune males to cohabit with the Lethe females and create their children through physical reproduction. Metrin found the thought of sexual contact difficult to accept as she was sure her sister Overseers would too. She was getting ahead of herself, there was little chance of this happening soon and in any case once Bonded the commune people may be reluctant to cohabit with anyone else let alone have sex relations. She would have to find a telepathic male or more than one willing to physically impregnate several Lethean females, she thought not an impossible dilemma but a very difficult one. The only unbonded males Franil had come across who would be suitable were Bron and Horden, at this time not yet willing candidates to even consider leaving their communes

Metrin was unaware of the underlying sex drive of all commune males where the strong generally prevail, when selected by their Bond females the innate urge to pass on their genes to the next generation was very powerful. Man born of the communes were not technically as advanced as the Letheans but were born by natural selection the way nature intended. The commune people's innate instinct to mate would later let the elders and Metrin know there would be no real problem once the males were confronted with a willing Lethean female.

Franil had time on her journey to Three to wonder about the decisions of Metrin and her seniors. The commune people were friendly and happy, content with their lives; she enjoyed their company even though her visits were brief. She was always made welcome and her seeking to remove some of their youngest and brightest to Lethe for what was to be an experiment was an order she carried out reluctantly. She had been told the survival of her kind depended upon its success but had doubts concerning the real reasons behind the Science Masters endeavours. She would of course do as instructed after all the Letheans were a far superior people and her elders knew best.

Chapter Three

The wind from the east was no longer so cold, the winter almost over and the preparation for planting well under way. The useable terrain around commune Three was smaller and less fertile than others but still sustained around a hundred families, three to four hundred or so people, well above the Overseers considered minimum number of inhabitants for continued survival as an individual isolated community. The Overseers had to provide some intervention in the early days to ensure commune Three continued to flourish. There was no problem now, its people were skilled farmers, well versed in animal husbandry and the trades needed for a secure and sustainable life.

Gren made an early start, the dividing had given him the field at the far end of the land so more time was needed to transport the seeds and drill to the start point. The field was almost flat so not the most difficult to work just a long slow ride away from his home. The two oxen were ready, the cart was fully loaded so only one trip would be needed today. This field was used for chard last season so this time it would be maize. An easy crop to sew with the mechanical drill. This had been given to the commune by the Overseers when his Pa's Pa was a young man; his Pa had shown him how to use it as a young boy as he had in turn shown his sons Horden and Arak. The composted fertiliser had been spread at the end of last season, which was the job of each user of the previous season, it had been washed well into the ground by the winter rain; a good crop was expected. As the ox pulled the drill the seeds were deposited one by one a distance apart to ensure a good yield,

Horden followed behind his Pa covering the seeded area by hand with straw from the cart. Two good days work may see it done maybe three. The next rain would see seeds set and his work would be done for a while. With the rain came the weeds, the straw stopped some but not all, this is when the hard work would begin again. His Bond Limbina would help with the weeds and Horden, who was now almost full grown, was a great help too especially during the setting of seeds and the harvest. Gren's other son Arak was also able to help but only during the harvest, he was still young so most of his days were spent at the learning of songs with the elders during the day.

In the next season or two Horden would want to Bond, he already had eyes for one young girl named Jeska, but there was plenty of competition from those who would set their sights on her too. All eligible boys, though now more like young men, would present themselves to the girls and the girls would be the ones to choose. It worked well for all who were worthy eventually Bonded with someone of their choice. Horden may not win her as his Bond but it wouldn't be from a lack of effort. He was hopeful but unsure of success so he had visited other girls too. It was their duty to Bond and have children for the commune to flourish. Any of the girls would make a good Bond but Jeska was Horden's favourite.

Arak mind called Horden as he left the great barn after the days songs of the elders had been discussed and understood.

"Hey brother are you busy"?

"I'm working, what do you want"?

"Nothing really but Jeska is coming to our house later, I thought you'd like to know".

"How, why"?

"I know you like her so asked if she wanted to play the new game with the coloured bricks we had from Ma and she said yes".

"You're a real buddy Arak, I'm on my way".

Arak was just twelve seasons and Horden almost sixteen but the two brothers had mind spoken together since birth. They accepted it as normal and their Ma and Pa were well aware of what it meant but the rule was they always spoke aloud when in the house. Switching from one to the other came naturally as they had been using both for many seasons. They didn't always adhere to the rule, sometimes a comment would cross the void that neither of them wanted their parents to hear. Arak knew of his brothers feelings so decided to move things along for him, besides he liked Jeska and would endeavour to encourage her to be her brother's Bond. Horden's mind drifted to the image of Jeska; she was beautiful, still young even so quite tall and much thinner than she would become as she matured, her pale skin was smooth and shone like the petals of the white moon flower, her grey eyes held him captive framed by her yellow and gold hair which hung in natural curls down her back. Horden could hardly wait so called to his Pa.

"Hey Pa, can I go now I have something to do back home"?

"What's the hurry we haven't finished yet and there is plenty of light left".

He felt bad if he left his Pa to do the work alone; it was much faster with one person checking the drill and driving the oxen along whilst the other distributed the straw. On your own you had to keep stopping it took much more than twice as long.

"I'm meeting Arak he should be home soon; we are going to play the new game Ma gave us".

"Play comes after work, you know that Horden. Look let us finish this line it will not take long, then you can go. We have done well today. I will bring the oxen back on my own, the drill and hay cart can stay here ready for tomorrow".

"Are you sure"?

His Pa nodded as he drove the two ox forward with renewed vigour. Both boys were good and helped in the work when ever asked. He couldn't deny young Horden this request, he seldom asked for anything so allowing him to leave a little early was something Gren would do willingly as his way of showing love for his son.

"Thank you Pa that will be good".

Horden mind called his brother to start the game and keep Jeska at their home as he would be a little while yet. He stepped up the pace, he wanted this days work to be over as soon as possible.

He ran down the pathway beside the fields praying that Jeska would still be there. The work had taken much longer than he wanted but was grateful his Pa had let him go when he did. He would make it up to him tomorrow by working extra hard. He arrived at the front of the house completely out of breath with a pain in his side and covered in sweat. He couldn't go in like this, what would Jeska think. He stood bent over panting waiting to recover enough at least so he could speak to her. He would explain his dishevelled condition as a result of the hard work and not his headlong dash; he did not want to appear over keen, which of course he was. Perhaps she would wait whilst he washed and changed. With his heart still pounding he walked into the room relieved to see Jeska with his brother at the table playing the new game. They looked up and smiled, Jeska spoke.

"Hello Horden, come and join us this is really good game."

"Give me a minute or two I need to have a shower it has been quite hard work today".

"Okay, don't take too long I have to go soon".

Horden took the quickest shower he had ever had and was back at the table clean and free of sweat but still out of breath and a rapidly beating heart.

"Right this game is new to me you'll have to show me what to do".

The Overseer Franil visited the communes by a route not quite a circle with the furthest away being number Five. The numbers were originally given in the historical order they were established; when visiting however the order used was by the shortest route. The furthest away was commune four but it no longer existed as its people had taken to living in the forest. She started at commune one then two followed by Five, Six and Seven, finally commune Three the one closest to Lethe. In the early days a commune would be visited individually to assist its people if there was a problem but they were all well established now and could cope with most anything. Many communes had been started using people found to be living in small groups but most had failed in the early days because the people were unruly or preferred to live a nomadic life. Remnants existed in isolated pockets, mainly hunters or wanderers in the wide open plains dependent upon their animals for sustenance. A few smaller settlements remained but the Overseers of Lethe ignored these groups, they resisted all efforts to influence their way of life besides there was little to be gained for seldom if ever did mind speakers emerge from their midst.

Communes One, Two, Six and Seven had no mind speaking children above the age of seven seasons so were of no interest this trip she hoped commune Three would prove to be more promising. Franil arrived at number Three with the usual gathering of its people around the great barn, she entered the building as always to speak with the elder Brugan currently the most senior amongst those who lived here. Her first question concerned the fortunes of the commune as this was originally the main reason for the visits although hardly necessary now. She then enquired of any developments since the last visit some six seasons before. Her main reason for the visit was her quest to seek out children of the right age who had retained the gift of telepathic communication. There were five families who had children with siblings who showed they had the ability to mind speak but the majority who had this gift were still very young so of no interest at this time, the exception being the sons of Gren and Limbina. She asked the elder Brugan to call the family of Gren to the barn as she wished to speak with them.

Franil was excited by the excellent prospects presented by the four mind speakers she had discovered in Commune Five who were already at an advanced stage; now commune Three showed promise too with the brothers Horden and Arak. The other communes had no emerging gifted young people of the right age, those who had shown earlier promise when children, had largely lost the gift; they would be visited during the next cycle to monitor any new prospects. If these two boys were suitable and were added to those of Commune Five this visit would prove to be the best chance yet for Lethe.

Franil closed her mind in the presence of the family and spoke aloud to all.

"I am pleased you are well and happy but I am particularly pleased with the children here. Their ability to mind speak is a wonderful gift one which the Overseers wish to develop for the good of all. I know it is difficult for you parents to understand but if all in a commune could have this ability it would greatly enhance the lives of everyone".

Pa Gren spoke first.

"We are well here and thank the Overseers for their interest but why is my family brought before you"?

"In a season or so I would come again and if Horden and Arak are still gifted I will speak of wonderful things they can do for you and all in your commune".

Franil could sense the parents discomfort and the contrasting curiosity from the children.

"I will leave here soon so now go back to your home and remember the Overseers are only here to help you and the commune, there will be nothing to fear for whatever transpires it will be with your consent and true wishes in mind".

They left in silence, the parents bemused and still fearful but the siblings were firing questions at each other as to why she had shown a special interest in them and not others with the same gift. They decided it must lie with the superior strength of their ability. Franil was aware they had come to the right conclusion, so interjected with her own thoughts to cement the relationship and demonstrate the power they could possess.

"Horden, Arak your minds are strong and I know you are certain what you want to do in your thoughts. I will return two seasons from now and with the blessings of all here you will travel with me to my land. Your ability is to be nurtured and can only grow under the guidance of the Overseers, if you stay here and as always happens in the communes your gift will fade as you mature; you will no longer be able to mind speak. If in future you Bond, with practice you may be able to establish mind speaking with your partners. If that is so you shall bring them with you, if

not, when the time comes you must break from them and come with me alone. Make your Bonding decisions wisely".

The brothers were shocked to the core as the mind of the Overseer swept unabated through theirs. They assimilated the thoughts as one being, immediately feeling the power that was possible. The encounter was brief but having tasted the compelling rapture of total unity it ensured their determination to retain the gift, in so thinking they had made the first step to becoming fulfilled beings.

Franil remained in the great barn after the family left; a courtesy to the elders to accept their hospitality of food and drink a tradition not to be ignored. If there was to be a transfer of these boys to Lethe it must come with their blessing.

"I thank you Brugan for the time with the family and this fine fare before me. I will come again soon to see your communes excellent progress. You have a fine talent within the sons of Gren which must be cherished. We will endeavour to help them in this when they are older and can know their minds".

"You are always be welcome here Franil, the commune flourishes. Please finish your meal and enter the chamber and rest awhile before you depart".

"I will do so Brugan, till the morning when I will leave".

At first light Franil left, no need for goodbyes. Few were awake as she ran across the pathways by the fields to her waiting machine.

Chapter Four

All season long the four young people worked on their skills, they had realised Bron was the one with the strength to call them together as of one mind. Bron and Star could mind speak now as easy as if they were brother and sister. However Sala and Porta had only managed to establish momentary links by total concentration; Bron told them they were trying too hard and should relax, they tried to be casual but no lasting connection transpired except when Bron included himself in the link. The failures did not stop their endeavours with an increasing number of small successes spurring them to continue.

The breakthrough came when Sala cut her hand when chopping vegetables. She yelled out loud at the same time sent out a powerful burst of pain from her mind. Bron in the fields and Star in the great barn caught the distressing call even though they were nowhere near Sala, to his surprise so did Porta who was also working but in a totally different field. The flow of mental energy came from her emotional and physical reaction to pain. Porta immediately asked Sala what was wrong who told him she had cut her finger but it was only a small cut and not to worry, the first real prolonged mind speak between the two had taken place; Bron and Star listened in to make sure Sala was okay. They didn't know how but from then on the four could communicate at will with one another, to any of them as individuals or all together as desired; Bron was no longer needed as the catalyst. The Bonding between Sala and Porta was now a certainty; it seemed a likely outcome for Bron and Star too but neither expressed a wish to do so. They continued to mind speak but as time progressed whole thoughts were transferred in an instant till finally when they wished all four minds were one. Mind speaking was no longer necessary as any desired question, statement or image was transferred as a complete thought. They continued to speak aloud in front of their parents or visitors to preserve the natural form of communication within the home and commune.

The season passed slowly for Sala; eager to Bond with Porta and for the return of the Overseer, the waiting was testing her patience. She spent more time with her Ma than in the past, skipped some of her planned visits to the great barn in order to do so. She learnt of any important songs and interpretations from the mind of her friend Star so lost very little. Kelena noticed the change and although she enjoyed the growing closeness was concerned for her daughter's welfare; she thought missing the songs and teachings of the elders may prove detrimental to her development.

"Sala why are you not attending all your visits with the elders you will miss out on some important learning"?

"I don't miss much Ma; Star lets me know if there is anything important and I go to any session where the song is repeated it's a good plan as I get to spend more time helping you and Pa Regol".

Kelena couldn't argue with her explanation but was not sure if Sala was being evasive. Having mind speaking ability brought with it some degree of covertness so Kelena wasn't sure if Sala's answer was designed just to give her Ma peace of mind. She was sure it was a true statement, having no idea of the highly advanced level of her children's ability, she felt there was more to it than she was saying. Sala could sense her Ma's unease and knew Porta and she would have to explain what was going to happen sometime soon, they could not leave it till the time to depart was upon them, the families would need to prepare and adjust. It was still uncertain if Bron or even Star would join in their journey the subject had not been broached since their minds had fully merged as one. In fact all had avoided the thoughts around the subject knowing it may trigger the conflicting feelings once again.

Time passed as always with the harvest gathered and the food stores full, the hard work of all culminating in a celebration with songs of joy and the drinking of menga. Two seasons now had passed, the time for Bonding was approaching. Sala and Porta were now ready having waited the allotted time for the approval of the elders; they and others of the age who had also made their choice were to be joined together in one ceremony. They would meet in the great barn with all the elders in attendance, the families gathered in the square as witness to the Bonding of their children. The elder Ezekiel would sing the song of the Bonding aloud for all to hear and the pairs of young people hand in hand would recite the words as he paused at the end of each phrase.

The land and rain sustain our need
We harvest well with one accord
Our families grow seasons proceed
To reach the time to Bond our word

We come together side by side
For all we are right now bestow
For us will merge will ne'er divide
In all we do, we do to grow

Preserve for each the life untold
We now are one, one Bond entire
To nurture those whom we enfold

Till to air and land expire

With these simple words, which had been heard many times at each Bonding ceremony through many seasons, each pair were Bonded. Ezekiel concluded with a final word.

"The Bond you have made is good and true
Bring children of good heart into our commune
May the land provide, may your lives be as one".

A house, once used by people now passed, had been prepared for Sala and Porta as other homes were also made ready for all those who had Bonded this day. But before they embarked on their new lives together the celebration feast was soon underway, a time of joy that would continue through most of the day and into the night.

Chapter Five

The elder Overseers and especially the Science Masters held sway in the land of Lethe, their wisdom had never been questioned, all thoughts shared hid no secrets. Their individual private musings concerning a subject, when concluded, were shared with the other elders the final decision being a consensus of their thoughts. So it was with the decision concerning the children of the communes.

Metrin agreed with the proposals to use them as breeding stock except her private thoughts differed in one respect from those of her fellow Science Masters. Although she would never go directly against their combined decision to feed them the Waters, she would endeavour to preserve the memories of the commune visitors for as long as possible. She wanted to take control of these mind speakers, tap into their power at the same time satisfy the wishes of the elders by making sure they cohabited with the Letheans and if possible with their telepathic minds intact.

The river water before it arrived at the lake of Lethe was safe in almost every respect but once mixed it had an unexpected effect on those who drank it. All memories of the past would be gradually erased leaving the mind clear of all past events. A clean tableau on which to build a new untarnished beginning. Metrin knew from the science Master Ouisa that there were certain substances in the water which affected the functions of the brain. Over a multitude of seasons the Lethean people stayed well away as they were not immune to these effects. Any person who drank this water would succumb to its influence. It came from the seeds of the Pinson trees which grew close to the edge on one side of the lake and shed its fruit into the water every season, the upstream river of Lethe which fed the lake had no such properties and was the supply used by all.

Ouisa had studied the Pinson fruit and extracted oil from its seed discovering that even the tiniest amount would render even an animal as large as an ox immobile for days, its mind a blank. The drug would remove the surface or recent memory right down to the deep rooted ones of childhood, depending upon the dose given. Tiny amounts selectively removed the memories of a former life retaining fundamental functions such as language and simple living requirements. If given too much, the brain is emptied to the level of a young child or a new-born baby. An overdose causes death. It had once long ago been used regularly to control individuals who showed dissent. Today everyone is aware of the danger so not only do they avoid the lake they do nothing to upset the Overseers.

In order to overcome any inbuilt inhibitions of the soon to be expected commune people, it was planned to feed them sufficient of the waters to erase their memory of being Bonded and any other barriers there may be to cohabiting with the chosen Lethean people. Metrin was afraid the waters may also remove their telepathic ability, thus destroying the whole purpose of the inter-breeding and more importantly her desire for power. She had introduced this argument as a possibility but the others wanted to proceed stating in return that the seed of the males and the egg of the females wold be unaffected; even if Metrin was right they could still collect more mind speakers from the other communes and try again.

Metrin agreed it would be a way forward to remove the expected resistance but in her heart knew the children of commune Five were very special and may never come her way again. She was determined to keep at least one of them safe from the Waters. Unlike the permanently guarded minds of Letheans, the energy in a new untapped mind could easily be seized and once joined with hers a lasting transfer of some of the power would occur. With repeated extractions an intensity of mind control above all others would eventually be achieved; her power over all of Lethe would then be assured. Science Masters and Overseers would bow to her wishes, a new Lethe would emerge holding sway over this World for always.

Metrin cared not for the Letheans who had lost the gift, there were enough of the others for her to remain in control well into the future. Those of commune Three were promising but the mind of Bron and his sister Sala were superior to any seen before. She would call to the elders at the time of the arrival of the commune people to allow a delay in the administration of the Waters to see if they would comply to the breeding request by reasoning. She knew her position as the Elder of Age may not prevail but hoped her powerful mind and skills in manipulating others were enough. She would instruct Franil to sow the seeds of what would be expected during her next visit to the communes.

Chapter Six

Franil was preparing to leave very soon, time enough had passed, the prodigies of communes Five and Three were now full grown and 'ready to be harvested'. Not her words but those of Metrin and the other Overseers who had finally agreed it would be she who went to persuade the young people to leave and make the return journey with her to Lethe. Although it was felt Franil's sympathies were not quite as resolved as her elders; familiarity with the commune people would give her great sway over their decision to stay or return with her. She did not like the idea these youngsters were a crop to be picked when ripe but it was certainly the way the elder Overseers viewed them. She knew it was necessary they came back with her and hoped they would be treated as people and not a commodity. There would be resistance of course but with her prowess in the art of persuasion and a few withheld facts she was sure at least some of them would come freely and once in Lethe they would comply with little resistance. If not there was time enough to quash their defiance or always the ultimate way to make them pliant.

The flying machine was prepared with seating installed to carry up to eight passengers. Commune Three would come last as she knew they would be the easier people to deal with whereas commune Five might prove more difficult.

The journey to number Five took more than one full cycle so Franil arrived in the dark. She landed well away from the commune centre, in a place beyond the fields where the people never ventured. She shut down, stowed the power unit in its cradle and secured the hatch. It was still almost dark but soon the sun would clear the horizon whilst she made her way to the commune on foot. It would not take long and she would arrive just as the people would be awakening and making ready for their work and study.

Sure enough as she descended the gentle hill leading from the fields to the outskirts of the commune the land workers, who were always the first to rise, were making ready to leave for their daily endeavours. On seeing the Overseer they all stopped what they were doing and waited for her to pass, remained where they were for a moment then followed behind as she made her way to the great barn. The news of her arrival sped before her the square around the barn filling rapidly even before she had reached its outer perimeter. Franil cast her mind calling out to Sala and the others. The contact with all four was instantaneous, Bron had been awake earlier than usual and was on his way to the far left field when he was startled momentarily by the call. He had been too far away so had missed seeing Franil as she had come down the central pathway; unlike everyone else he was unaware of her visit until that moment. The realisation of Franil's presence in the commune and what it meant gave him and the others pause before they would acknowledge the contact.

In the time since Franil was here before, the development in mind communication skills of Bron, Sala, Porta and Star had steadily improved. All could now block any thought both in and out. This had become necessary as when their minds were fully open they heard what everyone else was saying as their thought processes formed every word, they didn't know it but hearing all thoughts was a similar trait as found with the readers of Lethe; left unchecked the cacophony from voices in their heads was like being in a crowded room where everybody was shouting at once. They had experimented as individuals and as a group where what seemed difficult at first became as natural as breathing. There was a difference in the range where the communication ceased. Bron the most sensitive could listen even at the extremities of the commune, Sala lost contact as she reached the far fields, Porta and Star a little closer before their ability ceased. Sala experimented often with the range problem and found the distance she could achieve grew with each day.

Franil was aware the four youngsters had blocked her the instant she reached out to them. It was clear their skills had advanced much further than she expected. She was not concerned in fact was pleased they had reached a higher level as this may be advantageous in persuading them to come with her back to Lethe. She sent another thought one of her pleasure in being here and was looking forward to seeing them all again. The response was one of welcome but Franil could sense the apprehension, especially in the mind of Bron. She kept this to herself and closed her mind as she approached the great barn.

Sala was excited and called them all to go to the barn where the usual formal greetings with the elders would take place. She knew why Franil was here, they all did; the seasons since her last visit passed rapidly and unnoticed, the time to make a decision had come upon them sooner than they imagined.

They met and stood to the side of the barn; the crowds, not privy to the real reason the Overseer was here, had gathered so tightly around the entrance it was impossible for the four to get closer. A path would open later to allow them to pass when they were called by the elders for they knew they would be summoned at some time during the visit.

Ezekiel remembered the last visit and knew he would have little influence over the decisions and conclusion, his regret being he would probably see the departure of some of the most cherished members of his beloved coterie. Regardless of the Overseers assurances 'it was for the good of the commune' he had grave doubts. The people here lived a life of harmony however he was well aware of human frailties and suspected there was more to the Overseers' ambitions than was being divulged.

Franil stood by the entrance, a cordon of people surrounded her but eased back afraid to come too close. She waited for the elders to come and invite her inside. Ezekiel appeared before her.

"Welcome Overseer Franil, it has not been so long since you were last here. I am not sure we have need of help but are happy for your visit; please come inside"

"Thank you Ezekiel eldest of the elders it is my pleasure to be here".

The formalities dispensed with, she stepped inside out of reach of questioning eyes and sharp ears.

"There is no need for divisiveness Ezekiel I have your true thoughts and concerns in mind and understand your doubts. I wish to speak with the four young people who have the gift".

"Before I summon them Franil please be assured I will not bend to demands from you with regard to these children. If they are even in the slightest unwilling to do what you desire I will not permit them to leave".

"Of course your intervention will not be necessary for I would not do anything against the good of the commune or its people".

Ezekiel knew her answer was evading the issue but had no idea how to keep his thinking from the prying mind of the visitor, he hoped the young ones would do what they truly desired. Their ability to mind speak gave them an advantage he didn't have, but could they see into the mind of Franil through to the truth. He sent for Bron Sala, Porta, and Star. Their names were called at the entrance whereupon the crowd parted to make a path for the four thus summoned to enter. They came from the place where they had been waiting to the entrance, paused a moment to face the people and went in.

Once inside and out of sight Franil made contact to each individually with a greeting, then to all four as one with a request to relax and listen to what she had to say. There would be no voice communication, the elders would have no idea what was being expounded here. This would be her primary act of persuasion; any resistance would be dealt with individually.

"I have come, as you are aware, to ask you to make a visit to my home, to the land of Lethe. I sense your abilities have developed beyond even what was expected and I wish to help you advance your gift to its full potential. There are many things in Lethe to amaze you we have sciences way beyond your imagination. Our elders will teach you of the ways of our people and the Science Masters different ways of controlling this land. I know you will want to come with me and assure you your commune will eventually benefit from the knowledge gained during your visit with us. I sense many questions from you all, I will answer each in turn".

She closed her mind to all and accepted the thought of each individually but expressed her answers for all to know.

"Sala I know you are willing as is Porta, this Bond is good and will be honoured as will the one between Bron and Star. Bron you are not so willing as you have concerns for family; losing two children when they are at the peak of their working strengths will place a heavy burden on your Ma and Pa, a load you are not wanting them to endure. Your adamant aversion of before is now

much weaker as I see you wish to take advantage of the opportunity to improve all your skills, but concern for family is strong too. I believe there is a solution to this dilemma Bron, be patient. Porta you have no concerns and will follow Sala everywhere but to tell you how long you will be away I cannot answer, it will be your choice. Star you naturally follow Bron in his thoughts. Your simple questions about the journey are easily answered. Lethe is far away on the other side of this world it would be impossible to travel so far on foot. We however will travel in my machine which flies like the birds; a day or so will see us there".

She closed the meeting speaking aloud for the elders to hear. It was close now they were all primed to decide in her favour just Bron needed a little nudge, some incentive to take away his resistance.

"I am tired and need to rest now, in the mean-time consider what I have said. I will ponder on what I can do to help the families so making your choice easier. Please Ezekiel if you have questions of your charges we have no secrets. I am sure they too will seek your advice".

"Thank you Franil please follow the young elder he will take you to a place for some refreshment and rest".

Ezekiel held up his hand to stop the four from leaving, he waited for Franil to be out of hearing range although he wasn't sure if it made any difference to her knowing what was being said.

"Please stay a moment I wish to say something. Come sit with me a while. I know we have not spoken in some time but I have been following your progress and have great joy in the Bonds you have made. From my observations you hardly ever speak aloud when you are together which I presume is because your mind speaking ability has developed to embrace all of you.

I sensed the Overseer contacted you in the same way, she will no doubt have been very persuasive in her arguments to oblige you to leave. All I ask is consider her message with some degree of doubt".

"Oh master I for one wish to go. She assured us we are to be educated in new ways so when we return the commune can only benefit from our new knowledge. Have they not always been helpful and given us the means to live a good life".

"That is true Sala but remember they are not like us, not so open in their hearts and may have motives unknown. I am sure they believe they have the commune's long term well-being in mind when taking you away but be prepared for significant changes in your lives. These people are very powerful and once under their roof your choices and freedom may diminish. Bron how do you feel"?

"My head says to go as I have felt the power of the mind of this Overseer Franil and wish to learn more of this. My heart wants to stay with my family so I am not decided. Maybe if Pa can manage the fields for a season or two, I could return to the commune later, I just don't know ".

"Porta and Star will follow their Bond partners I am sure but before any of you decide go now and talk together; it may be a great adventure this offer to travel to Lethe but be sure before you commit".

Ezekiel knew they would choose to leave it was an opportunity no young person could resist; he only hoped the Overseers were true in their assurances but still remembered the stories of the past where any who had left the communes before had never returned.

Franil accepted the hospitality of the elders and rested a short while before returning to the barn. She was concerned when she found Ezekiel alone unmoved from his place.

"You seem disturbed Ezekiel are my assurances not enough"?

"I am sure you believe you are helping our young people but I have sorrow to see them depart at their most productive and happy time. Being with family and having children brings joy to us all here; these moments will be lost to us if they leave."

"I understand but this opportunity will only come once; the choice is theirs to make, not yours and certainly not mine. All except Bron are ready for the journey but he has strong family ties and does not wish to burden his parents, do you have a suggestion Ezekiel"?

"His Ma and Pa are strong still; age has not affected their work nor will it for some time. Some families have three or more children growing fast who I know would be willing for them to share the load with Bron's family till he returned. It could be arranged".

"I have made my offer to all four so will now ask them to decide. I will leave you to tell Bron of your suggestion of providing support for his family, it may make it easier for him to resolve his dilemma. Please tell them I will leave in a day or two with or without them. I will accept their decision and when they are ready ask them to let me know. They will need to prepare and say farewell to their families".

This final step should be enough Franil was confident she would have a full complement from commune Five. Metrin would be pleased.

Chapter Seven

The four young people of commune Five, each with their small bags of personal items followed the Overseer Franil along the pathway at the edge of the field leading away from their homes.

The whole commune turned out to see the young adventurers leave. Tearful goodbyes from friends and family now turned to waves of farewell and good cheer. Franil never understood the tears of emotion she had never cried in her life; it was a strange reaction never experienced in Lethe. At the far field they turned into an area of woodland towards the high hill; they seldom came this far and never beyond its crest. The Overseer Franil did not stop but continued on into the next valley, they followed but stopped for a moment, turned to look back one last time at their home and the tiny dots of people still watching far below, wondering when they would see it or their families again. The clearing amongst the trees where Franil had left her transport was just a short distance from the top of the hill.

The machine glistened in the sunlight like a reflection of the stars in water. None had seen anything like it before, as they came closer its sleek shape and true size revealed a wonder of engineering beyond their imagination. Bron's amazement at seeing such a sight sent an immediate exclamation from his mind.

"Franil is this it! What....How....is this the machine we will travel in"?

"It is Bron, come we will go inside".

Franil placed her hand on a small plate on its side; an entry hatch opened to reveal the interior. She stepped inside and beckoned for the others to do the same. Once inside she allocated their seats and explained the machine would shortly leave the ground and slowly increase its height and be speeding them on their journey to Lethe. No one spoke but gazed almost stunned in wonder at this amazing machine, an unbelievable experience about to unfold. Once they were seated she inserted the power source and took her position at the control before addressing the four children of Five.

"*The journey will take some time so please relax and sleep if you wish. You can look through the windows of course I know it will all be very new for you. In a while I will stop to pick up some others from commune Three, it won't take very long, you will be able to get out to stretch your legs during this stop. We will then fly to Lethe; no more stopping. We should arrive by the coming of the light".*

As the machine rose Sala held her breath revelling in this new exciting feeling. Bron leant forward closer to the window to see the ground fall away beneath him his doubts about leaving were beginning to wane as the new anticipated experiences seemed to be vastly more promising than expected. Porta squeezed Salas hand and looked at her with a broad grin he didn't have to say anything, she knew. Star stared in wonder but a tinge of sadness remained, she was still thinking of her Ma and Pa.

No one slept; the machine lifted them through the wispy clouds revealing the sky above, blue in all directions. They had learnt in songs how their world was a ball of living things, one among many that roamed the sky; here it was plain and clear, they could see the curve as it stretched across the horizon, where the blue of the sky merged with the clouds and green of the forest below. None could sleep at first as the scene about them captured their minds. There was no sensation of speed just the faintest whisper as the air passed over the sleek body of the craft. Once at full height with the track to commune Three set, Franil relaxed. Soon the four too relaxed in their seats as the scene below remained unchanged, forest being the only view covering most areas of this part of the world. She sensed the change so to encourage sleep she darkened the windows and dimmed the interior lights. Her hand resting gently on the control she lay back in her seat glad that she had managed to secure all four mind speakers with little problem.

She knew she had kept back some of the more pertinent reasons for their journey and what was to come would not be all what they hoped for or were expecting. Survival for Lethe and maintaining the gift was paramount, for if Lethean control were to cease then the communes would suffer; it's what she was told by the elders but she was not sure it was what she believed. She had been tasked by the elders to bring these young people back so had little choice but to be lenient with the truth for if they knew of the Overseers intended plan they never would have come. Next stop commune Three.

The landing was as quiet as the rest of the journey, they had all slept and remained so until Franil brightened the lights and cleared the windows to full transparency. Like at commune Five she parked the craft some distance from its centre in an isolated but open area. Landing such a machine in full sight would cause a disquiet among its people and generate many questions she did not want to answer.

"You may go outside and walk a little but stay in sight of the machine, there is nothing here to present a danger provided you remain away from the forest. I will leave the hatch open so you can come back whenever you like, I won't be too long. The

compartment at the rear has all facilities with food and drink please help yourselves. If there is a problem or delay I will mind speak with you".

Franil disengaged and stowed the power source then opened the hatch. She marched off at speed across the open ground and into the woods. The path used before had grown over but she knew the way well enough to reach the field furthest from the commune in good time. As she progressed towards the centre commune workers in the fields stopped what they were doing and as always followed her a few steps behind. The procession finally reached the great barn. Franil waited as usual for the elders to appear and invite her inside, a tradition and a courtesy from both parties. Brugan the elder stepped through the opening and motioned for Franil to enter.

"Welcome Franil your promised return has come as expected, please enter and we will discuss your earlier surprising proposal concerning the family of Pa Gren".

"Thank you Brugan the time has passed quickly to where the boys should be ready. Would you please ask the family and the boys Horden and Arak to come here I will explain fully what we have to offer them in Lethe".

"There have been developments Franil which may change what you intend. I know it is their ability to mind speak that draws your interest but since you left Horden has Bonded with a young girl and established a new home here. Arak's ability to speak with his brother has faded as always happens when they become of age".

Franil had not previously probed the mind of Brugan so was unaware of the changes but having heard these fateful words did so and saw the truth of it. She had planned to summon the boys and would know their intentions straight away; she saw no problems convinced they would be keen to come with her. Now all her intentions were in danger of failure.

"It does alter things a little Brugan but I still wish to speak with them and also to the girl with which Horden has Bonded. Please ask them and the families to see me".

"Of course they will come and speak with you please wait a short while. In the mean-time I hope you will take refreshment in the next chamber".

Franil was concerned; the boy Arak was now of no use as he had lost the gift; she would check when she met him again. If Horden has Bonded with this girl who cannot mind speak and the link between him and his brother had faded as the Elder Brugan had suggested, then she too will be of no use, indeed Horden may no longer want to leave so her visit here has come too late. What a mess. She moved to the chamber for a cool drink, to relax and to close her eyes a short while. They would call her when ready she would fare better after a rest. In her reverie she probed for the mind of Horden but got nothing, perhaps he had lost the gift too.

Horden had improved his ability to mind speak and had established a strong link with Jeska; they had made their Bond the season before. His brother's skill had not faded as was thought by everyone, they kept this to themselves. Arak still communicated with him but spoke aloud when not alone. All three had developed the skill to block unwanted outside thoughts. They never used the ability amongst others and encouraged the Elders to think their gift was no longer an important part of their lives. He remembered well the Overseers amazing contact last time and had blocked the call Franil just made. He called Jeska and Arak to stay blocked till they were in front of the Overseer. He was now ready to meet her again.

His brother Arak had not yet Bonded as there were no girls of age he could communicate with in the commune; he was still young so plenty of time for him yet. There were two sisters who could mind speak, he had made some weak attempts to communicate however he would have to wait one more season before he could fully engage with them; they were not yet old enough to Bond.

Franil had been expecting to be taking Horden and his brother Arak with her; since she'd found out Horden had Bonded with Jeska her options had changed; she hoped the pair had the gift so she could take them and leave Arak for later.

Even before they had arrived at the barn Franil was aware of the minds now open to her, all three had come to an unexpected level of achievement which left all the doubts behind.

"Horden, Arak and now Jeska how wonderful, I feared you were lost but now it could not be better".

Their minds mingled as one, each ambition for the future was revealed to her. Franil's offer to transport them to Lethe to develop their skills was taken with no doubt. Arak too wanted to come however declined for this trip but only till he was older and Bonded with one of the mind speaking girls. Franil was now in a position most unexpected, a reversal of an anticipated failed extraction had changed to something much better. There would be four not two as thought, Horden and Jeska this trip and Arak and his partner next time. All she needed was the families approval and the elders permission. Franil left the rest area and returned to the barn where Brugan and the families were assembled. Brugan spoke first.

"Please Franil explain what are your intentions for the families and why these particular young people".

At first Franil spoke aloud for the benefit of the families but also directly to the minds of the three she wished to recruit.

"I came here expecting to see if the two brothers would consider a move with me to Lethe; a visit to advance their education in many ways. The situation has changed where Horden has since Bonded with Jeska, so I offer the same opportunity to them. I seek approval from the elders and the families and of course the willingness of the two young people".

Brugan was unsure why the change, was it because Arak no longer had the gift so questioned Franil.

"Please Overseer, how long will they be gone and what of Arak why is he now excluded"?

"I cannot say how long as the subjects for learning are many and will take some few seasons to complete, there is no limit it will be up to them entirely. Concerning Arak, he is still too young and although he may be keen to come with me I now realise how important Bonding is in the commune so would not want to deprive him of this. I have reconsidered my initial plan; he will serve his family better here and will be able to Bond soon which he could not have done if I take him now. We will come again and he may yet be able to achieve his desire to visit us".

The elders and families began to speak amongst themselves she did not bother to listen in as she was sure there would be no dissention, she then spoke her prepared speech directly to the minds of the three.

"I have come, as you are aware, to ask you to make a visit to my home, to the land of Lethe. Your abilities I sense have developed beyond even what was expected and I wish to help you advance your gift to its full potential. There are many things to amaze you, we have sciences way beyond your imagination. Our elders will teach you of the ways of our people and the Science

Masters the ways of controlling this land. I hope you will want to come with me and will assure you that your commune will eventually benefit from the knowledge gained during your visit with us. I am sorry Arak your decision to stay is understood, I will return for you in a later season when you have Bonded".

    Horden and Jeska were of one mind ready and willing. Arak emitted some reluctant thoughts but agreed his staying was a sensible choice. Horden and Jeska would each ask their Ma and Pa for permission and seek approval from the elder Brugan to go with Franil to the new land. Franil waited in the rest area whilst the families said their goodbyes and the two packed a few belongings to bring with them. Franil felt the strange and powerful sad emotions emanating from all at the pending separation but it was confusing for her cold clinical mind; she thought *'These people are still quite primitive'.* Her visit had taken no more time than expected. Her two charges were young and fit and so kept pace with Franil as she strode towards the machine's hideaway. Both Horden and Jeska stopped amazed when they sighted the flying machine but Franil called them to hurry as she was keen to be on her way. Pleased to find the commune Five group in their seats, she waited by the open hatch and motioned them to enter. There was no need for introductions as an immediate link amongst all present established as soon as they became aware of the newcomers presence. The joining of minds beyond their own small group and the Overseer was new and exciting, all six were now part of this great adventure. Sala was reminded of her youthful wish to meet one of the gold haired people, she now had two sitting very close by, this was strange and moving. They studied each other, the colouring of their skin and hair the marked differences although Sala saw they were a little larger in body than themselves but nowhere as tall as the Overseer. Sala reached out to the girl learning her name was Jeska and how she and her Bond Horden had been recruited as was she and her friends. None knew what was in store but trusted in the one named Franil.

The airship left the ground, the course set for the final lap of the journey towards her home; Franil obscured the windows once the newcomers had exhausted their curiosity following the sun's sinking beyond the horizon; starlight and darkness engulfed the vessel. A gentle slumber overtook the six passengers, Franil felt the tension slowly leave her body, she could finally relax for the few hours of flight remaining, mission accomplished.

Chapter Eight

Light had returned as they arrived but a mist surrounded Lethe, as was common at this time of the season, Franil could see enough through the fine haze sufficient to land without technical guidance, a manoeuvre she had done many times before, bringing her ship slowly into the large building constructed many seasons ago to house the flying machines. Her passengers were still sleeping but had missed nothing of the view of their new home due to the hazy conditions. A gentle thought from Franil sent to all ushered them awake.

A gaggle of sounds invaded their senses, a multitude of minds with thoughts and strange words crowding in uncontrolled upon them. As they came awake the blocking of these new and powerful minds took a deal of concentration. Franil detected the situation and waited to let them settle. The four of commune Five reacted at once, closed out all intrusive thoughts and became receptive to her very quickly, but Horden and Jeska having had little need to practice blocking at such an intensity, struggled in vain. Franil interjected.

"Horden Jeska, relax my friends, close the strongest mind first, then the next and so on it will come, no need to rush".

She remained in contact, encouraging as they excluded the thoughts of the Lethean people one by one until they had control. The others were unaware of the problem as they were excluded from this exchange so sat waiting for Franil to tell them what to do next. Franil left the machines control and went back inside to disconnect the power source before addressing her human cargo; she spoke aloud, for to open their blocks to her alone with the background mental noise they had just experienced would be difficult for Horden and Jeska at this early introduction to Lethe.

"Soon you will see many unexpected things and may want to ask questions, please be patient and wait, all will become clear in good time. Almost everyone here has mind speaking ability to some degree; as you have just experienced it can be a mentally noisy place so keep your blocks in place, it won't take long for it to become natural for you. I will now take you to your new homes, you will be housed in adjacent rooms in pairs, each room has all the facilities. Here in Lethe we all eat together, groups of twenty or more at a time however to begin with there might be food brought to your rooms, I'm not sure I will see what has been arranged. We know you are healthy but we must provide a degree of protection for ourselves as you may carry some infections harmless to you but to which we have little or no immunity. You will be tested individually and once cleared of any medical problem will be given the freedom to roam anywhere you wish and join with everyone here in all activities. An educational programme has been set up to cater to your special needs, we hope you will want to take full advantage of this facility. Now gather your belongings and follow me."

Mentally stunned and somewhat open mouthed the six did as requested and left the flying machine to step into their strange new world. The huge building in which the craft had landed was so much bigger than the great barn and appeared to be floating unsupported, flimsy looking arches held up a roof of material that shone like water, the side supports seem to be made of the same material as their ploughs and cutting tools, so unlike their buildings in the commune which were constructed from trees, straw and the earth. The floor under their feet was not the well-trodden mud of many seasons made firm by the constant pounding of leather boots, but a smooth and solid platform of an unknown compound. Once outside the city of Lethe rose before them its symmetrical and shining buildings constructed of metals and other exotic materials stood tall and strangely beautiful. The pathways were the same as in the air ship building flat and firm, linking all the buildings in one seamless surface. Every now and then trees and flowering plants grew from openings in the pathways, making pleasant natural breaks in the surroundings. Looking beyond the nearby buildings a large glass pyramid structure could be seen in the distance. The air machine building was situated away from the other buildings at the far end of the Lethe in full sun but protected from the wind by the hills beyond. They encountered a few people who acknowledged them with a nod of the head or a raised hand as they passed by but said nothing either aloud or in mind speak. A large green area appeared as they turned down a side path where young children were running and playing a game with hoops and sticks, they were watched by a man and few older women. They continued on a short distance when Franil turned and stopped outside a silver door with a strange sign painted in black on its front. Now they had settled their thoughts after the initial surprise of their arrival she reverted to her more natural mind communication.

"Bron, Star this is your home".

Bron stepped forward and the door opened without it being touched.

"Please enter, you will find everything you need inside, some refreshment is available, remain here I will come back later. The room is programmed to open to your two faces alone, it will close behind you. To leave just touch the green panel inside and it will open".

The two went in and the door closed behind them. She moved several paces along to face another door.

"Porta, Sala this room is yours, the same conditions as for Bron and Star, please wait for me here I will return".

Sala wanted to ask many things but remembered Franil's instruction to be patient, so entered with Porta in silence. Franil moved along but turned into another path which continued some considerable distance before arriving outside the door of a second identical looking building to that of the others. Horden and Jeska entered their room.

Once inside Porta started to explore; the room beyond the entrance was furnished with four seats, one low table, a small empty cupboard and little else; behind was a bedroom with storage in which hung some white robes, lengths of folded woven material and soft cloth shoes; there was a bathroom to one side. Sala was concerned feeling confined, there were no windows and at once went to the door and touched the green pad whereupon the door swung open as she was told it would. She wished there was a window and as she expressed that thought a panel in the wall cleared revealing the scene outside. Amazed that the house could read her mind she and Porta began to experiment with different demands. Very little else responded except they could turn the water in the bathroom on and off and control the light level in each room. Porta found there was a hidden screen where pictures of whatever he wanted would appear. He thought of the forest near his home in commune Five and it miraculously appeared on the screen. He left it on display as a reminder of home. They lay on the bed for a short while, it was softer than they were used to but comfortable enough, they then sat in the seats looking at their forest picture, impatient for something to happen. Sala reached out to her brother.

"Hey this is not bad Bron, have you tried thinking for things"?

"*Of course the drinks in the cupboard is amazing*".

Sala caught his thought and immediately demanded a drink of water. An opening appeared in the wall cupboard with two cups and a jug of water. She then asked for a cup of menga but there was no response it made her laugh. She discovered by varied requests that what the cupboard provided was limited to water, a fruit drink unknown to Sala and two small cakes, she did not like these as they were very sweet. Porta ate both without flinching. Their experimenting and sharing information with her brother continued for a while. She then sent a thought to contact Horden and Jeska, finding they too had discovered the thinking responses of their room, but not the screen with the pictures. Their patience was growing thin with the waiting for something to happen when a strong thought from Franil invaded all.

"*I will be along in a few moments please wait outside your room, a slight change of plan, we will go and eat together, I and another Overseer will then answer your questions*".

Franil arrived with Horden and Jeska following, collected the others to proceed in line passing by the now empty green where the children had been playing it was becoming darker and the temperature was falling causing Franil to hurry towards the eating hall. They entered a large room through an open archway the doors of which closed automatically behind them once they were all inside. It was warm, the only furnishings were three round tables with ten chairs around each. A tall and older Overseer was seated at one of the tables, Franil motioned for the six to be seated at the table and joined them sitting next to her senior colleague who opened her formidable mind to all.

"Welcome to Lethe; I am Metrin an elder of the Overseers and Mind Science Master, I am one of those who brought you here. You all have the gift of communicating through the mind, *but unlike us here it remains a weak force amongst your people. It is my desire and all the elders here for you to develop these skills and endeavour to integrate with our people for the future good of us all. Your communes will grow stronger as a result of this amalgamation of our minds and bodies. I know you must be hungry following your long journey; this will be the place where you will eat; there would normally be others here but we must wait for the health checks to be completed before we allow full communal contact. I will leave you to eat before you pose the many questions I am sure you have for Franil. I will follow your progress with avid interest, we will no doubt meet again".*

The overpowering woman with yellow skin, black hair and penetrating dark blue eyes, dressed in the deep purple silken robe of the senior Overseers stood tall as she transmitted her final thoughts. She bowed her head to the seated assembly turned and left. A few moments later a group of young Letheans appeared from the rear of the room with plates of food, flasks of juice and all the accoutrements of a fine meal. They filled the table and disappeared as quickly as they arrived. Sala noticed the people and children she saw on her short walk from the airship were similar in colouring to Franil and Metrin but seemed smaller somehow and were dressed in various ways mainly white and a few in brown. The table attendants were dressed in simple white half-length trousers and tops, they wore white gloves and had masks across their faces, presumably as a protection from possible infection. Sala noted they were all female. Franil continued to explain things as soon as Metrin had gone, she spoke aloud keeping her mind closed tight not wishing to accidentally reveal hidden information during questioning.

"We grow almost all our food in the pyramid shaped buildings you saw in the distance. They provide enough for everyone; the system runs a continuous process which is largely automated. We all take turns tending to the large variety of plants we grow there including gathering the produce and delivering it to the eating halls. The same applies for the preparation of meals; again a highly automated system which you will soon see. You will all take your turn helping in both tasks, everyone here who is able shares in the work. Please eat now I will come back in a while to explain what will happen next".

The food, although not what they were familiar with had some similarities. Mostly green leaves and root crops, various nuts with fruits and some baked items similar to their home-made breads and wheat products. Oils and a kind of milk made from small fermented seeds were used in preparation and cooking. A minced and crisp brown crumb like substance had a strong flavour, it looked like the ground ox meat of home but less so. It appeared foods derived directly from animals were not on the menu. They found later the eggs of birds were sometimes gathered from the forests along with some wild fruits and nuts. Fish were occasionally taken from the river situated some distance away from lake. These additions to the green produce were saved for special occasions. The ox was an animal used in the past but were now left to run wild in the forest, they were sometimes trapped and used in experiments. There were no domesticated animals for food here, not even pets. Sala remembered fondly her little dog she had as a child and felt sorry the children here missed out on the joy of a pet. They finished eating and within a moment of the last mouthful being consumed the same girls who delivered the meal appeared and cleared everything away. Bron mind spoke first.

"This is weird don't you think, it seems like these people are here to wait on us like we are elders or infirm".

"Its new for us, we live and care for each other in family groups; you heard what Franil said, here they all share in the work, a bit like we do in the fields but in different ways. I am sure we will have our turn in preparing and serving the food for others".

"I don't mind them feeding me, the foods not bad either and if I don't have to work in the field ever again I'll be happy".

"You lazy so and so Horden they'll have you digging ditches just wait and see".

Jeska ribbed her Bond with the prospect of the worst job they ever had to do back home. The simple banter went on for a while filling time with ever more exaggerated verbal images of the tasks ahead, all really wondering what was to come next. Quiet prevailed as each became immersed in their private thoughts and misgivings. Franil returned to the silent group who shrugged off their introspection on her arrival.

"I hope you have had enough; you will eat again here next time; you must find your own way about from now on, you will soon get used to where everything is. There are other eating halls you may use, choose any one close to where you may be working or studying ask anyone with you, they will help. I hope you have had sufficient rest after eating as you must now follow me to the Body Science facility where you will be checked for unwanted infections, it will not take long".

They all left the table and followed behind Franil along a route similar to the earlier path, wondering what hidden infections they may have even though none of them were ill and what would happen if they found something nasty. Most buildings looked alike as did the pathways; it was the symbols on the doors which differed, Sala guessed this was a way of identifying where you were, she'd ask later. They continued until they arrived at a much more imposing door which opened automatically as Franil stopped and turned to enter with the six following behind.

"This is the hall of the Science Master Soma; we will go to the rooms above where you will be examined by one of the helpers. It is a simple and quick process where she will use a device to look inside your body for any problems you may have".

There was a sound of surprise from all six as the sloping walkway which led to the floors above began to move a soon as the last one stepped upon it.

"Sorry, I should have warned you, there will many new things here which I take as normal, don't be alarmed they are all here to make life easy".

The young man was alone in the room, Sala was curious as this was the first male she had seen up close since they arrived. He was quite thin compared to the females a little taller with the same blue eyes and very yellow skin. He spoke aloud when asking Sala to open her mouth; he then used a tiny spoon to scrape inside her cheek placing it in a glass tube. Next he gave her a white liquid to drink. She stopped him there asking what was in the drink. He explained it would enhance the pictures he was about to take of her insides; she supposed it was okay so drank it all. He said to stand facing forward in front of a black screen, with her arms raised hands placed on her head. He moved away out of sight saying for her to hold her breath and keep still. She awoke sitting in a chair not knowing what had happened. A moment later he said she could go.

"Did I pass out"?

"Yes it happens sometimes the drink and holding your breath can cause you to faint, it was only for a moment".

"Is that it"?

"It is. Send in the next one please".

They all went through the same process before Franil led them from the room where they had been waiting their turn, back to the moving walkway and outside, feeling a little giddy from their experience. It wasn't until very much later Sala found out all of them had been unconscious for longer than the few minutes they had been told. While undergoing the tests there was more done to them than they knew.

"Next we will go to the hall of The Science Master Enno the place where you will study the Science of the Senses. Here I will explain the programme we have planned for you".

They followed her to the next building a replica of the previous hall of the Science Master Soma entering a similar automatic doorway. This time they passed by the rising walkway and entered a room with many seats all facing a central table obviously set out to display or demonstrate some subject or other. A super version of the great barn where the elders sang their songs to the gathered commune. Franil invited them to take a seat.

"This is where the Science Masters impart their wisdom to those who study here. All but one of the halls have a similar room we would like you to attend these teachings according to a programme which I will now explain. There are seven Science buildings three you have seen already. The science of the Body where you were just tested and this the science of the Senses run by the Science Master Enno. There is the science of the Mind, run by the Science Master Metrin the Overseer you met at the meal earlier. The Science Master Kalli is the head of the Science of Agriculture. The Science Master Ouissa is the Master of Substance and the temporary Master of Physical. Overseer Praes is being trained to eventually become the newly appointed head of the Physical sciences as the previous elderly Science Master Katis passed recently. Finally the Science Master of the Air, is the Overseer Peto. His domain is next to the large space where you first arrived in the flying machine, a building very different from the other six".

"Are we to learn all these Sciences Franil, it seems an impossible task and will take a lifetime"?

"No Bron the programme is to give all of you a sample of each science, give you time to study with the Masters and your fellow students the subject as best you can in the allocated time. One person will go to each science hall for a brief period of learning, then move on to the next till you have covered all seven".

"What happens then"?

"I expect you will improve your abilities with the language and retention, even so by the time you reach number seven what you learnt of the first subject will be forgotten so there will be periods when you can go back to any or all if you wish to refresh your experience. At the end of initial period of about two seasons you will have covered all seven subjects and be able to choose what science you want to study in depth".

"Are we here just to study and why can't we stay together when studying"?

"Oh no Sala, study occupies only part of your time, you will be assigned duties like everyone here. Most tasks are automated so the work is not difficult. You will prepare, serve food and clean, help maintain the buildings, assist with the children, tend the gardens, I could go on there are plenty of tasks to keep you busy, you will find out soon enough. Don't worry you won't have to dig ditches Horden. To answer the other question think about it. If you stayed learning one subject together you would become too reliant on the one person in the group who understood the subject, the rest wouldn't bother too much. The only way is to apply yourselves to the best of your ability and do it alone. When you eventually cover all the sciences you will be able to help each other decide which way to go. Our main aim is for you to integrate fully".

For what purpose, what does 'integrate fully' mean, Sala wondered, Franil never mentioned their mind speaking gift or attempted to mind communicate once during the period since landing, yet this ability was the main reason they were chosen to come here. Franil was obviously listening in covertly to what they were thinking for she made the remark about Horden digging ditches when they were apparently alone. It all seemed too organised, too one sided for them to be given all this without some kind of objective, what did they want in return.

Two days later the allocated lessons were given out, Sala to Substance, Porta to Air, Bron Physic and Star to Sense. Horden and Jeska were given other tasks, he to the Pyramids to tend and learn about the plants and she to the food preparation areas. They were told their science lessons would begin later and the others would also have to learn about the work routines in their turn. Horden and Jeska's hours of work were different to those of the lessons so Sala's group were unlikely to meet them at the food halls and not at all in the houses. Another anomaly to add to her growing unease, were they deliberately keeping the two communes apart?

At first they all struggled to follow what the lessons were trying to achieve there was so many new words spoken by the Masters as well as mind concepts transmitted to them, they remembered almost nothing. There were young Letheans, barely more than children, who seemed to have no problem for they had pads of small sheets where they could make marks as the lessons progressed. Their fellow classmates said the marks were to aid them to recall what was said sometime later. When Sala asked if she too could learn to use the pad she was told that part of learning will follow soon; she did learn to read and write much later, not in Lethe but from a very different source. The songs of the commune were the memory aid she was familiar with so used songs of her own making to remember the lessons. Once she perfected this technique learning came easier. After class and during the meals the four of commune Five discussed the lessons each giving the other help with their personal memorising techniques, the language differences and the unfamiliar.

Horden and Jeska had drifted from their thoughts and were no longer part of the group.

Routine took over, the morning visits to the eating hall, the lessons and breaks for food, then more learning after and the end of class followed by even more food. Sitting in their rooms watching the screens before sleeping.

Almost two seasons gone in study, moving from one subject to another till all seven disciplines had been covered to a basic level. Day after day the same habitual routine only relieved by the days when you were either tending the plants in the Pyramid gardens or preparing and serving food. The times when they came together and played games dwindled each couple spending more time in their rooms. The monotony was broken by mind speaking every day, expanding their skills in blocking and listening in to others undetected. Discussing the lessons with each other took some time too and occasionally when the weather was fine taking walks together. Sala never lost her feeling they were waiting for something to happen; the Overseers were long lived which led them to be very patient, she felt she and her colleagues were being prepared for some unknown event. The word 'Integration' spoken when they first arrived, stuck in her mind but had still not worked out what Metrin had meant by it.

The time to choose their preferred subject to study in detail had arrived. For Bron it was Agriculture and had been from the beginning, Porta was unsure but the Body was his initial choice. Star said she had no idea but would like to go back to the first thing she was allocated which was Sense before choosing. For Sala the Mind was her elected choice, she didn't know why she chose Mind because her real preference was for Air and in particular the flying machine; for some intangible reason she kept this interest hidden deep within the recesses of her thoughts.

Facilities outside of the lessons and the eating halls were few, some green areas for relaxing and playing ball games were used mostly by the children and their guardians, there were small pools at or near these areas with water kept quite warm where you could immerse your whole body, a favourite of Star. Bron used one of the garden workshops to make the game with coloured bricks Horden had once shown him. We played it together at mealtimes and some of the Letheans joined in too. It became popular amongst the students who made several copies of the bricks, you would find someone playing it in any food hall almost every day. It seemed that after study and work when the meal was over most everyone returned to their houses alone and watched the screens. The screens not only had pictures of your choosing but music and stories much like the songs of the elders back home but concerning the life here instead. Sleeping took up a large part of the peoples time much more than Sala and the others needed. Sala was never bored as she moved about the whole community asking questions when she met people outside or in the food halls, revisited all the Science halls even though she had completed her allotted time there. Salas choice of Mind for further study she finally admitted to herself was mainly to remain close to Metrin; the leader of the Science Masters and the eldest of the Overseers. Her skills with telepathy were growing slowly, she could feel the changes and wanted to keep this fact away from Metrin, she had no idea why but did not trust this Overseer even after nearly two seasons without any problems, keeping her close was a constant reminder to be vigilant and the best way to protect herself from her prying mind.

    Her most enjoyable time was spent with Porta in their house and in the hot pools on their evening walks through the green spaces. They walked to the edge of the settlement where the paved areas stopped and the forest began, often making a circuit around the Pyramid gardens; no one was allowed to enter unless working there and everyone had to go through a cleansing process first. Once inside protective clothing and face masks were required, a precaution against introducing unwanted disease to the plants. They spoke little, the two minds joined as if they were one being. They thought of having a child but decided to wait till they were back in the commune, afraid if they had one here it may be removed from them and placed into a care group; not something they relished. Their education had been an amazing journey having learnt more than they ever dreamt was possible. Life for the ordinary people was near perfect when it came to comfort and ease of living but everyone seemed to be on edged all the time and the elements Sala and her colleagues treasured most, family and companionship, were missing.

    The days drifted by, soon a third season would be upon them; the group had settled into a routine and an easy life. Their work duties in the dining halls and gardens were few and simple, attendance at the Science halls dwindled, they had not really integrated making only a few acquaintances from amongst the other students none of them real friends; they had become complacent melding into the idle life and attitude of the Letheans. Sala was not as settled as the others, her advanced mind skills could sense a change was coming, the real reason they were here would soon rear its ugly head.

During the time they had been here even though the four had been allowed, indeed encouraged to join the teaching of the elders and to study the ways of the people, there was an undercurrent of holding them back, they had never been given the opportunity to learn the skill of reading and reproducing the signs and the question of when they would return home was avoided or ignored.

Sala had attended all the lessons she could fit in, many more than the planned education programme designed for them, the others were less enthusiastic but did go to most of the planned lessons. The programme included instruction on how food was produced and prepared, the planning of task rosters so that everyone had a fair share of work and rest time. They visited the green pyramids and studied how the plants grew and the properties of the many varieties. Bron even travelled once in the small flying machine to the forest to be shown how to collect the herbs and leaves used for medicine; these were gathered from huge trees or plants which did not grow well in the artificial pyramid environment. Lectures on the science of energy production were not well received, abandoned after two failed attempts as they all lacked basic mathematical skills with complex calculations and physical concepts. Sala did not give up so attended other classes to try and understand the basics of maths and the sciences. Certain teachers were very helpful but the Science Masters and those who were Overseers less so.

The codes of behaviour, and how the people interacted were very different from those of the commune. Uninvited physical contact was considered disrespectful, occurring only when colleagues were working together or the very young and elderly needed help. There was no greeting in the form of hand shaking, no Bonding or anything resembling a real relationship between men and women probably because there were so few males, it would have been impossible to form a cohesive society with more than three quarters of the females unable to have children from within a Bond partnership. Reproduction was by artificial insemination from a donor bank; the resulting children being nurtured by the birth mothers only briefly before being cared for in small groups of approximately the same age. It could not have been like this in their past, no family, no Ma or Pa no brothers or sisters it was all too much for Sala to accept, it was not the way it should be. The only time she noticed any hint of positive social behaviour was during meal-times. The mind speaking conversations became more relaxed and even personal; sometimes games were played and there was occasional laughter but once in class or at work and most certainly in the presence of the Overseers the people became withdrawn and humourless.

Chapter Nine

Their education and life continued well beyond two seasons punctuated by visits from Metrin and other Overseers who mind spoke of what a great service it would be for the commune people to be included in their breeding programme. Metrin had bided her time before pressing towards her ultimate goal waiting to see if the results of their attempts to produce children from the three commune males . They had no idea that during their medical examinations, when they first arrived, the female eggs and male seed had been harvested and used with selected Lethean girls. After innumerable attempts none produced any fertile results. It was now the Overseers intention to persuade all six to physically cohabit with the Letheans.

Here it was, the true purpose of the Overseer's elaborate scheme; they were here to breed. Although Metrin wanted the breeding to go ahead her real ambition was to extract the exceptional potency from Sala and Bron, their companions gift was much weaker and of little interest to Metrin; she made numerous covert bids to invade their minds but met a strong and permanent block. Sala responded to any direct call from Metrin but the invasive attempts worried her so she kept a solid block in place and warned her brother to do the same.

Constant reminders of an obligation to offer themselves to the Overseers for breeding were made, each time urging them to consider what they had been given, did they not see their life here is far superior to the life in the commune.

The commune Bonding and its associated song was a deeply established code Sala and Porta would not break, besides her brother Bron and Star were too emotionally attached to agree to such a profane and impersonal act. Even though she had not seen them for almost a season she knew the two mind speakers from the other commune Horden and Jeska had similar misgivings. Sala had looked into their minds when they first met and knew their Bond was strong too.

Sala had fears they may all be forced to comply but could not see how. Her trust in the Lethean Overseers intentions wavered; so decided to find out as much as she could about this place and its people to see if she could discover the truth. Sala made her way towards the science area, her mind blank except for thoughts of her intended purpose. The freedom of movement allowed to all who live in Lethe played to her advantage. When she first arrived, any time those who were curious about the commune newcomers would access her mind and know exactly where she was and what she was thinking but she had learnt to block the intrusion. Most of the Letheans did the same to each other in order to have some peace and quiet time so her eventual total blocking was not considered unusual. If someone desired contact, you would be aware of the call and unblock. The process was as natural as breathing for them but for Sala it had to be learnt.

Deception was unknown here, or so she had been led to believe, the concept of lying could not exist, when everyone was of one mind how could it; she would soon find out she was very wrong in that assumption but not until it was too late. The people were friendly and answered any question asked within their knowledge and ability. The Overseers were different somehow, they could be very evasive seemingly without realising it, just by blocking their thoughts or failing to pass on information. During her studies she found out about the nearby lake. Water from Lethe lake were avoided by all who lived here, Sala learned, soon after their arrival, from Ouisa the Science

Master about how if consumed it caused the memories of people to fade. Those who drank had a new beginning to their lives with no concept of what they had done before. The elders were unaware of her ability to listen in to their thoughts undetected; she overheard their discussion about how the Waters should be given to her and the others so they would not have memories of their past and their Bonding, removing their reluctance to breed with the chosen men and girls of Lethe; Metrin was against doing this so for now had been allowed to spare those of commune Five from the unwanted violation until the others from commune Three had been tested to see if conception was successful or not.

Sala and her group had spent a short time with Horden and Jeska from Commune Three, in the beginning they often ate together and were becoming friends but they had not been seen for this and most of last season. They could mind speak with each other and with Sala's help, had mastered how to communicate exclusively with others, they too had similar reservations concerning cohabiting with the Letheans having only recently been Bonded. Physical contact with them was lost soon after they arrived and she was told they were on a different program to the group from Five. The last attempts at mind speaking with Horden had been brief as if he was unwilling to develop the initial affinity that originally existed between the two groups; Jeska was even less communicative. Recent attempts to re-establish contact had been met with silence.

Sala would try to find them, warn her friends to be wary but unbeknown to her she had missed the later arguments of the elders where only commune Five was to be spared. The Waters had already been given to Horden and Jeska without their realising.

Sala had not seen either of them for such a long time and her recent search had proved fruitless so was more than surprised when her friend was seen coming from a class and walked straight by her without speaking, when she mind called her name there was no response. She ran after her and touched her shoulder, Jeska turned and just looked at Sala without recognition and spoke.

"Yes can I help you"?

A perplexed Sala noticed her protruding tummy, she was pregnant. Whilst she was speaking Sala realised something was not right, this baby should have been Horden's but instinct told her it was not.

"Jeska what have they done to you. Where is Horden"?

"I am sorry I don't understand what you are saying I am confused, when I don't understand I have to ask my Overseer for help, I have to go now, goodbye".

Jeska's voice was a monotone, her face expressionless, she turned away and walked off leaving Sala shocked and angry. They must have given her the Water Sala thought and probably Horden too; she must find Porta, Bron and Star now, warn them of the danger.

This chance meeting between Sala and Jeska had been immediately noticed by the Overseers as both Horden and Jeska were being closely monitored. As soon as Sala stopped to talk to Jeska the elders became aware of the possible ramifications so decided to act at once. Metrin who always stayed close came at once to intercept Sala keeping her away from her family. Sala shocked by what had just occurred, remained standing where Jeska had left her in a daze, when Metrin unexpectedly appeared beside her.

"Hello Sala, we must talk".

Metrin took Salas arm intending to lead her away, keep her occupied and away from her friends but Sala pulled free of her hand sharply and probed deep into the mind of the senior Overseer. The ever present block wavered for just a moment revealing Jeska and Horden had been given the waters.

"It seems you are aware of Jeska's condition. Let me explain. When we discussed her co-habiting she said she really wanted to help but it would be difficult, as did Horden, because of their bond, when we said we could help by letting their recent memories of boding be erased they agreed".

Sala did not believe a word, rising anger surged, her heart pounded in her chest her feelings of despair given vent by blasting her thoughts at Metrin with full force.

"You gave them the waters! They would never have agreed to that, you are not what you pretend to be, I see into your false heart lying to cover this awful thing you have done, I know what is happening here, I heard the elders planning this".

"Don't be upset Sala it is for the good of everyone".

"No it is not, and you know it. I must find my friends now".

Metrin reached out and held her arm again; the Overseer's mind block slipped again as Sala aggressively pulled away revealing Metrin's true intentions of this conversation; she was being delayed so as not to warn the others.

"I fear you are too late Sala the deed is done".

She reached out to Porta but there was only a garbled response like he was drunk on menga. Sending out mind messages to Bron and Star as she ran not being able to see where they were, first to the accommodation rooms, empty, then on to the dining hall finding them all sitting together eating and drinking. They all turned as she entered and Bron's weakening mind spoke these fatal words aloud.

"Hello Sala, come and join us this is a special party before we all go home".

She screamed in full voice.

"No, no, stop you must stop".

She knew it was too late, this was no party, their glasses were half empty and they were not going home. They had been induced with the promise of a journey home to eat and drink in celebration when no one else was around. The changes happened so fast; she moved to Porta who looked at her and smiled but then screwed his brow as her projected thoughts of her love for him faded from his floundering brain. She turned to Bron who's normally smiling face became vacant whilst she watched, he tipped his head to look at her more closely but it lacked recognition. Too late indeed; her three friends stopped their fateful meal just sat unmoving, unthinking, empty, lifeless. Violent anger and hatred welled in Sala's frame, emotions never perceived or experienced before, she wanted to hit out in revenge but she was standing in the dining hall alone.

An amnesia most profound had taken them; no memory of people place and upbringing remained with Porta, Bron or Star, they had no knowledge of Sala or of their home in the commune; Horden and Jeska had already been taken, strangers all; she attempted to speak to them but there was no response to her questions, not knowing their names, none had any memory of past events. Like animals with empty minds they were now ready to be schooled in the ways of Lethe then forced to breed like the oxen. Sala wept, her ability to mind speak with her family was lost, she wanted to die.

Sala was devastated, so traumatised she could only stand and watch as three Overseers came and led them away, it was the last she saw or spoke to them for a very long time. They had been taken, moved somewhere unknown to Sala and placed with an elder to educate them in a totally new way. Sala discovered this much later following their re-education programme; whilst learning about their new home and its inhabitants they had become fully indoctrinated with lies, believing it is where they came from; finally induced to cohabit with those chosen by elders as being a normal part of their lives.

Metrin avoided Sala ignored her outrage knowing it would pass with time; she made no attempts to enter her mind leaving her to adjust to the loss she was faced with. Once the Overseers were confident the transformation was complete Sala was finally allowed to speak with them, her first endeavour was to give them back their names; they believed she was one of the educators so accepted her word concerning their names but they thought she was a bit odd so failed to respond to her strange questions and statements about a past they had no memory of. The meetings were painful and going nowhere so she decided to leave them in peace to live their new lives, sad and still very angry at her great loss, the persons they were before had gone, they were like strangers, more, they were indeed total strangers.

She saw whatever it was in this water was powerful and had erased Porta's memory in just a few moments, so from then on she only drank in the dining hall what she knew was safe and from the same source as others. If it ever came to be her turn by force she would not swallow but allow the offending liquid to run unnoticed down inside her tunic to soak onto the material below. Her pretence of drinking, when in fact she hadn't, would be hidden deep in her mind. She never knew how the drug had been administered; it had in fact been extracted from the Pinson tree by Ouisa the Substance Science Master and given to her friends hidden in their food and if given to her in the same way she too would have succumbed. She never understood why she had been spared but assumed Metrin had something to do with that decision.

The days passed slowly almost halfway through another season, isolated from her friends, her reason to live had been destroyed; she was totally lonely in a strange land among strangers. Sala felt a dreadful sadness at the loss of her brother Bron, her Bond Porta and friend Star. They had not tried to feed her the waters as she thought they would, now she felt it might be a release from this wretched state if they did. She was so despondent, ignoring her former determination to conceal her deliberate spillage, she even thought about going to the lake and drinking herself. Metrin sensed the depressing thoughts so set a guard by the lake, knowing Sala would lose the gift as had the others; given time she still had hopes Sala would come round to her way of thinking.

Having been instilled with a new morality in complete contrast to their original upbringing in the communes and the isolated ways of Lethe, their underlying animal instincts were nurtured by the Overseers. The three boys, Star and Jeska were encouraged to mate with the chosen and similarly indoctrinated Letheans. Star became pregnant as had Jeska previously and three girls by Bron and another three by Porta. Only one of the girls partnered by Horden conceived. The Overseers had no idea if the offspring would be born with the gift or not they would have to wait several seasons to truly know and even longer to see if it was permanent.

Enough time had passed for Metrin to revive her plan she appeared at Sala's side almost every day, gently urging her to change her mind.

"Sala I am deeply sorry I was not honest with you and your people have thus been treated; I will make sure you and they have a good life with us. Their children may yet have been passed the gift of an open mind even though your colleagues have lost theirs to the Waters. They themselves may yet have the gift revived, our Science Master of the Senses is working to this end. It is my wish you cohabit with one of our men, one who has the strongest gift, your child may then become the saviour of our people and of your commune, for without the Overseers the communes are doomed".

She continued to feel angry in Metrin's presence never trusting anything she said again but hid her suspicions well; anger an emotion still unfamiliar to Sala she found harder to hide. Metrin was not fooling her, she said she was sorry too but as the Senior Overseer, she could have stopped it from happening. The communes would survive and grow regardless, probably even better without interference from the Overseers, for Sala's people were resilient and hard working and all this science has not given the Letheans any real improvement in their lives. She had been lied to from the beginning and had no second thoughts about doing the same, she could be as convincing in her lies and fine words as this Overseer.

"Let me think about what you ask Metrin. I have lost my Bond Porta as his mind is no longer as it was, he no longer knows who I am, but by our custom we are required to remain for life as one. To Bond again or cohabit with another is not conventional till one or the other has passed. However because as he has made children with another I feel he is no longer with me either physically or mentally. I may yet consider him to have passed and be no longer Bonded. I would like to have children so if I can come to accept this premise I may yet agree to your request, just give me a little more time".

They had taken away everything she had cared for all with their expressed *'for the good of the communes'* as their excuse, used people like breeding animals with no thought or care. To Sala, any life without compassion was not worth living. The Overseers thought they were the answer to man's ascendency towards a better being, to become true man but their manipulation had revealed some underlying real ambitions that were a step back from the ideals they were supposed to believe in. Sala felt helpless, they didn't even realise what they were doing was wrong. She had no intention to concede to the demands of the Lethe elder Metrin, she must find a way to leave, to get back to her commune and warn them of the true objectives of the Overseers. Her words to Metrin had bought her time.

Chapter Ten

Mind Science had been Metrin's subject of study and teaching for most of her adult life, there was nothing about the human brain she did not know. Her control over the other Science Masters had developed unintentionally at first. Her age and superior telepathic ability led the others to look to her for advice and guidance. The genuine guidance given initially was benevolent and helpful but gradually erred towards promoting the personal desires of Metrin herself. Now advice was seldom sought but was given unsolicited in the form of a command to be obeyed without question. The Science Masters enjoyed the benefits of pandering to her demands but most did so with reluctance. In the early days of her rise to power those who dared resist mysteriously lost their minds to the Waters, no one in recent seasons had suffered such a fate, her control was absolute.

During her time in Lethe Sala's chosen subject had been The Science of Mind under the guidance of the Science Master Metrin. Most lessons were conducted by helpers and other Overseers with rare appearances from the Master. Her main reason for opting for this subject was because she thought it important to learn more about Metrin even though she really wanted to study in depth the Science of Air.

The thought processes used during mental transmission from one being to another were not understood by even the Science Masters. Accepted as another sense, but unlike sight, taste, smell, hearing and touch, which were physical and chemical well understood functions of the body, telepathy was an unknown quality. The recognised five senses were linked to the brain by nerves and receptors, the sixth, telepathy, was an exception. These were all analysed during her brief period of study at the Senses Science classes. The telepathic receptor, for it was thought there must be one, to link the brain to the outside world and the receptor of another person, was a mystery. Sala pondered on the problem whenever she was resting, searching within her special mind for a moment of revelation; it never came. She finally came to the conclusion there may never be a solution to the conundrum, the brain itself could be the receptor, or maybe there was no receptor at all or even the need for one. To make contact with another being something must move from her brain to the brain of the other person; was it something physical like the stream of vibrating air waves when transmitting sound? Sound requires air or another substance to move from one place to another, what do brain waves need? Sight required light part of a spectrum of radio frequencies, energy which travels in free space, could thought be a frequency wave of some kind? Tests showed no measurable frequencies emanating from two subjects whilst transmitting their mind speak. Why do siblings have the ability and not others? The questions came thick and fast, she stopped all thought of the impenetrable subject and finally slept.

Her lessons at Mind Science included studying the areas of the physical brain itself. Dissection of the brains of small animals were conducted in the laboratory by her and the other students. Each part of the brain and its functions were discussed. It was not until the second season when the brain of a human was used that Sala's interest peaked, she never knew where this brain had come from and never asked. The dissection was carried out by the master with each stage explained in detail, apart from size the differences between man and the higher animals was less than Sala expected but there were areas where its real function was unknown or inconclusive. Areas of interest to Sala in trying to discover where her telepathic gift lay were difficult to determine. Of all the basic functions of the major areas the Hippocampus which involved awareness and spatial memory seemed to be the most likely candidate. The other functions were also considered but there was no real conclusion. The Cerebellum which synchronises other brain systems seemed a good possibility but proved not to be so. Having spent many days learning the names and details of the brains many parts and functions she was no closer to an answer to where her gift lay than she was during her first lesson. Most of the nerves which served the brain and through which it controlled the body sent the information in and out via the spinal column. Perhaps the sensor for telepathy uses the spine itself as the receptor, Metrin and the other elders thought it was the dome of the skull; but with no conclusive proof. The ability to mind speak had a limited but variable range dependent upon the individuals. Intervening structures like buildings had no effect, whatever signal was being transmitted it either passed through or around them. Everyone tested could be contacted within the confines of the city and a short distance beyond but not much further. The Elders who had the most potent ability never offered themselves to take these tests. Sala suspected they had a much greater power in this respect and did not want it to be known; she later found this was indeed the case, some like Metrin had an almost unlimited range. Her own range had not been tested but she was sure it extended well beyond the confines of Lethe.

All the while she slept, meditated or was awake the development of her gift grew. A new sense of a power within her seemed to come from her whole body and not just her mind. Security from invasive thoughts of others came naturally now, it was permanently in place without effort and impenetrable. Her fear of the Overseers waned as their comparative strength diminished while hers grew stronger.

Metrin kept close watch on Sala, where regular covert attempts to enter her mind were rebuffed every time, a natural reaction not unexpected. Very few had the power to resist Metrin's pressure. When her name was openly called Sala accepted the request, again a normal response followed by reasonable conversations between them. The subject matter was irrelevant to Metrin, she was just assessing her prodigy's ability to resist her probing.

Metrin's need for Sala to breed with the male she had selected at the moment was uppermost amongst her desires. The young man was of good body stronger than many, one of the most powerful minds amongst the males. Yona was deliberately made part of the Mind student group in order to be near to Sala. Metrin avoided mind contact with him as she knew Sala would quickly detect her presence in him and find out her intentions. She was trusting in the gregarious nature of the commune people to develop an accord with others. The students often operated in pairs when experimenting and Metrin made sure the instructors put these two together as much as possible. Sala never suspected the reason Yona and her were so often a team, she found him to be clever, a real practical help with dissection and he guided her through the language and writing difficulties with great patience. The initial physical attraction she felt faded fast for he seemed devoid of emotion; never laughing or smiling, her banter and quips were ignored, he just didn't understand them, her efforts to be friendly were lost on this passionless boy.

Metrin herself had little understanding of Salas reaction to this male, it went very well at first, she could see by \the way Sala looked at him she was attracted and could not see why the partnership was not progressing further. She left things as they were in the hope of an improvement. Her conversations on the subject of cohabiting always met the 'Bonding for Life' promise as a barrier, but recently Sala had hinted she may change her mind now Porta was no longer physically with her, he was a renewed being, a different person not the one she was Bonded to, saying she may be able to consider Porta as truly gone from her life given more time.

Metrin never grasped the concept of Bonding, it was so alien, the whole idea seemed unnatural to her, the exact opposite of what it truly was. Cohabiting was not something Metrin would ever consider, the thought of intimate physical contact she found abhorrent but these commune people seemed to enjoy it, they did it all the time so why is Sala being so difficult. The cohabiting of those who had been subjected to the Waters was a complete failure, as Metrin feared the loss of telepathy went hand in hand with the loss of memory, the resultant children had no sign of the gift. She was becoming impatient with this primitive girl of the communes she was the only one left who could transfer her telepathic gift to others; her mind abilities were exactly what was needed to inject some new life into the population of Lethe but she was not cooperating as wanted, still she had indicated she would consider changing her mind soon which gave Metrin some hope. It may not be Yona she cohabits with; no matter there were other suitable males, Metrin would seek another male who may develop a better affinity with Sala.

Chapter Eleven

Long before her plan to escape Sala had been amazed by the flying machine. Since her first journey to Lethe she spent considerable time in researching its history and development. She also studied other scientific subjects related to genealogy and the insemination techniques developed to procreate their species. She showed interest over many areas of the sciences in order not to draw attention to the fact she was overly interested in the flying machine. She didn't know why she acted this way some instinct to do so took hold.

There were three machines which operated using two principles from nature, gravity and momentum. The subjects were explained to her by the Science Master Peto, although she understood some of the concepts little of what was said about how it was used by the machines was absorbed. Gravity Inversion allowed it to rise above the ground and the Earth's Rotational Momentum allowing it to travel forward, how the machines used those forces remained a mystery to her. There were limits to the height and speeds it could reach. When the gravitational pull of the earth matched the inverse force generated by the machine it could go no higher and the velocity of the rotating earth at ground level was the maximum speed at which the craft could move; again not really understood. She said little during the lessons just nodded and smiled now and again, the teachers could see in her mind that she did not always understand, so would explain again in more simple terms. They must have thought she was stupid but did not show it.

The original ship and by far the largest, the one in which they first achieved flight, was on display in the science centre; it had not moved for a very long time. The second and the smallest with only two seats and a box shaped separate storage area was still used during local flights for the harvesting of special crops of flora and chemicals used in medicine and occasionally the trapping of small animals used for research. The third, in which she and the others had travelled to Lethe, was designed to carry up to eight people, now used almost solely for visits to the communes with the occasional search for any new groups of man which may be emergent. It was magnificent, the smooth body of a silvery metal she had never seen before that shone in the light and reflected images of whatever was around it. Clear material moulded seamlessly into the body allowed the occupants a view in all directions. The interior could be arranged to carry anything, fitted with storage pods or plush seating as needed for the task in hand. How and where these wonderful machines had been made was not revealed; both were kept in a large building adjacent to and part of the main Air Science centre.

    Sala used to go there often just to look and wonder, remembering the journey from Five to Lethe as a highlight of her experiences amongst these people. Sometimes she sat on the low wall along the perimeter of the room dreaming of when she and Porta would go back home; she had learnt so much and wanted to share it with her Ma, her Pa and all the others at her commune. Her visits had been observed by a young male who was responsible for the maintenance of these machines, he kept out of sight at first too shy to approach the small stranger with bronze skin and silver grey hair. One day Sala spotted him in the hulls reflection as he ducked out of sight behind the machine; she never attempted mind contact but called out to him as he crouched below away from her view.

    "Who's there, my name is Sala"?

She knew he was still there but he didn't respond.

"I just like this spot it is quiet away from all the others, I hope it's alright for me to be here, what's your name"?

She wasn't going away and as he was getting cramp crouching down so low was forced to stand revealing himself above the body of the machine. He looked directly at her and smiled his yellow skin had turned slightly orange with embarrassment unable to speak.

"Have I disturbed you. I'm sorry I'll go".

He didn't want her to go, no one hardly ever came here it would be good to have someone to talk to apart from the Overseers. He called to her as she rose from her seat and began to leave.

"No don't go It's okay for you to be here, I'm not busy at the moment".

Sala noticed the orange of his skin had faded back to the more normal ochre yellow. She returned to her seat on the wall.

"Do you study here? err..... I don't know your name.."?

"Oh no I just look after the machines; my name is Lunn. Oh dear I have forgotten yours I'm sorry I know you told me but I was a bit flustered."

"Don't worry its easily done; my name is Sala. Hello Lunn, I came from the communes to study here".

"I know where you come from everyone does".

This was the beginning of a true friendship, the first between a Lethean and one from the communes. She spent many hours with the young male Lunn whose work was to maintain the two machines. He told her everything he knew about the machines and his role at Air Science. She learnt their source of power was from a cylindrical cell the size of a man's arm, using a gas and a crystal substance. This had not been part of the Science Masters lesson so Lunn tried to explain its function with drawings and symbols but Sala had not been able to learn the language well enough yet to understand fully. She did closely observe Lunn whilst he removed and refitted the cell after recharging.

Following their initial voice contact conversations were now in the mind as was common here, there were very few occasions when anyone spoke aloud.

"I have to replenish the cell with new gas after each journey; there is enough energy for many journeys but if allowed to stand idle too long the gas goes stale the cell dies and cannot be revived. As long as you keep flying and replace the gas it will live for many seasons".

"You mean the power to drive this machine is alive"?

"Of course all power comes from the living it's a basic science fact did you not know this"?

"What if it dies when you are a long way from here"?

"It's not likely, all the power sources have an unlimited life, I have never known one to fail under my care. If away or idle for a long time I believe it is possible to replenish the energy by generating gas through the power of the sun, it takes quite a long time and you would need good weather I think. No one ever has had to do it in my knowledge; I'll show you how if you like".

Lunn then removed a pack from a storage locker at the rear of the machine and demonstrated how to set up the sun capture device on the roof and its connections to the power source. It was simple enough she could do that.

"You would have to cover huge distances and be away for at least two seasons before emergency measures like that were required; besides replacing the gas, like I am doing here, is done in a few moments and is all that is ever needed."

"What is the gas where does it come from"?

'It is made in the pyramid gardens, they use left-over rotting vegetation in closed vessels the gas is given off as the material decays and collected in these bags, it doesn't smell very nice".

"Oh so that is what it was, I've noticed the smell sometimes but didn't say anything. We only learn the ways of the land and animals in the Commune all this science is new to me".

He didn't want her to leave. He wasn't a teacher but her interest in the machines might be a way for him to extend her visit.

"Don't worry I will instruct you if you want Sala".

"Thank you Lunn that will be good".

Over the following season he taught her all he knew. He started with the mind linking device which was at the heart of the machine; the person designated to fly had to communicate with the device via the hand control set in front of the central seat, in combination with the mind; the wishes of the pilot would be processed by the link and the machine would follow the path desired.

"How does it work Lunn"?

"It's not easy Sala, it has a to be practised for some time before you could be successful. Remember it is not the control handle that actually controls the machine it is your mind. The handle it just the link to isolate anyone other than the person holding it from influencing the machines movements".

"But what if you got it wrong wouldn't the machine fall to the ground and be destroyed"?

"Well not exactly it won't let you do anything to cause a problem and if you let go the hand control the machine slows to a stop, if the pilot does not recover in a set time it searches the nearby terrain and will automatically land in a safe place or hover above ground if nowhere safe is close".

"What happens if the pilot doesn't recover his position at the control"?

"An emergency signal is generated, I don't really know, probably we would send the small machine to see what was wrong. I seem to remember from something I read or heard about the Overseers being able to bypass the control and use their combined minds to bring the machine back, that may be just a story though. It has never happened in my life Sala, no one gets to fly for real until they are ready. Follow me".

Lunn moved out of the building housing the machines and his workshop along one of the many corridors to another building where they entered a small room. At first it seemed completely empty until Lunn went to a small console behind the door. He pressed his hand against a wall pad and the room became like they were inside the flying machine. It was not real but a projected image, however a real physical seat and control handle rose from the floor.

"Here we have the trainer Sala where all the Overseers come to learn how to fly. They can make mistakes as many times as they like here and won't do any damage".

"Can I try it Lunn"?

"I don't know if it is permitted, it's really for the Overseers, I'll have to call Peto and ask".

"Come on Lunn it won't take long, anyway he is not around to ask and probably busy, you know he won't like you to interrupt by mind calling and it may take ages to find someone else who can say yes, then the opportunity will be lost. Overseers aren't the only ones who fly; you do, and there are others too I have seen them; besides I know you want to show me how it works. Please, I won't tell anyone, we can keep it to ourselves".

"That is true I suppose it will be okay after all its not the real machine and can't do any harm".

He began by explaining the thought commands. The initial command RISE was always the first which would lift the machine just clear of the ground, the command LIFT would raise it slowly up until it reached the height you wanted and set in your mind when you would command HOLD. Then AHEAD or BACK would move it in the desired direction at ever increasing speed until HOLD again would maintain the speed. Turning used the Commands LEFT or RIGHT with the HOLD as the terminating command. Lunn then led Sala to the control showing her how to grip the handle at the same time as thinking a specific command.

"It is easy enough Sala just sit, take the control in your hand, relax and let your mind communicate with the interface. It will get to know you and what you want; as time passes you will hardly have to think the commands it will gain a rapport with you and follow your desired direction speed and height There are many safety features like I said, if you let go it will land, also it will not let you fly into any object or land too quickly. It will not go too high or travel beyond a safe speed. The training program will let you fly in what appears to be the outside. It will present problems; objects like trees when you are low down and hills when you are much higher will appear at random. Clouds, bad weather too such as storms and mist will be generated to test you; even I never know what will be presented, it is different every time. Right I will turn it on, remember start with the RISE command let's see how you get on".

She couldn't believe how real it seemed or how easy it was at first, but as time progressed she was presented with a sudden storm which threw the machine about, even the floor she was standing on moved trying to dislodge her grip on the control, concentration was broken and the machine slowed to a stop.

"Regardless of the conditions Sala you must stay in mental contact with the interface or it won't know what you want. Try again".

It took four more tries before I could continue without losing control, I used all the commands and dealt with obstacles and bad weather eventually bringing the simulator machine back to land without a hitch.

"Very good Sala you are a quick learner, but we must go now a lesson is scheduled soon so we must not be here".

"I enjoyed that Lunn, can we come again another day"?

"Maybe let's go. The Overseers are near".

"Okay; do you not like it when they are near"?

"Not much, when they see you up close they look deep in your mind, you can hide nothing, they will know you have been in the trainer and I let you use it without permission".

"What would they say, you did nothing wrong"?

"Don't ask. Let's just leave and return to the workshop".

One more insight into this place, even its own people live in fear of these Overseers; another good reason to leave. Of all the people here her friendship with Lunn was not as hollow as it was with others, he was almost normal.

She had the opportunity to use the simulated flying machine one more time but after that Lunn became reticent, saying one Overseer had asked about Sala's presence. Fortunately the Overseer did not probe his mind beyond accepting his answer of her casual interest so he had managed to block the fact she had been in the simulator saying she was just curious following up on her Science Master lessons. She did however enter the real machine again when Lunn fitted a newly charged power source to which she paid particular attention. One thing he'd never mentioned but Sala saw it in his thoughts as Lunn was working, was the normal practice of removing the power source when leaving the machine unattended. Sala didn't know why, but she would remember to do the same if ever she had the opportunity and need.

She missed her visits with Lunn, a friendship had developed between them he even showed signs of empathy lacking in most others she met. He filled to some extent the lonely periods which dominated her singular life here. There was no way she wanted the Overseers to suspect her motives by spending too much time with Lunn so moved on now to study other things, interest shown here, more than with other subjects, was bound to draw unwanted attention, she would bide her time, the perfect chance would come her way sometime soon enough, when it did she would be ready.

Her nights here were the worst periods of loneliness; sleep was difficult and often dogged with dreams of her life as it might have been. Only the songs of the elders and the ones her Ma sang to her as a child lulled her into a more restful slumber as she hummed the familiar tunes to herself in her worst moments of despair.

Little oil lamp burning bright
See me safely through the night
When the darkness covers sky
Your sweet shimmer lights my eye
Sleep will see me until day

Your jaded flame then fades away

She was very keen to learn anything new and sought to study the specialist subjects of each of the Science Masters and understand their symbols and drawings. Lunn had become a friend, despite his very different background there was an inherent rapport between them, he was a good source of information but she avoided him when he was at work so as not to draw attention to her fascination with the flying machine. She saw him on occasion in the food halls and would sit and talk about life here in general; he helped to fill the void left by the loss of her family at the same time advancing her knowledge of his complex society. The limited knowledge she had gained about how to fly the machines would have to be enough, afraid to return to the building that housed them as it may invite ill-advised scrutiny. She would ask him questions when she met him whilst dining, her interest would not be noticed amongst so many, everyone there would be conversing in small groups, minds blocked to everyone else, she would do the same with Lunn. She failed to understand how the live crystal worked and had never seen it up close; fascinated by this device which controlled the machine Sala decided this day to find out more.

"Lunn, I've been wondering what you do all day. It can't take long looking after just two machines".

"No it doesn't. I do go through some tests now and then; I give lessons in the simulator which breaks down often enough to need my attention most days; apart from that and gassing the crystal power source I read a lot".

"How many crystals do have to keep recharged Lunn"?

"Only six, one and a spare for each machine. Before I came there were several more but whoever looked after them did not understood about the gas and replenishment so all the ones stored away have been neglected and no longer work; there must be fifty or more dead ones in boxes back there. It was lucky in the old days they flew the tree machines regularly and rotated the spares or there may have been none".

"Where do they come from"?

"Nobody knows, it is not recorded anywhere. There are tales of lands where the crystals were formed in great fires thousands of season ago, but they are just stories I think".

"Can I see one up close"?

"If you like, there is not much to look at. Actually that's not strictly true I see them so often I no longer take notice; you'll see".

Lunn went inside and came out with a source its crystal inside its protective gas filled chamber. He opened the end to reveal the glistening stone, it was not just reflecting ambient light but a multi coloured radiation emanated from within.

"It looks like it really is alive".

"Yes quite spectacular, unlike the dead ones. I must close it now Sala as the gas is escaping, I'll have to recharge it again before it is put to use".

"What do the dead ones look like"?

"They are plain black, still reflecting light a little from the shiny surface but nothing from within. I tried to regenerate them but failed".

"That's a shame, still you still have these. What about the big old machine, can it fly".

"I don't see why not; I mean it will probably need a good clean and a full run through of the test process first. All three machines were made long ago but never seem to age; as long as the power sources are gassed and the maintenance procedures of some moving parts is kept up all should be okay. I have a workshop full of spares there are never any problems, well nothing I can't fix anyway".

"How come the big one is left where it is".

"No idea, there are never more than a few passengers so its not really needed, I imagine it's a bit of a beast to manoeuvre in a confined space; it's been standing there gathering dust for as long as I have been here. Why do you ask, you don't want a ride it that old thing do you"?

"Of course not. You know me just interested that's all".

There was danger in studying one subject more than another, the Overseers were always watching and probing. If they had even an inkling of what she had hidden deep in her mind they would act for sure.

Sala had a small bag usually used to keep her personal items, it now held two water containers and some dried food saved from her rations over the past few days. Time was close now, Sala was ready to leave, although her last lesson from Lunn in the trainer was some time ago, it had gone well and was well remembered too; she felt confident enough to fly the real thing. There would be only one opportunity, if it failed they would certainly not let her have the freedom she had enjoyed so far and would probably just feed her the Waters and be done with her. She had one small regret; her friendship with Lunn had become real, which at first had been a pretence in order to find out about the flying machine. She had not confided in him her true intentions as he would not be able to hide it if confronted. Although she feared for his safety when they found her and their precious machine gone, his mind would show he had not been aware of her objective. She had little choice but to leave him to deal with the Overseers for Metrin was losing patience with her delaying tactics.

She left her bed late in the night well after the dark sky had been over the land for some time. The whole of Lethe was sleeping, she had practiced the route many times with her eyes closed but carried a small light just in case there were some unknown obstacles since her last check. The building housing the large machine was a good walk from her sleeping quarters but she hurried undeterred by the darkness towards the building entrance. She had not been here at this time of night during her practice runs and was surprised to find the door where she had entered originally was not only closed but locked, it was opened during the day by Lunns palm on the sensor pad she didn't realise it was closed at night, she tried it did not recognise her hand. She turned on the light briefly to see her way and moved to the front of the building to the large opening where the machine's exit was located. Her pulse was racing, if this was closed too she would have to abandon her attempted escape for now. The large exit gates were not closed she breathed a sigh of relief, slipped inside and approached the entry hatch. Again with bated breath and pounding heart she pressed the unsecured entry pad, the hatch door slid silently open; she stepped inside, the door automatically closing behind her. She had chosen this moment as she found out from Lunn he had recently replenished the power pack and no new scheduled flights had been ordered, a time when there would be no one in the area of the airship building.

    She sat in front of the control, shaking fingers reached out and lightly enfolded the handgrip, RISE was in her mind; nothing happened. Panic at first but then remembered that Lunn always removed the power source when the machine was not in use. She moved to the rear of the cabin having no idea where the source would be stored or even if it was on board. What if it was locked away somewhere or back in the workshop she would have to to abandon her attempt; she shone her light around the cabin catching a sparkling reflection emanating from the container's shiny surface as the beam swept by where it lay; stowed safely in a cradle right next to its connection point. With shaking hands she inserted the crystal power unit into the socket and returned to the control. She could feel her heart pounding in her chest, held her breath as the machine lifted at her command to RISE; this was it no turning back now, the feeling of movement was real and alarming, unlike in the simulator where a mistake could be rectified; she had to be extra careful when leaving the building's unlit exit. Transition to the slow forward motion was smooth and silent, once outside LIFT took her way above the ground and although she could see nothing in the dark ahead a feint glow from the pyramid gardens far below let her know she was well clear of any obstruction. No longer reliant on the machines inbuilt safety features, Sala gave the machine the go ahead speeding away secure in her escape believing it would not be noticed till the light returned the following day.

Metrin was furious when he discovered the Flying Machine was missing. She knew immediately who was responsible and chastised herself for not seeing it coming. She invaded the mind of Lunn to discover he had been allowed to show her too much but was saved from her wrath when she saw he knew nothing of Sala's intentions.

The power to deceive confirmed one thing this girl had gifts way above all other communers, she was glad to have saved her from the Waters. Now no more equivocating she would bring her back and start breeding her by force if necessary but would later accomplish her real objective by sucking her mind dry blending all of Sala's energy with her own; ultimate power would then be hers.

She called upon six Overseers to join together and target the living crystal of the flying machine, to constantly apply pressure to bring it home. The technique had not been tried before with these Overseers but a much younger Metrin had been part of a group to bring back a machine when the Overseer guiding it had become ill and died whilst on route to a commune. She instructed them on what to do and sat with them during the initial attempts. Once they were adept in the technique she left them to it, only returning when it appeared to be working and they were breaking through. Again another sign of Salas ability for whenever the signs of weakening were seen the power source was removed and the Overseers lost contact. She persisted in the hope Sala may weaken or be less vigilant; one time with her guard dropped would be enough.

Chapter Twelve

The flying machine no longer responded well to Sala's wishes, her hand grew numb with the constant gripping of the interface arm, her demands to rise and turn reacted sluggishly, much slower than when she first took control. She was tired and contact between her mind and the machine weakened with each passing moment, she wasn't sure if it was just fatigue or an influence of some force she suspected may come from elsewhere. There was little choice, she must land somewhere, anywhere, as soon as possible. She must disconnect the power source and gather her strength whilst she still had some degree of influence over the machines path. There were no open areas she could see, the forest below extended in all directions. She flew on, all her will needed to keep some safe distance above the never ending canopy.

A river winding its way through the woodland came suddenly into view as she passed over and was gone in an instant. She willed the machine to slow and turn back, its reluctance now confirmed as a force emanating from outside reached out overshadowing her efforts. If she let go now the force would take over and bring her back to Lethe. The sweat poured from her brow as she endeavoured to block the outside attempt at domination, all her energy poured through the tightly gripped interface. The machine answered her desperate plea turning slowly to reveal a silver ribbon of water ahead and below with a small lake beyond. She had no idea if the machine would float so tried to avoid any deep looking water; too exhausted she could do no more than descend towards the only area free of trees she could see. The machine came quietly to a stop, half on the bank and half in the water of the slowly flowing river; it seemed sound enough, there wasn't much she could do about it if it wasn't.

Sala let go the interface arm her hand deadened by fatigue, hurried to the power cell, lifted it clear of the socket carefully placing it in its cradle. She was secure now; the minds of the Overseers could not reach her here whilst the power source was not connected and the machine was inactive. Her mind block remained active, strong enough to keep her safe. The earlier story told by Lunn was not a myth, the Overseer's minds could combine and control the machine at a distance but not whilst she was at the control and strong enough to resist. What little daylight was left filtered down through the trees, its pink glow revealing very little but green all around, the lake now out of view with the river behind and in front as far as could be seen. She would eat and drink a little from her meagre rations try and sleep in one of the passenger seats, regain her strength and continue on when the light returned. She had been travelling for what seemed like days and was completely lost but Sala was determined to find her commune or would die in the search.

She woke with a strange feeling something was not right, there were people close by she could hear their thoughts but they made very little sense; words she had not heard before all jumbled together with many that were familiar forming in several nearby minds. The light had returned but there were strange noises and a flickering across the glass canopy. Sala rose from the reclined seat at the rear of the machine and began to move forward. She saw two faces peering through the glass, big dark brown eyes with blue tinted skin framed by shiny black hair streaked with silver, the eyes were darting from side to side scanning the interior but had not yet seen her in the darker recesses at the rear of the cabin. She moved closer towards the window and as she did so the eyes widened momentarily as they caught sight of her, in a moment the faces and their owners disappeared into the green.

Sala looked through the glass in all directions but could see no sign of her visitors. Her immediate thought was to venture outside and search but held back unsure if whoever was out there would be happy to see her. She was not afraid, the feeling of real fear she had not known at any time during her life in the commune, there had never been any kind of threat to her or her family until her recent encounter with the Letheans; even then her reaction was one of indignation rather than apprehension. She would wait by the window low down ready for when they returned, out of sight from prying eyes; they would not see her unless whoever came back moved close enough. She could sense their curiosity so knew they would come back soon, whenever they did in her current position she would see them well before they spotted her. She did not have to wait long, a single face appeared looking towards the rear where she had been seen before, she crouched lower still out of sight so she could study the face more closely. A second then a third face appeared followed by six or seven more. One clambered on to the top of the cabin clearly visible through the glass canopy. None so far had seen her, she stayed perfectly still thinking if she showed herself they would scarper like before. They appeared to be quite young, mostly children of maybe twelve or so seasons and were clothed in what appeared to be animal skins crudely fashioned, their exposed arms and legs, like their faces, were blue, not like the sky but lighter almost white but not quite. The hair of the youngsters was black, with two older adults showing streaks of silvery grey. She couldn't tell if they were male or female but felt by their soft facial features, which were not unlike hers, the majority were more likely to be female. They were talking to each other but although she could not understand all the words their thoughts conveyed wonder and a little alarm. She rose slowly smiling, as her face came into view several of them shrank back out of sight but the one on the roof remained unmoving as did the two with grey streaked hair. Sala looked into the eyes of the grey haired woman and directed her thoughts to her alone; she knew immediately she was female and although the languages were a little different Sala's gentle friendly mind spoken words were understood and her thoughts were immediately reciprocated. She mouthed and mind spoke her name to which the woman excitedly shouted back "*Sheff I am Sheff*".

Sala had no fear as she moved to open the cabin hatch, the minds of these people showed nothing but wonder and kindness. As the hatch door released they all moved away from the machine and stood on the bank of the river close to the treeline, the girl on the roof scrambled down as Sala emerged and ran to the one named Sheff to cling to her arm, with a tinge of disquiet emanating from her young mind; Sala sent a though of comfort and her name directly to her. She let go Sheff's arm and waved to Sala mind speaking her name in response, "*I am Kitta*". With a calmness in her mind she stepped down onto the sandy bank to become surrounded by all their bodies. Suddenly they were all around her touching her arms and legs, pulling at her clothes and roughing up her hair. She almost fell back through the open door feeling trapped unable to shift from the spot where she stood, uncomfortable at first but realising it was just the novelty of them seeing someone so different, she relaxed and let them satisfy their curiosity.

She put her hand behind her back and closed the hatch with a touch, allowing her to lean back supported by the closed entry and waited to see what transpired. Their initial interest soon satisfied, the group surrounding her stepped back a little giving her room to move; Kitta left her mother's side approached boldly and took Salas hand leading her away from the machine towards her Ma the one named Sheff who smiled and took her other hand. Sala felt quite safe so allowed them to lead her away from the machine. They continued along the riverbank for some way before turning in towards the seemingly impenetrable forest. An opening appeared that was not visible until you were almost upon it; once through the gap a pathway opened out with plenty of room for them to move freely under the canopy of green; very little light filtered through but there was enough to see where you were going.

The young entourage followed, all chatting away about the strange visitor and her amazing machine. All the while she listened; as they continued on more and more of the language became understood. It took a while to settle to its rhythmic tone very different to her own but with a novel accent where they used their tongue to make a hollow clucking sound to punctuate their speech, some new words but with many the same. Through her mind the initial awkward sounding pronunciation became irrelevant, she knew what they were saying and more importantly what they were feeling; even some of the completely new words gained meaning when used in context.

They continued on for a distance of at least two of her communes longest fields when suddenly the light changed as the path became wider; here the overhanging trees were less dense. The first building appeared partly hidden amongst the greenery but with plenty of open space in front; it was made of wood, as expected but was more sophisticated in its construction than those in her own commune. To start it was very tall, as tall as the great barn back home and had openings way above the ground as well as those at ground level. People were leaning out of openings looking down at the group as they approached, obviously this building had at least two levels, something never seen in her own commune, although multiple floor levels were common to all buildings in Lethe. The people waved from above as she came level with them shouting down asking who this strange person was. They continued on with similar buildings appearing at intervals along the winding and ever widening path eventually coming to a halt outside one large building with a much wider frontage than the others, it also had a substantial entrance at ground level. Sheff let go her hand and pointed to the opening and spoke.

"This is the hall of the old ones please go in; the leader will wish to speak with you".

Although their voices were not easy to understand, Sala used her mind as well as ears to listen. Her own words by mind speak combined with her spoken word were understood by Sheff; it was clear to Sala these people were really unaware of the mind contact believing it all to be spoken aloud, the images being generated within their minds of their own making.

"My name is Rinn I have been given the task to speak for the people of the Outerworld; you are welcome here. I am told you came in the flying machine like some had come before you, but you are different, you speak with us kindly and have good temper towards us, unlike the tall yellow faced ones who came to influence the minds of our children and take them away by force".

"Thank you Rinn for the welcome, my name is Sala. I am not from the yellow people you speak of but have been confined by them for several seasons. I recently broke free from their land, a distant place they call Lethe, I escaped by taking their flying machine one night and have been seeking ever since to find the way back to my home. My journey has been very long, eventually I became exhausted and could not go on; I had no choice but to land near here, the river-bank being the only clear place in this vast green forest. It is by chance and my good fortune that you and I have found each other. You said the Lethean Overseer invaded your children's minds and removed them by force, how did this happen"?

"Our history shows these yellow people came many times and cleared the forest for us to plant crops for food but the forest would grow back each time, besides we were a hunting people and did not wish to plant seeds and sit waiting for them to mature. They gave up trying to help and left us to ourselves. They came one time pretending to be friends; they moved amongst our children giving some of them sweet drinks and telling stories. The children became sick and could no longer remember who they were and before we had any notion of what to do they took them from us and were gone. They returned another time but we were ready with our hunting spears and chased them into the forest, we have not seen them since. Did these people take you away from your home too"?

"They did but by subtle coercion not direct physical force; my family, friends and I all went with them willingly at first, having been persuaded it would be of great benefit for my people. They were false; their reasons were not as promised; like your children my Bond, my brother and my friends have had their minds stolen. There were two others from another commune gentle people with pale skin and golden hair; we had only brief contact before they were also stripped of their memories. I for some unknown reason was spared and have been living a lonely existence in their midst. I could no longer stand the isolation and loss of my friends so decided to find a way to leave. I learned many things during my time there including how to fly their machines".

"They allowed you to do this"?

"Oh no, it was not with their knowledge; when in their presence and during conversation I hid my true sentiments; I maintained a friendly untroubled appearance, giving the impression I was happy to be there, they thought I was inferior to them and no threat so they gave me the freedom to roam and learn their ways, they had no idea of what I really felt or had in mind. I built a friendly relationship with some of the teaching masters and in particular with one of the people who takes care of the machines and from them I learnt all I could".

"How did you escape?

"I went during the darkness; they all sleep for long periods at night so I waited till all was quiet and went to where the machines were kept. I carried a small torch …."

"What is this torch"?

"Oh Rinn, they have many things you and I have never seen before, all from the science of the past. The torch is a portable light with no flame, I can't explain how it works but it gives a bright glow lighting the dark spaces ahead for as long as you need, it helped me find my way to the machines".

At this point Rinn held up his hand to stop me.

"Excuse my furrowed brow it is not a reflection of my thoughts about you. I am becoming confused by your words some of which I do not understand so I now have many unknowns. I will try and follow your story as best I can. Sala do continue I will ask my questions when you have completed your speaking, but please speak more slowly".

"I am sorry Rinn I will but can only speak the words I know, I will try to use your words, the ones I understand many of which are new to me too, I will explain later, If I can. Anyway to I simply took the machine and left, no one noticed as they fly without making a sound. I had no idea where I was going but tried to fly in one direction for about the same time it took when we first came to Lethe hoping it would at least give me a valid starting point. I then made a one quarter turn and plotted a winding route either side of the path at the chosen range hoping to see some place I recognised, but up till now nothing has appeared familiar. I must have slept much longer than I thought on my first journey so have misjudged the distance and time, I fear I am completely lost. Their elders have power over the machine from a great distance, they are trying to take control and bring it back home. I have been able to hold them off for now but became too tired to continue. Now you can ask me what you want to know".

"The questions can come later Sala you look so tired; your bronze skin has become paler even as we speak; have you eaten"?

"I brought plenty of drink and a little food with me but the real food has been finished for some time, I only have sweet cakes left, I am quite hungry".

"Then we will stop now and continue after you have eaten and slept; it will give me time to think."

With that the old man Rinn stood and left the building, a few moments later Kitta and her mother came and led her away to what Sala found out was their home. They sat her at the table and gave her some bread, not from the fine maize flour used at her home but with a deep brown coarse consistency. The bowl of stew had a strong tasting meat of some kind with strange root vegetables and leaves resembling those of the chard they have at home. She ate heartily as the fare was tasty and more than welcome, finding the bread difficult to chew was a source of amusement to young Kitta, she laughed at Sala's attempt to do so. She took a piece of the bread and dipped it in the stew allowing it to soak up the juices, she then offered it to her which she took finding it much more palatable. With a full mouth Sala nodded her approval, Kitta laughed again and sat close next to her on the same bench and leaned her head against her body. Their conversation was through the spoken word with Sala using mind contact at the same time to help her with the language differences.

'What is your age Kitta"?

"I am twelve seasons and seven noms".

"I don't understand what is this nom"?

"It is the big round light in the sky it comes and goes each season many times more than ten I think".

"Ah I see now we call it laune; it cycles each season about twelve times; I learnt this from our elders songs".

"You learn with songs how is that"?

"The elders have many songs which they learnt from their elders and their elders before them. We all go and listen and learn the words. The elders then explain the meaning with stories; everyone knows many songs before they are full grown. It is how we come to know ourselves and each other. It helps us choose what our place in the commune will be".

"I like that; we too have teaching but it is different, we listen and learn the words spoken by a master from the books. We have to write it down from memory each day. I think I would prefer to learn from songs".

"What is write and books I do not understand"?

"You don't read and write! I can't explain in words, I will have to show you".

Kitta left the room and came back a few moments later with what looked like a box. She placed it on Sala's lap and opened it to reveal the pages. Sala looked in wonder as Kitta, turned the pages and read aloud to her; the shapes on the thin sheets were strangely familiar, she had seen similar during the science lessons in Lethe but had never had a chance to master their complicated patterns, the Science Masters were not willing to spare the time to explain.

"This is a book; it is where we keep many words it saves us trying to remember long complicated stories".

" Do you know what to say just by looking at this"?

"Yes, each shape joins with another to represent a sound, it is a visual way of speaking".

"Will you teach me this I would like to make a write".

"I am still studying myself; you will need a master Sala for it takes many lessons to learn the skill to read and write. I think you will not be with us long enough but I will show you how it works, you will then have to practice on your own".

Kitta put her arm around Salas shoulders and squeezed gently towards her, she looked up into her eyes and smiled; Sala was moved almost to tears, no one had been this affectionate or physical since she had lost Porta to the Waters of Lethe.

"Do you have siblings Kitta, also I have not seen your Pa is he working in the fields"?

"I have a brother Terr, he is only one season. We have no fields, all green plants are too strong here, except for the houses and the nearby pathways to the river the trees keep the land for themselves. Pa Frag is out hunting with the other men".

"Will your Pa be home soon I want to thank him for letting me stay in his house"?

"Not for a long time at least one nom, they search for the food animals and will not return until they have enough for a half season at least".

The concept of hunting was strange to Sala, in her commune livestock were domesticated and always available along with the field crops as a source of food; in Lethe they had their pyramid gardens as their food supply. She understood, through Kitta's thoughts, what seemed brutal to Sala, was normal to sustain life amongst the trees. Here there were no field crops on which to feed the animals so it was necessary to seek and kill the wild beasts in the forest. Sala realised people adapted to the conditions where they lived but her commune had been completely influenced by the Overseers where many seasons before they had cleared the land to provided the means for them to thrive. The climate was much cooler than here so the trees were not dominant at home, leaving the fields free for cultivation. Her commune did not have to adapt, they had unwittingly accepted subtle subjugation and had lost the motivation for self-development. The location of Five usually meant a cold end to the season, often the winter crops failed when it snowed and the ground froze; a hard period then followed living off the limited stored produce and the dried ox meat. Now more than ever she was determined to find her commune. They had been denied the wonder of books and words to write; this she would change, all in her commune had more to give than learning songs, feeding themselves and producing mind speaking children for the Overseers breeding plans.

Sala woke with the light from a window on her face, remembered being led by Kitta to lay on a long soft bench after her meal, where sleep came quickly. Kitta was standing over her with a cup in her hand; she sat up and took the drink offered it was similar to the hot teas they had at home.

She was sipping silently and suddenly realised they were speaking but in a way not used before, it wasn't just Kitta picking up Salas's thoughts and responding with spoken words they had communicated directly through their minds. Kitta was very aware of this and explained the old men said they were not allowed to use the mind speaking as it was this skill that had taken the other children away but with Sala it seemed so natural she could not resist. When asked who could speak like this, she answered saying most of the young ones had the gift, telling her it can fade when you grow but they all work together which is keeping it active beyond childhood; Sala was the only one she had spoken to like this who was not a young person.

"Kitta to be safe and comply with the elders wishes we should only speak aloud from now on".

Sala did not want to jeopardise what had clearly kept them secure all this time or upset the elders by breaking their ruling. She thought, perhaps we should have done the same. Sheff entered the room.

"Sala please be ready soon the old wise one wishes to speak again;, I will take you there".

On arriving at the place where they met before Sala was faced with not only Rinn but two other male elders.

"I think you are recovered now Sala you look much better. I have my friends here to help my understanding of what you say; they will listen and confer with me but not speak with you till you have finished".

"I am fine thank you Rinn the family of Frag has been most generous, please ask your questions".

"First you spoke of your Bond what is this we have no word".

"He was my life partner; his name was Porta we joined together by our elders in the Bonding ceremony when we were of good age. He was my Bond and I his".

"Ah I see, we call it the Merging celebration. We have words different but the meanings can be the same. The more you speak the clearer it becomes. Now more important to us you said these people are trying to bring you back, is it possible they will follow you here"?

"They do have one other flying machine but it is small and not made for long journeys so it is unlikely they will use it. I have disabled the one I came in so they cannot take control or know where I am. I would do nothing to bring them here, in fact I will leave straight away if you would guide me back to the riverbank".

"From what you say it is not necessary for you to go so soon, we have no need to be concerned for now. We wish to learn more of your home and the land of Lethe. If you want to find your home I believe a plan for your onward journey would be better than wandering around aimlessly; maybe we can help".

The conversation continued for some time with Sala describing the life in their commune and her knowledge of other similar communes across the land. The coming of the Overseer to visit every few seasons. The telling of the endeavours of the Science Masters took some time for many questions were raised as the words and concepts were unknow.

She explained about the toxic drug from the Pinson tree pods dropping into the lake and how it affected the mind. How the reluctance of her commune people to break their Bonding and breed with strangers led to them being fed the tainted Waters. Details of the indoctrination of those who had been stripped of their memories.

She was loath to mention her own significant telepathic powers but knowing the elders were aware of the phenomenon did say how young children in her commune and especially siblings could mind speak. She told them of the Lethe elders powerful mind control ability, but how it was slowly being lost amongst their people with passing generations. The reason why they wanted the young people from the communes with the gift to breed with their own was their hope to restore their power with new breeding stock. Having opened the subject she knew there would be telling questions, she wasn't wrong.

"You and the ones from the communes who had the gift were taken from your homes unaware you were to be induced to breed with complete strangers".

It was a statement and a question at the same time demanding a response, she had to explain.

"Yes that is so, we had been contacted by a visitor from Lethe, an Overseer named Franil who could read our minds; they encouraged and helped us, when we were quite young, to improve our skill with the gift. She came again later and as young adults we went with her not realising her elder's intentions".

"How is it you were never given the drug"?

"I am not sure, the leading Overseer called Metrin was against the giving of the drug altogether. She believed the waters would not only destroy the memory but also take away the gift. She was forced to concede to the wishes of the majority. It seems she was right for those who were drugged lost everything. Somehow she was allowed, or deliberately decided to spare me the treatment".

"Yet they still continued with the breeding"?

"Their elders are certain the gift is in the structure of man's seed and the female ova not the construct of the mind; only time will reveal the truth, when the children from the cohabiting grow they will know".

"Do you still have the ability to mind speak"?

"I do Rinn. I don't know why but is has developed to be as strong as the Overseers. I have also the ability to partially close my mind from outsiders making it appear my gift is weak; this has enabled me to learn so much about them and their science without their knowledge. They felt I was no threat so gave me free access to most things. I led Metrin to believe that in time I would consent to breed with one of their own. My escape however has revealed my true intent and the power of my gift".

"Sala we thank you for your openness, we will discuss how we can help you in your quest. Now return with the family of Sheff we will speak again. One more thing before you go, we have many children with the ability to mind speak, we hide the fact so as not to attract unwanted visitors. Some of us here too had the gift as children but it faded as we matured, a sad loss for me, I am glad for you to have remained a whole being, truly as it should be".

'A whole being' The expression voiced by Rinn felt so right she had not thought of it before but without the gift she would be not be complete. All the senses combined were what made a complete person. The loss of any would make her as if blind or deaf.

Not unexpectedly Sheff and Kitta were waiting outside, the young girl took Sala's hand as they walked slowly back to her house.

"You are good with the youngsters my Kitta likes you a lot, do you have children of your own"?

Sala remembered the word Bond had no meaning here so used the term Rinn had used.

"No Sheff, my man of Merging has been taken from me. I live in hope".

"I hope too that you find him again; don't wait too long you will make good babies. Please sit I will bring you some drink".

These people and their simple comments were making her think. 'whole being' and 'don't wait too long' were particularly pertinent. Here she was far from home, far from Porta, escaping from what? The truth was she had deserted her Bond, her brother and friends; even if she did return to her commune she would never be happy or free. The Letheans would come eventually, if not for her then at least to retrieve their flying machine. Telling herself she was leaving in order to warn her commune about the Overseers was true but hidden deep within her an underlying motivation for self-preservation, fearing they would force her to bear a child by giving her the waters. She felt ashamed, another new emotion; one that would persist if she did not try to help her friends, her brother and Porta even if they never regained their memory of her. She would wait to see what Rinn had to say before considering what to do next.

Sheff returned with a drink she had not seen before, a clear liquid with a red colour and strange odour. She took a sip, it was sharp to the tongue but a little sweet at the same time, very pleasant. She drank it all, swirling the juice around her mouth so as to enjoy the contrasting flavours. She thought this is similar to our fermented menga but red instead of yellow and tasting much nicer. Sheff smiled when she saw Sala had drunk the whole cup in such a short time.

"You should take this more slowly, it comes from the juice a tree fruit called Juanda, it can make your head spin and if you have too much you will sleep even if you do not wish to do so. I gave it you to help you relax; your brow is deep lined with too many thoughts in your head, this is not good for you".

"We have one such drink called Menga, I will be careful. You are right my head is spinning but not from the Juanda, I have a big decision to make, it occupies my mind".

Sheff took the empty cup and poured more Juanda until it was half full.

"Then take another sip or two and sleep a while Sala, I will wake you presently".

Sala sipped the calming nectar more slowly this time, the spurious plans and scattered thoughts melted away as each drop drifted her to the promised slumber. The next time she woke she was refreshed anew; no disturbing notions had interrupted the recovery a good sleep brings. Her first intent was to seek the advice of Rinn. She wondered where Kitta was, fully expecting her to appear with a morning beverage but all was quiet in the house. Although there was light it was only just showing itself; her time rhythm here was askew as she had slept such odd hours; sitting back and relaxing till the family awakened was an easy decision. She waited a while but decided to walk to the building where the elders assembled before the commune faced the day. It seemed Rinn was expecting her even at this early hour.

"Rinn I have decided to return to Lethe but will make one more effort to find my commune before I do. I want to be with my Bond Porta and my brother, it may not be possible but I have to try".

"You must go back of course; I am glad you can see why now. You must stay with us a little longer we have some ways to help you in the search for your commune".

"If I do get back to Lethe they could force me to take the waters or, like they did with the others, hide it in my food, in which case I would have failed but would never know. For that reason I would still like to go home first to make my peace with my family and warn our elders of the menace posed by the Overseers of Lethe".

Sala had seen writings before in Lethe but they had not been given lessons in this skill in her official learning periods. It had only been when she attended lessons outside those of the planned programme that writing was used, she had never understood or been shown how it worked, now believing it was a deliberate exclusion by the Overseers. What little she did know came from Lunn. There were many things here with writings and drawings and was fascinated how such simple marks on thin flat sheets could hold all the words of a great number of songs.

Travelling back and forth over the ground time and time again looking for a piece of familiar terrain was slow and exhausting. When Rinn had promised he could help she had glimpsed in his mind images drawn on sheets of the land and the pathways she knew held the answer to her navigation problems. She also understood he needed time to find the right one and as there were so many drawings she would have to be patient.

Two long periods interspersed with sleep, learning from Kitta the way to understand the writings with breaks for drinking and eating helped to pass the slow passage of time. The call from Rinn came, at last.; Sheff woke her gently.

"The master Rinn wishes to see you Sala, shall I take you"?

"Thank you Sheff there is no need, I know the way".

She hurried to the meeting place. Rinn had laid a large sheet covered in pictures and writings on a table, as she approached she could see some of signs she had recently learnt, significantly the number 'FIVE' at the top of the ancient object.

"This is one of the many picture sheets left here by a visit from the yellow people many seasons before I was born, we have no idea why they left them here it could even have been a mistake to have done so. They show our world and where we all live within it. There are many sheets one for each commune and other places where people have been found, its position is clearly marked with the land between them and the home of the yellow people. More than sixty sheets, with the Outerworld shown as number 'Four'. There are stories of conflict between us so they may have been left during that time. We have kept these objects hidden and if they ever return to get them back they will find us ready; we have chased them away more than once and will do so again".

Rinn unrolled the sheets and laid them out in order, on top of each corner some weights to hold them flat.

"As you can see Sala the land of the Lethe is shown here at the bottom and my commune is marked near the top but how these will help you get from here to where you want to go I am not sure. The symbol and number combinations written at each location are positions in the World, every place is unique. You see here commune Five is marked with NW 75.44 and our commune here is ESE 82.13".

"I don't understand these Rinn how will it help me"?

"These sheets and markings were made by these people for a good reason, I think it enabled them to travel anywhere in this World. You said you control the flying machine with words and thoughts, I believe it may be possible, if you use your mind speaking skill, to send an image of these symbols and numbers to the flying machine. It could use them as an instruction. I don't know if it will work, you will have to try".

"Do you have sheets for number three commune and one for Lethe too"?

"Yes, all communes and more but there are no numbers for Lethe, why do you need them"?

"If it transpires to be the answer to finding my home I want to learn the symbols for your place here so I may return some day. Commune three also lost two children so I want to warn them of the danger posed by the Overseers".

Rinn laid out each of the sheets in turn where Sala set about learning all the symbols for each location, still unskilled in writing she had Kitta write them down on a small sheet so she would not forget. She picked a location marked by symbols close to her current position and went to the machine to test if this would work. Kitta wanted to come with along but she would not let her in case it failed and she could not return.

She placed the power source back in its receiver and immediately felt the presence of the Lethe elders but being well rested she blanked their force with little effort, realising her telepathic ability was becoming stronger with every passing day; gave her confidence that despite their relentless pressure she would prevail. With the symbol of a what was once a clearing a short distance from her current position in her mind she grasped the control and thought RISE then LIFT, she ship lifted and moved forward turning to her right picking up speed as it climbed. Within a few moments the vessel slowed and came to a halt above the canopy. The marked clearing had obviously grown over since the sheets had been created so they could not descend or land. She then simply thought of the place she had recently been, immediately the vessel returned and landed with precision at the exact spot left just a short while earlier. It had worked better than she could ever had hoped; it seemed the controller was linked to her mind in such a way it memorised every location of her past journeys. She only had to think of a place or the symbols of its location from the sheets and the flying machine would know the way. Maybe even returning to Lethe may be possible without the symbols if the crystal already had the position stored. The symbol for commune Five, was embedded in her brain NW 75.44. She was going home soon.

Suppressing the force generated by the combined minds of elders imposing its will upon her was gradually taking its toll. The block she set when rested was easy but Sala knew she would not be able to resist if she became over-tired again. To maintain the block and continue to fly the machine at the same time was difficult for long periods so the journey would have to be undertaken in stages so she could rest before continuing. If she tried to rush and exhausted her energy they would surely find her and take over the machine bringing her back, a failure with no future, the fear of the dreaded Waters ever present.

She was ready to leave having spent several days studying the sheets and learning the symbols; and the need to recuperate fully; before doing so she moved the machine from the unstable river-bank, where it had lain since her arrival. It had rained daily for some time; her vessel had shifted from the sandy bank into the path of the faster flowing river and was now at risk of being washed away or flooded by the rising water. She landed her craft in the small clearing a short distance from the houses where it drew interest from all who lived here, a constant procession of the curious passing by inspecting this strange machine.

The location symbols provided by Rinn would guide her to the area of the fifth commune, once close she is sure she will recognise the hills and fields of her home. The sheets showed some areas over which she would pass where Rinn said she must not land. Areas where contaminations existed on her route, where nothing lived or grew, which would cause a painful death to those who came too close. She wold have to plan her stops for rest carefully to avoid these dangerous places. Some of the songs she had heard in her youth told of a great upheaval in the ancient times when man covered the whole world. She couldn't remember the words but they told of a weak minded people who did not understand the ways of nature and in trying to control the very earth which gave them life they destroyed it and themselves. Badlands remain, it is said, as a warning to all who may come after.

    She removed the power source in case the elders were able to control the machine even without its pilot. It also blocked the power of their force as they were using the machines living crystal to focus their energy on her. She stayed nearby, lay on the soft grass mound prepared for her by Kitta and closed down her whole being forcing herself into a deep sleep; in this state she would have some respite from the relentless calling of Metrin and her sisters and will endeavour when rested to find a way to achieve her desires.

    Now awake Sala found Kitta asleep beside her, she gently removed the hand resting across her shoulder and rose quietly so not to disturb her young friend. She looked fondly at this young woman wishing she could forget all that had happened and embed herself in this wonderful community but forgetting was not the way it should be. Intransigent memories marked your role in life and should remain with you till you die. Good or bad they are a lesson to learn where the best of them should be told in songs to your children so nothing significant is forgotten.

    The farewells were to be said this day for she was rested and ready to depart. She woke Kitta with a soft touch from her mind, who realised what was about to happen.

    "Do you have to leave now please stay a little longer".

"I am sorry you know I must go, but if it is within my power I will return I promise".

"The Letheans will keep you there I will never see you again".

"Kitta I will never give in, be happy in your life, you will make a good merge, Bond as I did with a fine young man and have many children".

Kitta laughed slightly embarrassed but with tears in her eyes at the thought of Sala's imminent departure. Hand in hand the pair walked down to the centre where Rinn had been waiting aware of what was to come.

"Goodbye Rinn, thank you for your kindness, I wish you good hunting and will see you again, if not in this season or the next but when I am a free being once again".

"It has been a revelation for me Sala , return if life allows. Safe travels and good fortune".

They smiled at each other, Sala turned without further words and headed for Kitta's home. Ma Sheff and Pa Frag were waiting somehow everyone here knew she was leaving.

"Your home has been my sanctuary for so long, happy times spent here were a joy for which I thank you."

Sheff stepped forward and hugged Sala as if she would never let go. Pa Frag just smiled and made a small gesture of a wave to acknowledge her words.

"I have made a food package for you Sala it is of dried meats and fruits which should keep you going far a good while. Don't forget the water too in the flask by the door, Kitta will carry it for you."

Sala too had tears in her eyes and could not summon her voice to speak further. She nodded her farewell and left before the emotion overtook them all. The walk back to the ship with her food pack and Kitta carrying the heavy water flask was deliberately slow both delaying the final moment. The hatch now open she leant through and placed the water and food inside.

"No more tears Kitta you know I must go".
"Goodbye Sala I will never forget you".

She stepped back through the doorway and closed the hatch and her mind to further contact, proceeding immediately to the control not wishing to prolong the agony she was feeling. The craft rose from the soft ground clear of the tall trees, Kitta visible through the side window, a slowly diminishing image seated on the ground with hands in her lap and sadness in her heart. This to be remembered vision of the Outerworld left far behind the instant Sala mind transmitted the position of Commune Five to the machine.

Chapter Thirteen

Sala's plan to return to communes Five followed by Three and then on to Lethe would not be as easy as she thought. She wanted to return with dignity, in full control and be seen to do so under her own volition. Whatever else she wanted to achieve going to her commune first took priority.

The flight began at a pace, height and direction totally out of Sala's hands; by simply transmitting her desire to go to Five, using an image of the symbols extracted from Rinn's sheets, the machine was set in motion the moment she was seated and her fingers made contact with the control arm. She no longer had to be constantly vigilant when guiding the ships passage, leaving her to concentrate on blocking the Overseers ever present attempts to take over. She settled back in her seat looking in all directions at the forest below, there was nothing but trees as far as could be seen. The machine continued to gradually climb and accelerate finally reaching very close to the machine's limits; higher above the surface and at a speed way faster than any she had ever attempted when it was directly under her command. The darkening sky slowly obscuring the curved horizon told her she would most likely have little or no view of the terrain below at least for the next part of the journey.

Sala awoke with a knot in her stomach, something was wrong, her hand still rested on the control arm so it had not been loss of contact that had brought her craft to a standstill, something else had caused the lack of motion. She leant forward to better see her surroundings, the machine had stopped a long way from the ground, the green of the forest had been replaced by a red and grey rock strew landscape immediately ahead and into the distant horizon, to her left and right the remains of the green could be seen but short stubbly yellowish brush had replaced the magnificent trees now far behind. She urged the machine to continue but felt its reluctance to continue. What was it Rinn had said about the Badlands, was this it, an area so dangerous to venture in would be the end of life. What to do, she couldn't just sit here high in the sky for ever? She gripped the control and thought of the coordinates for commune Five again but also mentally asking for a route to avoid the ominously looking wilderness which lay ahead. The vessel slowly turned and moved back the way they had already been and climbed ever higher till the ground below became a blur; imperceptibly the craft gradually edged its way along the outer rim of the waste contaminated land eventually by-passing its lethal effect to later re-join their original path. Sala had no idea what had caused such an inhospitable area to exist and why it was to be avoided, but the dying vegetation at its outer rim was convincing enough to verify the elder Rinn's warning. She was certainly grateful the living crystal which controlled the machine had a close enough rapport with her, to have stopped and saved her from exposure to whatever danger may have been lurking in these Badlands.

 Sala never understood how the power driving her airship functioned even after her friend Lunn had explained it more than a few times but she now gained insight as how the life force within the crystal was at one with her and all living things around them, when at the control it became an extension of her mind aware of all that made her who she was; convinced an empathy existed between them with a natural need to protect her like a mother would her child. Sala took comfort in the thought as a calmness spread throughout her body and mind, feeling a confirmation coming from the crystal as to its truth.

No more Badlands and a reduction in height opened up many new vistas as the journey progressed. A return of the forests, green grasslands, high hills with the colour of many different plants, rivers and lakes all appeared in turn, each wonder quickly gone to be replaced by other more diverse areas than she imagined were possible. They flew over mountains covered in snow, and finally an ocean of blue water that spread in all directions until a band of green hills appeared in the distance before her. The ship reduced its enormous pace and slowly descended as it passed across the shoreline over the hills and in toward the land of commune Five. She did not yet recognise her home but knew they were close and her voyage would soon be over.

Returning to the very hidden spot left so long ago the machine gently set down and she let go the control. Sala had no ulterior motive, no need to hide the machine away from the eyes of the commune people like the Overseer Franil had done at each visit. She touched the control for a moment with her wish to move closer, the ship rose and drifted across well recognised fields towards the centre of the commune setting down in the square outside the great barn.

Songs had been sung about the Overseers being able fly like the birds but none of the people here had ever seen such a machine. Sala thought maybe the elders had done so but it mattered not for now everyone would know the awful truth.

A crowd gathered along the paths leading to the barn not coming close, very wary of this unknown, unbelievable shining machine that dropped from the sky. The airship occupied a large part of the area outside the barn. Sala waited a while observing the barn entry for her old mentor the elder Ezekiel, once she saw him appear at the doorway she moved to disengage the power source before opening the hatch and stepping out.

She avoided mind contact and spoke directly to Ezekiel in the ancient formal way as she approached the old man.

"I'm pleased to be in your presence old master Ezekiel and hope you are in good spirits. May I speak with you alone"?

"You are welcome here always Sala please enter".

The crowd now less timid, for some having spotted and recognised Sala as she exited the ship, drew closer. All were overcome by curiosity and awe at this strange and wondrous machine standing before them; soon some were looking in through the windows whilst others were running their hands over the smooth metallic surface. She left them to it, they could do no harm, stepping through the familiar portal to join Ezekiel inside the great barn.

Sala waited till they were seated at the rear of the large space away from the ears and eyes of other elders. Ezekiel spoke first.

"This is a great but welcome surprise Sala; I am more than curious to know about what has happened to you and your colleagues over the last two or three seasons. I never expected to see any of you again. Your arrival in the flying machine of the Overseers is even more intriguing; is the one we known as Franil your guide, is she inside"?

"No, I am alone, I will explain later but first it seems you already knew of this machine"?

"Oh yes. As a young man I sometimes ventured into the land beyond our commune, it is wild and a difficult terrain to travel over even a for a short distance. I often wondered how one person, seemingly alone, arrived and departed carrying nothing with them for such a journey. Many years ago I followed the Overseer during a visit and watched as she reached its hiding place beyond the high ridge. I was more than surprised to see such a machine but even more so when it left the ground and was gone at such speed".

"You never said anything or never told anyone"?

"No, I felt it would create an unwanted curiosity amongst the people and unsettle them. Now tell me your story why have you come back and why are you alone and not with Porta"?

"The story is a long and sad one, we were deceived, as I think you may have suspected; the Overseers from the place called Lethe are not what they claim to be, the good of the community indeed all communities, for there are many, is not what they had in mind. What I am about to tell you will change everything, how we teach our children and how we live our lives. It will take all your knowledge, wisdom and experience to find the way forward to manage our community in the right way. The changes will be slow but without interference from the Overseers changes there must be. I am sure they will come again so you must defend yourselves against them".

Sala paused to see if Ezekiel had any questions before she continued; he indicated for her to continue.

"They have advanced technologies you will not believe but their motivation is not benevolent like we thought, we have been nurtured as we do our animals, to be harvested for our bodies, fed and watered to provide them with new human breeding stock. They want the mind speaking ability from our children, yes children like Porta and me, to be injected into their population by forced breeding with as many of their kind as they can. When faced with their demands to breed we of course refused, so they poisoned the minds of Bron Star and Porta with chemicals along with people from another commune, destroyed all memories of who they were and where they came from and set them like the oxen to impregnate their females or be impregnated by their men".

"Oh Sala, my heart cries to hear such dreadful things, how come you were not also mistreated in this way"?

"I believe by good fortune, the gift of mind speaking was the main reason for our abduction, but when given the drug this ability was lost. They want the gift to be transmitted to the children of this experimental breeding but they are unsure of the outcome and will not know of success or failure until the resulting babies have grown. I was spared by one of the more astute Overseers as she did not want to destroy my mind as befell the others, I led her to believe I would comply and agree to breed once I had accepted the loss of Porta".

"You obviously escaped using one of their machines will they not come after you, are you in danger, are we in danger"?

"You are safe for now; they only have one viable machine and this is it. The current generation did not make these flying machines and I am sure do not have the skills or materials to build new ones. It is very many season old inherited from ancestors long dead, they do have two others but one does not fly and the other is too small for such a journey".

"How did you learn to fly and why did they let you go"?

"So much has happened whilst I was away It will take much time to tell you everything, please be patient I will reveal all I know. Although the Lethe elders are devious and have their own nefarious motives the ordinary people even though somewhat dispassionate, are clever and can be friendly. Almost all can mind speak so there are no secrets or so they say, however the Overseers can block their own private thoughts and seem to hold the ordinary people under strict rule. There is a feeling of trepidation when they are in the presence of the Overseers, a sign of dissidence exists within them but they are physically weak and so controlled they will do nothing".

"I still can't see how they gave you so much freedom you could learn their secrets and technology enough to fly and escape".

"Even though they never mind speak things untrue Ezekiel, they are well able to hide what is really in their minds. Whenever I asked a question concerning their intentions, if their true answer would be not what they wanted me to know they just remained silent. They believed they had access to my mind at all times but were unaware of my ability to block them unnoticed when I wished. Their egoistic attitude placed me beneath them in knowledge and intelligence I was considered to be no threat, they gave me the freedom to roam and study whatever I chose, my true intent well hidden".

"Why have you come back Sala and how did you find your way here"?

"I came to warn you of course, my journey here and my reason for doing so is complex".

"Why do you think we need to be warned"?

"They will come again and again taking our children from us, I wanted to tell you what will happen and warn you to never trust these Overseers".

"When you were taken I knew it was not for what had been promised but you were all too insistent and full of what was to come for me to influence you to stay. We the elders never expected to see you again. We have since found the ones amongst us who are gifted and warned them against communicating in this way. If ever the Overseers returned again we would have hidden the children away urging them to close their minds. I would have told the visitor Franil we had no children with the gift and sent them away empty handed, even if she tried we would have physically refused her access to the children, what could one Overseer do against a whole community".

"It is wrong to stop them from using their mind speaking Ezekiel you must encourage the children to develop their gift as a group, it is only a strong combined mind which will protect them against the invasive thoughts of the Letheans. Overseers minds are powerful and could penetrate your thoughts` and the gifted children's and know of the true situation. Your vigilance and physical safeguards will probably work for they are weak and unlikely to use any kind of force if strongly opposed. They control by stealth and deception so being aware of this and with the combined minds of the children repulsing their efforts you are in a much better position to defend against them".

"I have no experience of mind speaking but understand how powerful it can be. I will do as you say and assemble all here who have this gift to join and develop their skills".

"Combined minds can resist almost any deceptive thought; it is the only way to truly protect our young. I met people in a similar situation in another very different community where they repulsed the Overseers and now live a life they have developed in their own unique way free of interference, their children safe from abduction".

Sala then related her story, their journey to Lethe, the first arrival and the wonder of the place and its sciences, the meeting with Horden and Jeska from commune Three. The gradual pressure to cohabit and the final poisoning of their minds when they resisted to mating with the Letheans. All details of how life functioned there, its buildings, the Science Masters schools, the power sources, the pyramid gardens and the food processing rooms; all aspects of her life there were told to Ezekiel and the elders.

She described how Metrin and the other Overseers had complete power over all the people; explaining the effects of the deadly Waters; of her despair when she lost her friends, family and Bond Porta to its insidious mind transformation effects and her eventual determination to escape and warn the communes. She expressed her gratitude for the help given by Lunn the engineer in showing her how to fly the machine and her good fortune in getting away undetected. Finally her accidental finding of the Outerworld people and the role of Rinn and his sheets with their symbols in her being able to locate the communes. The story was long and as detailed as needed for the elders to understand without the need for many questions.

"Your resilience under the circumstances is remarkable Sala but our hearts are heavy learning of the terrible fate of the others. What are your intentions now"?

"My first intent is to see my family; I sense their presence outside and will join them now with your permission. I will stay here awhile and explain to you and the elders details of the sciences particularly about the writings and symbols for learning and remembering, you will soon realise the songs are not enough. The skill was deliberately withheld by the Overseers to repress our natural development. I am not expert in these matters but our children are clever and will learn quickly under your guidance".

"Go now, of course we will meet here tomorrow; I and my fellows have much to ponder".

The old man's mind was most unsettled, the Song of Light appeared to be coming true, the fateful journey mentioned in the song had been made but the promise of its final phrase,

'The one True Man will then embrace. Eternal life and light to grace' seemed an impossible task for this young girl.

Ma Kelena hugged her daughter with tears of joy running unchecked down her face. Pa Erin too had a tear in his eye as he enfolded the pair in his strong arms; they stood thus for some time the crowd around them easing back to give them space. The huddled trio released their embrace walking arm in arm towards the family home. Sala had her parents minds within hers and knew their unspoken question. 'Where were Bron, Star and Porta? She would have to tell them soon but would think of a way to soften the blow.

Ma made her sit at the table as she always did for a guest, brought food and drink placing them before her, withholding the question at the forefront of her mind with an effort so not to spoil the occasion.

"Thank you Ma, I know you want news of the others, they are alive and in good health, but could not travel with me this time. They have fully integrated within the community of the Overseers and are living their lives as one of the Lethean people".

"Porta did not mind you leaving him there and what of your brother did he not want to come too"?

"I came alone Ma; the others were not allowed to come with me there are rules very different from the way we live here. They are now fully part of that community so will be unlikely to return any time soon".

"But you found a way and came back, are you not part of their community"?

"No Ma no not really, anyway not like the others. Although I have been living there I chose to remain as I am and not integrate fully. I came here without the Overseers knowledge".

"You flew that thing on your own"?

"I did and although I wish I could stay I have to leave in a while".

"Of course I understand you must be with Porta you should not be so far away from your Bond. Will you come again"?

"I will do my best Ma but you are right, I have to go back to Porta and the others, next time I will try to stay longer".

"Tell your brother when you see him to get back here too for a visit at least, we miss you all too much".

Sala's leniency with the truth, to some degree had put her parents mind at rest for the time being at least. Now she could relax a little and catch up with local gossip, very aware her Ma would not hold back on telling her all the comings and goings of her friends and neighbours. Pa looked on smiling but Sala's glimpse at his thoughts showed a deep sadness for his lost son.

Much time was spent with Ezekiel and the elders, details of the Lethe way of life particularly the method of food production and the other sciences enabling them a life free of the hard labour experienced by the commune. She told the elders about writing and recording information on sheets with symbols and pictures, her knowledge here was weak but the concept opened the beginning of a new way of learning for her commune, the young elder demanded details on how the sheets were made and how to draw the symbols. He spent several days with her until he believed he could replicate the material used in making sheets and make writing. He never came back with the other elders for a long time and when he did he had made a sheet from a piece of clothing material stiffened by soaking it in boiled maize water and drying it in the sun. He had scribed some marks with a burnt stick which he said was the name Ezekiel; no one doubted him, how could they. She knew it was a small beginning; the songs would remain and was happy they would continue, but the addition of this alternative way to retain and pass on information would surely open new avenues for the next generation of children.

The problems of the Overseers were also discussed at length; their breeding by artificial means, the lack of male children, the slowly dying mind speaking ability. Their weaknesses and strengths were sought out, Ezekiel believing the most important weakness being their lack of empathy. He said if they don't care for each other then their selfishness will lead to their demise.

Sala thought their common mind was their strongest point but the underlying covertness in its use was a weakness. She related how friendship existed among the ordinary population and was possible in a limited way with some Overseers, citing her relationship with the Franil as an example. Her friendship with the engineer Lunn she said was very real so she believed it was true for anyone given the opportunity. Describing how they lived under a strict regime with obvious fear of the Overseers and how they could not be seen to have any feelings of empathy when in their presence; there were signs of resentment when unobserved also an element of underlying radical dissent, another weakness to note. So it went on, time after time from morning into the darkness, relaying every memory, every thought until there was no more. Almost a half season had passed during this visit, too long a delay, for the journey was far from over.

A period of rest and some treasured time with her family were in order before her inevitable departure. She sought out the young mind speakers and spend time teaching them how to spread their communication to more than just their siblings. Great results occurred each day as more and more began to connect; their combined minds now able to resist Salas testing them with sudden powerful attempted disruptions. The time spent here stretched to more than originally intended for she did not wish to leave. A new journey to seek out commune Three called to her, the sad news for them, a burden she had carried for a long time, must to be delivered to families as yet unmet.

Her Ma cried as Sala stepped aboard the machine, her Pa resolute, held back the tears but Sala knew he was hurting deeply, his radiating desire for her to stay cut into her, weakening her resolve to do what was right but she too held fast with the need to continue her quest.

Her work at Five complete she would now go to commune Three in the knowledge her power would continue to develop with each passing day. By the time it came for her to leave commune Three for her return to Lethe she hoped she would be strong enough to open her mind to Metrin and her sisters without being completely overwhelmed.

A wave of goodbye through the glass to the people surrounding her air machine was probably to be her last contact with home for a long time. She sat and allowed the machine to rise slowly until the commune buildings and its people were a mere speck in the landscape below. The remembered image of the symbols for the location of commune Three were transmitted to the living crystal, at once the machine swivelled to its new direction streaking off into the bright sky.

≈

All the time she had been away Sala had been preparing for this moment. Her next journey was to commune Three; the inevitable return to Lethe soon after was also a certainty. Once she realised returning unhindered would not be possible if she used a remembered image of Lethe to guide her, for to do so she would have to unblock and pass the image to the crystal; once unblocked and as she came closer to Lethe, Metrin and her sisters combined minds would grab the opportunity to overpower her. Maybe there was another way but she had no inkling of what that might be.

When first learning the symbols and numbers for Five and Three from the sheets locating the position of the communes there was a sudden and irresistible force directly impinging on her mind as each location was committed to memory; did they know about them? Was absorbing these unique numbers a clue to her own location? It seemed Metrin was there ready waiting for this moment. She shut it down immediately but even if she had found Lethe's missing numbers and symbols the slightest thought of them were never going to be something she could use to go back on her own terms, she was just not strong enough. Allowing the Overseers to take over and direct the machine may be the only way back. Her plan to return and remain in control would not happen unless she found an alternative.

Chapter Fourteen

The flying machine fell slowly to the ground, the location a hidden ravine out of sight, the place Franil must have chosen previously before descending to the commune on foot. Sala considered taking the airship right into the heart of the commune as she had done at home but being an unknown here thought the peoples reaction to the machine might overshadow the purpose of her visit. She was unsure of its exact location so reached out for which way to go from the mind of one of the people nearby.

An unexpected shock as she made contact with a powerful mind fully open, for Sala was immediately inside the mind of Arak and knew who he was. He mind spoke to her but she had an automatic block in place where he knew of her presence but nothing more.

"I know you are there, who are you what do you want"?

Sala opened the link but only enough to mind speak avoiding total immersion at his stage.

"My name is Sala I am a friend of your brother Horden and his Bond Jeska, I have come from the land of the Overseers to bring you news".

"You are an Overseer"?

"No, like you I am from a commune similar to yours and in the same way as your Brother I too went to Lethe many seasons ago. I will come down to meet you".

She had seen where he was and the route to take to his home, a similar walk she had made many times before at her own commune; over the ridge hiding her ship, along the pathways skirting the fields full of the crops of maize and edible grasses. The similarities to Five were startling.

Arak was on the way to meet her as she approached the outskirts of the settlement. They stopped a short distance from each other, he held out his hand to her, she stepped forward and gently placed his proffered welcome palm in her own and smiled releasing her block enough for the two minds to blend as one.

"Wow. I haven't know this feeling since my brother left, I mind speak to many here but not like this. What of Horden and Jeska, I cannot see them in your mind, you are holding back I can tell, what is wrong"?

"Please Arak take me to the commune centre. I can tell you now your brother and Jeska are alive and well but are changed people. I will explain all I can to you, your parents and the elders together".

Sala remembered the pale skin and curling fair hair of Horden; Arak was a younger version of his brother, he turned and led the way through the pathways of the commune with houses, not unlike her own, on either side; the path followed the easiest route winding through the uneven terrain. All the buildings were of a similar construction to those at home. The commune centre again had the ring of familiarity, for the great barn was so like the one she had recently left, again realising how much the Overseers must have influenced all the communes in the past. She waited outside whilst Arak entered briefly before returning to her side. His thought indicated the elders would be here shortly. Sala told him she would speak aloud to the elders and to him avoiding mind contact until she had judged their reaction to her story. The elders came to the doorway and the leader stepped forward.

"My name is Brugan, I welcome you stranger to our commune".

She avoided mind contact and spoke directly to Brugan in the formal way of the commune.

"My name is Sala. I'm pleased to be in your presence Master Brugan and hope you are in good spirits".

"I am happy you are here Sala please tell us the purpose of your visit".

"I am originally from a commune like yours and have recently been living amongst the yellow people. I bring news of Horden and Jeska. May I speak with you and your fellow elders alone"?

She mind spoke to Arak asking him to be patient as some of what she had to say should remain with his elders, it being up to them what was made general knowledge for all. He understood and stepped back moving to the rear the square outside as Sala entered the great barn to face Brugan and the four elders of the commune.

"What I have to say here will be disturbing to your people so I will leave it for you to deal with as you see fit. The news concerning Horden and Jeska will be greatly upsetting for their families. I will explain to you first and if you wish I will tell them the fate of their loved ones in my own way so as to make it easier for them to accept".

"We are concerned for our children who left us with the Overseer Franil, she was very persuasive so they left with our blessing but we the elders had doubts at the time eclipsed by the young ones eagerness to follow the Overseer to the land of great promise. I presume you have knowledge of Franil"?

"I know her well, she has a good heart but her Master's orders as envoy to the communes have induced her to become deceptive and manipulative, one who never lies but avoids the truth. I, my Bond Porta, my brother Bron and his Bond Star went to Lethe at the same time as your Horden and Jeska; travelling in Franil's flying machine. At first it was all a wonderous adventure but the real reason for our abduction was more sinister and became clear much later. We were there, not for our benefit or for the good of the communes, but to be used in an experimental breeding programme".

"An experiment you say, but why these particular children and why you and your family"?

"Our ability to mind speak was the real reason for us being chosen".

Sala went on to tell the whole story of Metrin and the sisters plan to restore their people's weakening telepathic sense by breeding with the gifted commune people like animals. The final act when the Pinson fruit toxin was secretly given, destroying their memories and thus their reluctance to breed with strangers. She touched on her own relationship with Metrin, a brief description of her escape, and the reason her flying machine was close by but out of sight. She was strong in her warning to prepare to resist further advances from the Overseers.

"We are fully aware of our young ones ability to mind speak but did not realise how far this gift could develop. Your tale is more than disquieting for us Sala, I have many questions but will deliberate with my fellows before we continue. In the mean-time go with Arak to his family and that of Jeska. Use soft words to tell them of their children's fate with the least anguish. Return here tomorrow, we will ask our questions then and decide what to do".

"I have had to pass the same sad news to my family with some degree of mitigation and will do the same for Horden and Jeska's Ma and Pa. I will return at first light".

Arak led Sala to his home holding back on the question burning at the forefront of his mind. He spoke briefly with his Ma Limbina and Pa Gren saying he was going to get Jeska parents to come over as I had news from the land of the yellow people. Ma Limbina made Sala sit at the table, as was the custom she brought food and drink, which was most welcome; all holding back from speaking until Arak returned with Jeska's Ma and Pa. Sala knew what she was going to say having rehearsed it in her mind several times. The truth in many respects but the loss of memory through the Pinson Tree's poisonous extract would remain untold.

"Thank you Ma Limbina for my meal and to everyone for your restraint in delaying your obvious question. I know you want news of Horden and Jeska; what I can tell you is they are both alive and in good health but could not travel with me this time. What may be difficult to accept is they have fully integrated within the community of the Overseers and are now living their lives as one of the ordinary people. It is a strict regime where all thoughts of their earlier life and of their old home are discouraged. They are learning new things never imagined in the communes and are deeply involved in their new lives. I am sorry to tell you it is very unlikely they will be able to make the journey back home".

Everyone began talking at once, all with a different question, but really asking different versions of the same one, the very thing she could not answer, WHY? There was no answer, she had told them the truth but felt ashamed, even so could not reveal what had really happened without breaking their hearts. She spoke at length describing the homes they lived in the schooling they were undergoing, the food they ate. Trying to make life there seem so good the parents would be happy for their children in their new environment. Evading both the Ma's question concerning possible children from the Bond by saying 'not yet', when Sala knew there were several young ones born out of Bond with no likelihood of there ever being one born within a Bond no longer remembered.

Eventually a calm shrouded the household each lost in their own thoughts, Sala sensed an acceptance coupled with sorrow; she too felt saddened by the hopeless situation, but glad sharing the awful facts had been avoided, unsure if she could shield against Arak learning the truth concerning his brother and Jeska; his powerful mind was capable of penetrating hers if at any time she remained unguarded, she probed his thoughts.

Arak was calm; what Sala had said was not what he had expected of his brother and he knew there was something she had omitted to tell them. If Sala held back certain details she must have had a good reason; he had no wish to find out what they were. Sala slept in an unoccupied house next to Gren's, the quiet, only interrupted by a relaxing rhythmic swish from the nearby trees braced against the night breeze, allowed her tired frame a deserved respite.

The soft tap on her shoulder from Arak woke her from the much needed sleep, refreshed and ready to tackle whatever came her way. Today it would be the elders of commune Three. She thought living with a number rather than a name was deliberately uninspiring, all communes should have a name, one to reflect their location or its people or a combination of both. She wondered what name could be assigned to commune Three and her own home commune Five. She knew if it was proposed there would be as many names put forward as there were families, a big conflab would occur with the elders finally choosing something completely different from any of those on offer. She'd like to be there; if ever she went back she'd suggest it; for now the name Five would suffice. Her brief reverie left her fully awake, alert and ready to meet the elders once more.

"Did you sleep well Sala"?

"Yes, thank you Master Brugan and in anticipation of your next question I have given the families the news of their children without mentioning the loss of their memories. They seem to have accepted the situation; I regret I can do no more to salve their sadness".

"That is good I did not relish the task and will keep the secret of their plight safe. From all you have told us it seems we have a great period of adjustment before us if we are to ward off any attempt by the Overseers to take more children".

"The knowledge of their true intent is your best defence; they are unlikely to use physical means it is not in their nature and their mind control will not break down your young people who have the gift if they combine their efforts. It is important to be wary as they are very persuasive you must reject all Overseer's propositions; they will always seek ways to deceive you. There are many more communes with no knowledge of their true intentions so the Overseers have alternative supplies of young bodies apart from here. When I return to Lethe I will let them know you are no longer an easy source I believe you will be left alone".

Sala continued her long story speaking to Brugan and the others about all aspects of her recent life and her covert self-education as well as the open one offered by the Overseers in which she became fully involved. Her discovery of the sheets and symbols in the Outerworld and its importance in her being able to come to commune Three.

"Will you be leaving soon"?

"Not for a quite a while yet, I want to spend time with the younger elders to show them how the sheets are formed from the weaving and coating of fine cloth and how the pictures and symbols are made. I must pass on as much of what I have learnt as possible. My return will come soon enough for I have a fear the Overseers response to my actions may be harsh".

"It is good you will spend time with us, it is also obvious you must go back to seek justice for your loved ones".

"In returning my original aim was to seek retribution for what they have done but have since pondered deeply on their reasons. I was making judgements based solely on my own commune's expected behaviour and did not consider the history of Lethe and what they think of as quite normal. They believe they are doing no wrong , they are abiding by their own codes of conduct so who am I to say otherwise. I hope they will give me the time to explain how I feel and we can resolve the differences between our cultures in a way to benefit both. I have some wild ideas but no real plan yet even so I must go back and deal with whatever I find".

"We the elders will be pleased to learn new things but will reserve judgement as to their being an improvement for our people before passing them on. We will speak again here tomorrow; I will assemble the elders for your teachings".

Sala left the barn and walked back to the house of Limbina she needed to prepare a plan for the education of the elders of Three as she had done in Five, the rest of the day and probably part of the night too would a busy time, but one to savour.

Many days merged into another half a season all spent with the elders where Sala passed on her limited knowledge but in so doing the foundations of a written record was established, as well as continuing with the songs. These elders were wise with age but understood they were mere children when it came to the technology used every day in Lethe; she did not attempt to go further than explain about the different Sciences and what was possible. Their interest only peaked once, asking questions when she told them about the pyramid gardens but soon realised there was nothing to be gained when the structures required were way beyond their capabilities.

Education by songs would remain the way it will be for the time being; the keeping of record through sheets and symbols will be studied and improved on until developed to a practical and valuable level before being added to the elder's way of teaching. The elders realised how far removed their commune was from the way of life in Lethe but more significantly they now knew why the Lethe Overseers had deliberately held them back.

The evenings spent with Arak and the family were without doubt most pleasant and a welcome rest from the daily grind spent with the elders, however she had imparted all she could, the rest was up to them, all too soon the time to leave arrived.

"Goodbye Brugan; my true wish is for all people to come together and if it becomes possible I will return. I hope to survive whatever Lethe has in store, if not remain vigilant and enjoy the life you have. Whatever advantages lie in Lethe they are as nothing to the joy I found resides here".

"Farewell Sala, good fortune".

Chapter Fifteen

The symbols for all the communes well embedded in her mind and the location of the Outerworld and its image never forgotten; Lethe's location however remained an unknown. The flying machine now high above commune Three remained hovering waiting for a direction from Sala. The instant the thought of Lethe appeared in her mind a surge of power from the Overseers, tangible enough to almost touch, invaded the space around her. Her periods of rest and relaxation at Three had lulled her into a position of vulnerability, her earlier constant rebuttal of invasion had long been idle whilst the source was disconnected; her most powerful rebuttal instantly revived at the ferocity of this new attack. She was strong enough for now but had many hours ahead to sustain the effort required to stay safe. She didn't know what would happen if she failed to keep them at bay, perhaps they would not be able to take over the machine so maybe they were just worrying her to force the return.

The image of Lethe she held in her mind waiting for a response. She hoped it would be enough to allow the living crystal to find its way back home after all it had made this journey an untold number of times before. It seemed to be working as the machine climbed high above the clouds and headed off with a purpose.

Their initial attempt to take over faded soon after which made keeping the Overseers away much easier. Sala to sank back and relaxed in the chair her hand resting gently on the control arm. She had no idea how long the journey would take or indeed if the ship was even on the correct course but trusted the crystal to protect the craft and its lone pilot. Her semi sleeping state was interrupted as the machine slowed to a crawl, her eyes focusing ahead and below saw the barren land mass like the one she had seen once before. The obvious path was to go ahead but the same reluctance to cross these Badlands again halted the ship from continuing along the direct route. Sala wanted to see more so urged the machine forward slowly; she felt the hesitation but the craft crossed the line from lush green forest through brown shrub into the dark reddish rock strewn wilderness spread before her as far as could be seen. She pressed the craft to drop lower which it did very slowly but still resisting the command ever present in Sala's mind; an attempt by her to go even further met such strong resistance the ship halted progress both downward and ahead; the limit had been reached. She peered through the window at the ground below hoping to see some sign of life, looking intently for the reflected light from anything but dead rocks but there was none. Was this the deadland of Lunn's ancient tale? probably not, but then again maybe it was; for sure it looked like a very unsafe place. Her curiosity tempered but not satisfied, she reluctantly allowed the machine to return to the green rim, where it skirted around the edge of this forbidden terrain and then continued on the intended path.

She wondered why the machine halted at the Badlands border and wait for instructions to continue. Perhaps long ago the route was safe to cross and this direct path is heavily imprinted in the crystals memory, the safeguards now in place won't allow it to cross unless instructed, even then it was impossible to urge the ship to encroach too far. She felt she could have forced the issue and made the machine continue but decided not to take the risk; whatever had taken the life from this land in the past appeared to still have dominance.

No sooner had she ceased thinking about the Badlands and the sight of familiar green forest had returned, when another interruption in her search came unexpectedly, for the ship slowed and descended towards the trees below, Sala scanned the landscape this was not Lethe but prompted an impression she had seen a landscape like this before. Recognition dawned as the river came into view, she was approaching the Outerworld and the home of Kitta. Although her intention was to return to Lethe dreams of her travels must have been floating through her mind as she sat half asleep with the machines control in her hand. Her fond memory of these people had influenced the crystal enough for it to bring her back. Maybe her instructions to return to Lethe had a tinge of unease which allowed the crystal to act in this way. It seem to have an intelligence of its own. Did it think? It certainly made decisions. Who knows what it was capable of, whatever Sala felt protected by its presence.

Sala was not in the least disappointed for her sensed trepidation concerning her original plan was not unfounded. The craft had landed in the exact same spot found during her first visit however today a safer place, for the river level was low and moved slowly under the green canopy; this time there was no welcoming party. She disconnected the power source and made her way along the riverbank to the remembered opening in the tall trees which led to the houses. The gap and pathway opened out as she knew it would but since her last visit the route had become quite overgrown. With not much room and almost no light under the looming leafy cover, she pressed on head down, the path underfoot still visible from its well-trodden earlier use guided her through to the edge of the settlement. Her view of the first houses showed no obvious changes; there was no one around all was silent. Sala had lost all track of time but realised it was still very early in the day and nearly all would be sleeping. She approached the house of Kitta and her family certain there would be someone stirring soon. She sent a gentle thought to Kitta not wanting to alarm her if she was sleeping but enough to wake her and make her aware of her physical presence.

"Sala, Sala! Are you really here"?

"Yes Kitta I am, look out your window."

Kitta's face showed briefly from the opening above and at once vanished to reappear an instant later at the lower doorway as it flew open. During almost two seasons since she was last here Kitta had grown, no longer a skinny child, she ran the few steps to where Sala was standing and flung her arms around her almost knocking her over. Sala reverted to speaking aloud as they had agreed during her first visit as the reasons for doing so were still needed.

"You can let go now Kitta, I need to breathe".

She released her tight hug but kept hold of Sala's arm with both hands, afraid she was not real and would disappear if she ever let go.

"I'm sorry Sala. It's just I never expected to see you again it has been so long, I thought you were gone for good. Why have you come back is everything alright"?

"I'm fine Kitta let's go inside I will explain".

"The machine brought me here without my asking I don't know why, or maybe I do in some strange way. Look it is difficult to explain. I am trying to get back to Lethe but don't know the way".

"Did you get to go home like you wanted, did the codes from the sheets take you there"?

"Yes they did and I went to commune Three as well".

"Did you warn them as you said, why did you leave your home, I wouldn't have; what about your Ma and Pa, now they know about what has happened you could have stayed, why go back there it's not safe is it"?

"So many questions, slow down Kitta, I will endeavour to tell you everything. Firstly I do have to go back, Bron, Star and my Porta are still there I cannot leave them. I must try my best to bring them home and even recover their memories if it is possible".

"Now you have their machine the Overseers cannot leave or come after you, if you go back they will take it away and will destroy your memory or even worse kill you like an animal. Please think again Sala you will have no chance once you are in their hands".

"They have other machines Kitta; the one that works may be small and less powerful but they can certainly go anywhere in it. The old one is large but as far as I know it is not working but if it can be made to do so they do not need the one I have taken. If I don't return they could easily come to recover this one and take me as well if they so wish. By going back I have a chance to put things right. The minds of the Overseers grow weak whilst mine grows strong, I have the power to protect myself from their invasive thoughts. As for killing me it is not in their nature to take life, the worst they could do would be to feed me the Waters, if so I will be at peace which I could never be if I stayed at home".

"You said the machine brought you here without you asking, there must be a reason, you hinted as such".

"Yes I did, but I am not sure. I was trying to memorise a vision of Lethe as an instruction to the crystal to which it immediately responded but during the journey it stopped at the Badlands like before, then continued to what I thought was towards Lethe only to find myself here instead. I thought it was because I was dreaming of this place half asleep and the crystal interpreted it as a command. I am not sure though; this crystal is an integral part of whoever is piloting the craft and seems compelled to protect both. Perhaps it knows the danger of my returning too soon and has brought me here to ensure my safety".

"You said your power is growing perhaps us mind speakers here can help by making you even stronger. We follow the guidance of the Elders by always speaking aloud when with others not gifted but all of us are aware of the other's presence. Our power is enhanced when acting as a group; it is much greater than when you were here last. With a little more practice I am sure our combined minds can repulse the Overseers".

"I am pleased to learn of your continued expansion of the gift, it is good news as you may be right about repelling the Overseers and if they ever come I hope you will be able to do so. I wasn't expecting to be here so I am quite unsettled, I am wondering why it brought me to you and not to Lethe as I asked. Right now I need time to think about what I will do next; let's go inside I want to see Pa Frag and Ma Sheff".

They walked hand in hand through the door to be greeted like a daughter coming home. The baby Terr now a little boy toddled away from his mother's side aiming for his sister, he held on to her shirt tail looking up at Sala wondering who she was. Had she been away so long or do children grow that fast. Ma Sheff in her usual way sat her down at the table and produced a cup of Juanda and a small cake, it was her way of saying welcome.

"It is good to see you again Sala I never expected to... err....well not...... Is everything okay"?

"Of course Sheff, thank you, I'm fine. I know you are surprised, I never expected to be here either. How are you and Frag"?

"Good, good Sala, we are both well, Frag is still sleeping, they were hunting for three days without rest and returned very late. I'll go wake him he will want to see you".

"No Sheff, leave him be he obviously needs to sleep, I am not going anywhere, I'll see him later".

"Just as well I suppose, he can be a bit grumpy when he's tired".

They laughed at the thought of Pa Frag in a huff and settled into a period of small talk seated around the table. Sala, with young Terr ensconced on her lap, gave a watered down version of her visit home and to commune Three.

"I think I should show my respects to the elders and go to see Rinn, is it too early"?

"Yes it is much too early, the elders are what they are, old, so need to wake slowly and at a time of their choosing, a good bit later I would think".

"A reputation they encouraged about themselves I'm sure. I don't believe it, I bet they are up at first light every day".

"Probably".

The time spent with Kitta and her family brought home so clearly what she had lost already and what she would be missing by going back now. The images of her Ma and Pa's future daily life alone brought tears to her eyes; was this the reason the crystal had brought her here, a pause in the journey, time to reconsider. If she stayed in Five her parents would certainly be happier, or would they? Just by being there she would be a constant reminder of her missing brother; and an affront to Porta and Star's family too, always reminding them of their loss. There was no doubt now she could not go back home until…..until she knew what fate had decreed. She wasn't asleep when Kitta touched her hand, only sitting eyes closed deep in her own thoughts.

"It is time Sala, if you want to see the elder Rinn. Pa is still sleeping but he should be up when we get back. Is it alright if I come with you"?

"I don't see why not this is a courtesy visit I have no intention for any private interchange with him and even if he wants to talk we know each other's mind well enough for it to be an open discussion. Are you sure he will be there"?

"He should be, the elders usually meet in the hall at this time of day".

As always the formal greeting was met with smiles as Rinn came forward to take Sala's hand. He wanted to hug her but resisted such a familiar gesture. She was aware of his need so gripped his hand not letting go until they were seated close opposite each other, the intimate contact was pleasant for both.

"Not yet two seasons gone and you are back, sooner than I expected Sala, I thought you would not want to leave your home. Still you are most welcome, tell me what has happened. I can see you are in fine spirits so presume you must have seen your family".

"Yes Rinn it was good; sad to leave them but my travels must continue".

"Are you on your way to other communes"?

"No not now; I have already been to commune Three; because I have had no dealings with any of the other communes I am unsure if they would accept me or even I could be of any use to them at this stage. First I must return to Lethe, see if I can have them listen to my plan. If I fail at least I may get to see my Bond Porta and my brother one more time".

"You don't sound very positive".

"The Lethe elders are very entrenched in their ways and under the control of a powerful Science Master who has only one thing in mind. I will need to convince them to look to a different future and overcome any resistance from Metrin, not a task I have confidence will be achievable".

"Why did you stop here, do you need our help".

"I came by mistake or perhaps by an intervention from some unexpected influence, I am not sure why but very happy I am here whatever the reason. Whether you can help is another question; I don't see an answer unless the code numbers for the position of Lethe can be found by further study within the sheets".

"We have not looked since you went away, there are many so it will take time, I will task the younger of the elders to make a new examination of the text and search for others which may have information we missed last time".

"Thank you Rinn, I will stay a while as I enjoy my time with the family of Frag and Sheff. I find I need more rest than normal when I fly the machine, it seems to drain my strength somehow, so will take the opportunity to relax with them and give your elders time with the picture sheets".

Sala and Kitta were walking back towards the house when Kitta stopped her.

"I heard what you said to Rinn, I think I can help, follow me".

She grabbed Sala's hand turning her to move in the opposite direction, they passed by the rear of the barn and headed out of the commune towards the forest. A while later after several twists and turns they arrived at a clearing where the trees had obviously been cut down by human hands the stumps remaining naturally formed a crude circle as places on which to sit. She motioned Sala to take up a position on one of the stumps and left. Sala waited expecting a surprise of some kind, it's the sort of thing Kitta would do. There was a surprise but not what she envisaged.

Eight ...no ten young people.. or was it more appeared out of the forest and filled the makeshift seats, eventually Sala counted twelve including Kitta in the group; a mix of boys and girls but all very young. They reached out to each other holding hands and including Sala to complete a circle of thirteen. An instant later Salas mind was flooded with the most amazing sensation, all were chanting, a simple one note pulsating tone not audible to anyone outside but contained in the minds of all as if they were one being. It ceased as suddenly as it came whereupon Kitta mind spoke to Sala to explain. All those in the circle let go their hands but were still with minds open to hear the exchange.

"We have been practicing this linking of minds since you left and have found by joining hands and using the chant to blank all other thoughts, the energy flow is so much greater than when we are not in physical contact. Although we were told not to mind speak it became impossible as we naturally communicate in this way without thinking. To keep it secret from our family and the elders took a great deal of self-control. To release the pent up energy that holding back created we moved out of sight where we can mind speak freely hence this clearing, we call it our Circle of Light".

"You come here every day".

"Yes and the reason I brought you here is we have discovered something about a joining which may help you in your quest to overpower the elder Metrin".

"How do you know about Metrin"?

"It was in your mind which was open to me when you spoke to Rinn".

"I must be more careful about what I am thinking when you are around Kitta".

"Don't worry I won't tell all your secrets".

The group all laughed; Sala had forgotten they were all privy to this conversation.

"How do you think you can help"?

"A joined circle can target one mind within the circle and by chanting like we did, directing our thought towards just one, that individual's power is increased many times. It fades when we break the circle but some additional ability remains with the one selected".

"If some extra power remains with the one person do the others lose anything"?

"Yes but we all recover usually by the next day. Our power is growing slowly as we practice and communicate here but by each of us being the receiver from all the others in our turn we are growing much faster. The increases are small but over time will add to the power of the group".

"I see you want me to grow my power in this way. If I do join in your group I won't have time for it to make a significant difference".

"I didn't mean for you to take just one turn, we have all agreed, we will target you every day; although we may lose a little we can make up for it later".

"If you think it will work I am willing to try, when do we start"?

"We already have, did you not feel it"?

"Was that what I felt ? It was over so quickly".

"It is difficult to maintain a transfer like that for long but the improvement will be noticed and significant after a few visits. We will come tomorrow and try to maintain the chant for longer".

The group dispersed as quickly as it came, Kitta took Sala's hand and led her back out of the forest towards her home. The feeling she had experienced lifted her to a new level but now she felt deflated a tiredness slowing her down physically and mentally, eventually the need for sleep took over.

Awake early long before anyone else in the house Sala lay unmoving, musing over the previous day's events; she could not judge if there had been any permanent rise in her mental ability. The change in her body's physical sensitivity had been significant at the time but had returned to normal now; whether her mind had changed in the same way she had no way of telling.

To Sala's surprise the next time she came to the clearing there were seventeen others present including Kitta.

"Kitta are all these people gifted"?

"Oh yes and more too".

"How many of you are there"?

"Fifty four aged over fourteen seasons with others too young to know if it is permanent. Almost every child born here has the ability to mind speak. One or two have lost the gift when they became older but since we started the group sessions it seems we have stopped the loss. Come on let's get started everyone here has to either go to class or help with the work so we can't hang around. One thing Sala you do not chant, just listen and absorb".

The circle of eighteen was formed with Sala's hand gripped tightly by the two boys either side. The chant began and soon the overwhelming surge of energy began to flow to her, she felt as if she would burst as it filled her whole being. It lasted slightly longer than before but ended just as abruptly. The group dispersed in moments leaving Kitta alone with her friend.

"All I can say is where does it come from? I feel incredible like I could run like the wind or fly as the birds".

"Enjoy the feeling while you can Sala, It will pass soon enough but some of the additional potency will remain with you always. We will be here tomorrow with new people, give the others time to recover".

"Do they lose much by doing this"?

"A little yes, but it can be replenished in a few days, if we cycle everyone in turn the effects will be minimised. Anyway we can catch up when you leave, its important you gain as much as possible".

"Can we miss the next session, give them more time to recover I don't want to harm anyone".

"You won't, the next group have not been used yet".

"What about you; you have already been in the circle twice".

"Don't worry about me I am one of the strongest here and would be happy to give you all my power if I could. Look let's see how you fare after the next session, we don't know how much you are retaining, we'll assess the improvements then".

"Fine but if the changes are not sufficient to make a difference we should stop, besides I feel so tired, it leaves me weaker not stronger once the initial surge has faded".

"That is normal you will be fine after a rest. As for stopping, no way, not until you have given it a good try then we will see".

"We will Kitta, we certainly will".

The words came out not as she intended the thought had an aggressive tone, not a nice feeling, if this is what the new-found power is doing to her mind she will not allow this to continue. After the euphoria came the fatigue, she certainly didn't notice any difference in the energy level now only having felt the surge at the time of the chant. She had no idea if she was really stronger or how she could find out. Maybe tomorrow would bring answers.

As always they walked hand in hand back to the house, Kitta's need for physical contact a reminder of how different the Letheans were in this respect. Changing innumerable seasons of conditioning was not going to be possible in the time she had left, it may take several generations.

At home with Kitta, her parents and brother was always a good place to be, fun loving cheerful company great food and the odd glass of juanda ensured her a time to relax and put the questions aside. The soft bed, the sated body and the peaceful mind let her sleep till late undisturbed. She woke naturally as the light of day filtered through her eyelids. She took advantage of the fine wash facilities taking a long shower before dressing and venturing into the main room of the house. Ma Sheff was seated at the table with Terr on her lap.

"Well, well young Sala, you did need that sleep didn't you, if you need to eat there is plenty on the table here, come help yourself".

"I'm sorry Sheff, I didn't mean to sleep so long".

"Hey, you can sleep as long as you like it's no problem. Kitta is at class right now she said to wait for her she will be back during the food break".

Sala sat and selected from the different fruits on offer and some of the bread she liked along with some water, her preferred drink. The juanda which is drunk copiously here was always on offer but Sala was convinced it had contributed to her overlong slumber of the previous night. Rested, fed and now in a much less apprehensive mood from the day before she was ready for the next session, more than that she could hardly wait, it was almost addictive this rush of blood in her veins she experienced during the chant. She wondered how Kitta would test if her strength had really increased; she certainly said they would check so must have some already trusted method.

She passed the time waiting for Kitta to return by entertaining Terr with a ball made of grassy material, it brought back memories of her own childhood when playing with her little dog. No surprise when mental contact was made with him, not in words exactly but emotional bursts of joy when he caught the ball and grumpy thoughts when he missed. Kitta was right this place was special, this might be the place from where the new beginning would emerge.

Unnoticed at first, Kitta poked her head round the door and called out loud to Sala to attract her attention.

"Hey Sala, let's go I don't have long before I have to get back to class".

"Aren't you going to eat Kitta, you are always in a hurry".

"No Ma lots to do I'll have something later. Come on Sala".

"Okay I'm coming give me a chance".

She threw the ball to Terr one last time he caught it and waved her a goodbye, as she left she turned to Ma Sheff.

"Thanks for the food Sheff, looks like I must go".

"Hurry up there isn't much time".

The hand was grabbed once again pulling Sala along the path of yesterday.

"We are going to test you this time and come back later for another session".

"How do you test I don't see how".

"Well start with six of us in a joined block, see if you can break through, if not we'll reduce to five and try again, or increase to seven or more if you are strong enough to break the six. This will find the number of minds needed to block you in

other words your limit. After a few more sessions well repeat the test if there is no change then we know further sessions will be pointless, if the number increases we will continue. Most of us can break four some only three, when we started just one or two was the norm".

"Why six when you have only achieved four".

"I think you are already much stronger than us, it a good starting point anyway. Come on the others are waiting they have to go soon it will only take a moment".

They arrived at the clearing to find eight people only two she remembered from before.

Sala was placed in the middle of a circle of six holding hands. Kitta stood with the two spare people to one side.

"Okay Sala they have closed their minds see if you can break through".

She closed her eyes not to be distracted by any one individual, concentrated on the group using a pleasant thought a greeting. The block was strong she faced it head on imagined it as a wall of stones trying to find a weak spot a weakness in one of the group they were as one, no individual was vulnerable. Full energy at the group as a whole was too strong nowhere she might get through. It held firm, she relaxed opened her eyes.

"I'm not able to break this lot Kitta, too strong for me".

"By holding hands we find there are no weak ones it is the combination you are pushing against. Right let us try five".

Three stepped out and the two who had been observing stepped in leaving five. Following what Kitta had said about there being no weak individuals, this time she adopted a different approach; imagining the group as a shroud surrounding her pressing in on all sides. She let her mind expand the enveloping cloud with an imaginary explosive thought. She burst through, easy enough when you knew what to do. Once their minds were open she sent a mind speak message of thanks. Kitta was excited no one had broken five minds before.

"That was quick, so five it is. Let's say two more sessions and well try the six again. Look I must go Sala I have a class, see you back home later. We'll come here this evening".

The evening came and went, a session with twelve this time. The same sensation again, brief, stimulating but an unknow result as yet. Kitta wanted to make several more sessions before testing. She was afraid if she tested too soon and there were no positive results Sala would want to stop. Her own experience when testing her group only produced positive results after at least six sessions. Because they took it in turn there was a large time gap between each transfer, six sessions took a whole season for each individual to show a permanent improvement. This was agreed to be the best way for the group to grow steadily and evenly. Sala would have six sessions in six days, she had no idea the effect this may have.

Sala was unsure if the change affecting her mind was for the good, would all this power be beneficial, or would it alter her in ways she would not like? They argued that evening where Sala finally agreed to three more session before the next test. Sala was adamant if four injections of energy since the first test had no effect then she was done with it. Kitta decided to increase the number of minds in the circle hoping to compensate for the reduction in the number of sessions she would have liked; she didn't know if it would make any difference, they usually had between ten and twelve in the group; she would try and organise one with twenty or more.

The evening session was a tight squeeze in the limited room at the clearing, twenty three including Sala. Kitta did not join the group this time, she didn't say anything but was feeling the effects of too many transfers and not taking the time to recover. She was glad they were speaking aloud when in the home as it was difficult to avoid her weakness being sensed by her friend when their minds were connected.

The following day nineteen came to give themselves over to Sala. Every time the same pattern an elation during the joining and a deflation soon after but Sala noticed the lethargy felt this time was gone after a short rest. With one more session to go before the test, Kitta was determined to rally as many as possible.

Forty of the communes mind readers crowded in the small space, some had to step back amongst the trees to make room for a circle which now fringed the edge of the clearing. Twenty six joined hands with Sala, the largest union of gifted minds ever made; those outside the circle too concentrated their minds on the task in hand. The intensity of the transition exceeded all that had gone before her very essence seemed to separate from her body and encompass all the minds around her. The instant cessation of the earlier sessions was less sudden this time, a calm descended upon the group as each let go their hands the return to normality took longer somehow. The elation Sala felt remained with her for the rest of the day. These sessions for certain had made a permanent change in her, she had grown in a few days from being a young girl with a telepathic gift to become a grown woman with as yet untold psychic strength.

Kitta had remained outside the circle this time but felt what had happened today was significant enough to have confidence of a successful test.

"Those of you who were not part of the circle will be fresh and strong so please return tomorrow for the tests; we will know

then the true result of this venture. Come on Sala, let's go home I'm starving".

Another evening eating, drinking and relaxation with the family followed by a night of undisturbed sleep leaving both friends recovered and ready for what was to come. Kitta went to class as usual with the instruction for Sala to meet her at the clearing at her meal break. Nine gathered along with Sala and Kitta. The same as before with six in a circle and Sala in the middle. Sala adopted the same strategy which brought her success against the group of five. With eyes closed the group pressing in on all sides, her mind expanded breaking its grip with one single attempt.

"My that was fast and quite easy for me Kitta, it seems you were right".

"Stay there Sala we will add another to the group".

The group of seven fared no better Sala was able to break their combined block with ease. Eight proved the same, followed by nine. With all nine in the group the task took longer but they were still unable to keep her out. Finally Kitta wanted to join the group to make ten but Sala said to stop.

"I think if the group of nine had been fresh I may not have broken them down so adding one more to an already tired group will not prove anything. Let us have a day or two of rest no session this evening. I thank all of you for your time and giving up some of your strength. Come on Kitta, let's go, now its my turn to need feeding, I missed eating this morning".

Twenty days later and a dozen more sessions, a full circle of eighteen fresh minds was easily broken under test; no limit had been established. Sala had reached a point where she knew she could tackle anyone even the combined minds of the Lethe Overseers. The time to leave was fast approaching.

"Kitta I will be leaving soon but I would like to address all those who helped. I want to let them judge my plan for dealing with the problem imposed by Lethe Overseer's desire to abduct the commune mind speakers against their will".

"We can meet in the clearing if you like".

"I believe there are more than fifty, so not much room. A mind link with all would be good enough, in any case I would like to include some young ones say aged eleven or even ten. By the time we reach the need for direct participation they will be of a suitable age or very close. I don't know who they are without scanning everyone's mind and do not wish to openly call the whole commune. so would you inform them to open their minds and join me at a time you can decide. I will be ready."

"I will do what I can, some may be unavailable, commitments to work or family may exclude them but most should be free early tomorrow".

The calls came thick and fast as soon as daylight replaced the night. Seventy one minds were waiting all intent on hearing what Sala had to say. She stayed on her bed and remained there throughout.

"What I am about to propose and the things I will ask you to do may go against what you are feeling, however I ask you to hear me to the end. There are too many here to deal with questions during this joining so will ask you to select a group of say three or four to represent you all and I will confer with them later. Please inform those who are not joined today of this meeting of minds ".

A surge of minds interconnecting with each other began to settle after a few moments till an ethereal hush surrounded the group; Sala closed her eyes and began.

"The land of Lethe is a place of advanced science but progress in the various fields has left them bereft of what we in

the communes and you here in the Outerworld hold as an important part of life. They no longer truly live together, there is no Merging, Bonding or physical contact between males and females. Children are conceived by artificial insemination and as soon as possible are separated from their mothers to be educated in groups. A society of soulless selfish individuals. In the past all had the mind speaking gift but with each generation it is being weakened and often missing in the new children at birth. A significant reduction in the male population is another problem brought on by a side effect from faulty inseminating source selection. Many seasons ago they tried to stem the loss of mind speaking by using the commune mind speakers as a source of male seed donors, this failed.

Since then they have deceptively encouraged the communes to send their best mind speakers to Lethe with the sole intention of forcing them to breed with certain chosen Letheans in order to refresh their genetic line and halt the telepathic decline. Our people refused to break their Bonds so were given powerful drugs to erase their memories. The results were without success; those drugged lost the telepathic gift as well as their memories and the resulting offspring had no sign of the ability either. I have given you a brief summary of what went on there over many seasons but now want you to consider a way for us to grow and learn their scientific ways and for them to stave off their decline. It is my belief if Lethe falls we will follow soon after, I am not saying we are wholly dependent upon them but unless we advance and learn their science we will stagnate and slowly be swallowed up by the earth and its forests which now give us sustenance.

Their idea to mix our bloodlines is sound but the execution flawed. It is my proposal to bring gifted people of both sexes from Lethe to the Outerworld and I want to take some boys from here back to Lethe. I want them to learn our ways in the communes and for you young people to mix and learn alongside the Letheans. My hope is friendships will form and natural Merging will take place".

Sala stopped at that point as a murmur began to rise from the group. She forced her mind over their mental noise to conclude and terminate the joining of the group.

"Please consider what I have said as individuals and in groups, select your representatives who should call me with questions when ready".

She shut her mind to all as a crescendo of voices filled the previously silent space around her. She opened her eyes and looked up to see Kitta standing at the end of her couch.

"That was very direct Sala quite a shock for most of these youngsters, a lot to take in".

"I didn't see hiding the fact that the Letheans were not at all like us would be of help. It is a challenge indeed and even if everything went to plan it would be many seasons before we could see if the next generation of children have the gift".

"Lets see what transpires with this group; you still have to persuade the communes to do the same".

"I know, it won't work unless all agree to take a step into the unknown and believe".

The following day a young couple came to Sheff's house at first light. Sala was awake and aware of their arrival but Sheff and the others were still asleep so Sala asked them to wait outside.

"Everyone here is still sleeping let's not disturb them. It is a pleasant day; we can move to the green area by the barn I will answer your questions as we go. Why only two and why so early"?

"I am Josan and this is Evecia we have been talking much of the night with all those at the joining and they have asked us to speak with you, there was no need for more as we are all in agreement; one representative would have been enough but Evecia and I are soon to be Merged or Bonded as you say, which raises our first question. We had many questions at first but eventually just a few we could not resolve amongst ourselves. We accept your proposal is good and quite a few but not all, would be prepared to go to Lethe and all would welcome those of Lethe who wished to come here".

"Your first question is obvious and the answer is simple if any of you are Merged or wish to Merge with someone in your own community you cannot be part of this initial trial. If you wish to go to Lethe as a Bonded pair I see no reason why not but much later, maybe even several seasons later".

"You told us both male and female were to come here and to the other communes but we are sure you said only males were to go to Lethe or did we hear wrong"?

"No indeed you heard correctly. The Letheans are socially inept, not an impossible task, however it will be difficult to make friendships. If we send a mix of boys and girls it is most likely those from here will either already be friends or will become so to the exclusion of the Lethean, defeats the objective doesn't it. There are very few boys in Lethe compared to girls, an unnatural balance so we don't want to make it worse".

"That is a reason we did not consider; it makes good sense. How long will anyone who goes there have to stay".

"As long or as short as they like, a season at least I would expect in order to give it a fair try but there will be no compulsion to stay if anyone really wanted to leave. One thing even if you never make a friend or Bond with a Lethean you will still learn more science there in a season than in a lifetime here".

"The Lethe people never Merge or even cohabit in the same way we do, so will we still be able to have the Merging or Bonding ceremony if we do meet someone".

"Most certainly, you could come home with your partner for the event and stay here or you go back to Lethe as a pair if you wished. It may be possible to conduct the ceremony in Lethe we would have to see. I know it goes against what you have been used to but it is not a necessity to Merge or Bond in Lethe in order to have children".

"What if the Letheans won't come to us will you still expect us to go there".

" Your questions smack of insecurity you seem to feel unsafe and want assurances I cannot give. I do know of some Letheans who will want to come here; I accept it is a big decision for anyone from either community to do what I am asking".

"If we go and they come here, and it all works out as you hope there are certain to be at least some children as a result; how long will it be before we know if they have the gift".

"The results of any cohabiting will be children with unknown abilities, although we can sense if a baby has some ability very soon after birth, it is not until they are at least two seasons will we see its tangible presence by controlled contact with another and fifteen seasons beyond that to know if the gift has been retained. It will take many generations to find if man has become fully integrated and all with the ability to communicate through the mind; way beyond my lifespan and probably yours too".

"Thank you Sala we will deliberate with our friends and come with an answer soon".

"No doubt more questions may arise, call me direct no need to come here".

"It is a courtesy to come to the elder for talking".

"I am not an elder".

"You are to us".

Sala couldn't argue with that, she was certainly older but not enough to be an elder, anyway not for a long time. You don't become an elder by just being old, you had to be wise too, she didn't know if she was wise or just a dreamer; she hoped both.

She waited patiently for a communication from the young gifted people but the days went by in silence. She asked Kitta what was happening who said she was not included in the deliberations as she was too close to Sala and had a biased opinion. When the request to meet came it was Josan and Evecia who came as before.

"We have come to a decision where all the males in our community would be willing to go. Many of the females would like to go also but understand the reasons against their going this time, however if you can give assurances that they may be included in some future visit we will provide the names of six boys from the most gifted. There are eleven in this group so the six have been selected by the drawing of lots".

"Girls were never excluded from future transfers, only this first journey. Once an established integration has formed both sexes could come and go between all communities. There will be physical limitations in the numbers for transportation as Lethe and the other communes are far away. I can see now why I have been waiting, you have done most of my work for me, selecting the boys who will transfer was not a task I was looking forward to. There will be some considerable time before they can leave. I have first to return to Lethe and persuade them to the accept the proposed solution to their problem. If all is well I will come back as soon as I can. I will need to thoroughly brief the chosen boys concerning what to expect and how they should conduct themselves; this information and the possible extensive wait

before they leave may bring about a change of mind in some; if so please have alternative names ready for me when I return; I hope they are not needed but you cannot be sure ".

"Thank you Sala we concur, go ahead with the plan."

The positivity radiating from these young people was uplifting but Sala's return to reality came rushing in as she thought about her return to Lethe. It was not going to be easy to arrive and remain safe, and as for her convincing the Overseers and Science Masters to go along with her ideas, this was a task which presented a mountain of problems. She must not fail to persuade them to do as asked or all this preparation will be for nothing. Sleep came fleetingly as waking from invading doubts and dreams of Metrin with an army of Overseers standing against her, occurred several times during the night. She needed to go but was unhappy to leave this place; second only to her home, this was where she would like to live.

She was awake before light with no intention to try and sleep again. All in the house were asleep, Sala would like to have left quietly to avoid the emotional goodbyes but could not leave these good people in this way. She left her bed and went to the living area to make a tea and seek out some of her favourite bread. Sheff had laid the table ready for the morning, so not wishing to disturb anything she ate the bread dipped in the tea whilst squatting on a stool by the open window. The breeze rustling the leaves a reminder of the forest's constant endeavour to swallow the homes of these intrepid hunters. They would wake soon enough until then she watched the branches swaying in the wind, their leaves dancing to natures tune.

The hugs and tears over, the good wishes voiced, Sala stepped through the hatch with a final wave.

Her thought of Lethe held ready for her hand to reach out and touch the control.

Chapter Sixteen

This time the flying machine did not hesitate Sala instinctively knew it was on the track to Lethe. The force from the Overseers faded as they too sensed her imminent return. High above the clouds and at great speed she hurtled towards the unknown. No stopping at the Badlands this time, the living crystal some how knew this was to be her moment; she felt at peace.

A reduction in height and velocity roused Sala from her calm repose, recognition of the now visible landscape warned that arrival at Lethe was imminent. The craft fell slowly to the ground back to the place from where it had been taken during Sala's daring escape. Settling gently inside the large building at the exact spot left so long ago. She could see a dozen or more Overseers and others including Metrin through the machine's glass window. There were no active minds trying to contact her, she had the strongest block possible in place, any attempts to break through would be met with an impenetrable wall; they all felt her resistance so remained quiet. She left her seat and moved to the door which, to her surprise, opened revealing Lunn standing before her; he threw her a fleeting smile as he brushed by, quickly stepping inside to retrieve the power source leaving with it under his arm a few moments later. He was gone from view as she stepped from the machine onto the floor of the building. Did they think she was going to go off again, is that why Lunn took the living crystal power source before anything else? They had no idea what she had come back for so had reacted defensively and without thinking.

She intended to deliver her message immediately leaving them in no doubt as to her intentions. Whether they would be convinced was another thing but she would never give up trying.

No one moved towards her, they just waited to see what she would do. She sensed Metrin's desire to speak to her so opened her block to her and her alone.

"Welcome back home Sala".

"Thank you for the welcome Metrin but this is not my home, not yet anyway".

"You have been away far too long; I am at a loss to know why, if this is not your home, why did you return"?

"My Bond is here and my brother, I need to see them, be with them a while".

"You do realise you can't have them back as they were and you can never take them from here. You will never be able to leave again".

"I am no fool Metrin, I am fully aware of the situation, I do have other reasons to be here and one is to do what you once wished and have the commune people integrate fully".

"You are playing games with me Sala, 'integrate fully' you say when I know this is the last thing you intend to do, what is your real purpose in returning"?

Sala opened her mind and sent out her message to all the Overseers not just Metrin. Most minds were curious and ready to listen those who were not found their blocks fall away as the weight of Sala's delivery broke through.

"I have not been idle whilst away, I have learned to harness the power within me and within others too so I now have the will of the communes to attempt the integration of all our peoples. I have travelled this World and seen the strengths and weaknesses of all and have come to realise we need each other if any of us are to survive. The communes are full of many who are gifted, Lethe is full of many with scientific and gifted minds too, we must join these people together, not with force or by destroying their memories but though harmony"?

Metrin forced a cynical laugh.

"You want to take our people to live in the communes, you are deluded young Sala the Overseers will never agree, beside none of us will want to go and visit any commune let alone live in such primitive places".

"Maybe not at first but what I can do is bring many young males here to live amongst you, to form friendships and when of age to Bond and cohabit with your young Lethean females. A pure relationship which will bring forth many gifted children by natural means".

Metrin focussed her mind towards her doubting followers she felt the Overseers response to Sala was not what she wanted, there was a positive element in their combined mood towards Sala, she would have to put a stop to this at once.

"You took our machine by night, betrayed our trust, furtively left us with no idea why you went, blocked all attempts to contact you. You told me you were ready to cohabit when you had no intention of doing so, closed us off from all our efforts to know what you wanted; an affront to us all, lying with every breath, not very harmonious of you was it?

She waited to sense the reaction of the Overseers and saw a shift away from the earlier acceptance of Sala's ideas, so Metrin continued to try and make further gains.

"Now you come with this fanciful plan for mass cohabitation when before you were dead against any suggestion made by us to do the same. I don't know what your real intentions are Sala but I will not allow you to deceive us again".

Sala had an adversary here who was very adept with words, a battle she may lose if she was not careful; she would have to keep things simple if she were to win over the minds of all the Overseers; being side-tracked into public verbal arguments with Metrin was not the way to go. There were signs of some here who were, if not convinced, leaning towards listening to more of her proposal. She would make one more statement and then find a way to work on individual Overseers. She was not certain but did not expect to be whisked away somewhere and force fed the contaminated Waters, she was relying on the non-physical nature of the Letheans and the power of her mind to resist and retain her freedom.

"I have not come to deceive but to ensure the survival of Lethe and the communes. I want Lethe to flourish again revived by the injection of new young blood; strong mind speaking children will be born here and in the communes too. The natural balance of male to female babies established here once again".

Metrin felt the enormous energy of Sala's mind as she listened to her radiating thoughts. Her total concern was to safeguard her position here in Lethe, stem the proposed corruption of the way of living she helped to create, where she and the women Overseers controlled all aspects of what happened here and in the communes.

The inferior people of the communes had served their purpose in the past but were now rising against her. Fear grew in her mind as Sala spoke; Metrin's paranoiac perception of Sala's ambition was that she wanted to take over her role as leader, the false notion grew with each word; she did not listen to the arguments or reason but was seeking ways to prevent Sala from undermining her position further.

"I hear what you say but doubt it's what you truly have in mind. I will seek audience with the elders before any further discourse".

"What do you want me to do Metrin? Am I really welcome or did you just say that to impress the Overseers of your fair mindedness. Am I free or do you wish to secure me away somewhere"?

Metrin was riled by Salas astute observation, she would dearly love to rid herself of this girl but to forcibly remove her was not the way it would cause alarm amongst the Overseers for the code against physical coercion was paramount in Lethe. She had another way in mind.

"You know we have no inclination to imprison anyone, regardless of your previous actions Sala, you will be closely watched but not restricted. Perhaps you could seek out your former family, I have no objections, you may go where you wish. You will be here for many seasons and will eventually find your place amongst us so why not start now".

The assembled crowd and Metrin dispersed leaving Sala in the machine building alone. She sensed Metrin was quite disturbed, even though she outwardly appeared to be in control with her carefully chosen words of derision to belittle Sala in front of the assembled crowd; underlying thoughts showed fear and something quite disturbing; she would have to be most careful, for there was an unpredictability creeping into this confrontation. Her next thought was to go and find Porta and the others but was interrupted by her old friend Lunn who reappeared from behind the machine.

"Hello Sala, I am happy to see you, are you okay? I never expected to meet you again".

"Lunn, I am glad to see you too and even more glad you are still working with the machines. I am fine and so sorry I left without telling you but I......"

"Hey, no mind, I know why you kept it from me, my resistance block is weak, they would have known you were going if you had told me, I understand".

"Are we still friends"?

"Of course. I heard what you were saying to the elders what are you going to do, Metrin will not let you change anything here if she can help it".

"I do have a plan".

"Don't tell me"!

She laughed, even Lunn, who made the quip without realising it, smiled.

"I won't. In the meantime I will find Porta and the others, do you know where they are"?

"I know Bron spends time in the pyramid garden but the others I can't help with. I don't go out much".

"A good place to start, I will try their old houses too, I'll find them don't worry, can we meet again"?

"I'm here most days, come when you like. I've been working on the very old machine; they thought the one you took was gone for good, it's a big old beast and doesn't fly yet but I am close to having it ready".

"Okay Lunn, I'm so glad you are still here, I'll come by soon. By the way why did you take the power source from my machine"?

"Metrin said to lock it away, I think she thought you might try and escape again".

"Is it secure"?

"Oh yes, but the key is yours anytime you want it".

"Really"?

"Of course, she never said not to give it to you".

Sala left with a silent laugh, having returned the smile beaming at her from Lunn's happy face and his joke concerning the literal interpretation of Metrin's orders.

The search did not take long, she found Bron in the food hall by the lower pyramid garden. He had shrunk a little his usual muscular frame had obviously been lacking in exercise. As she moved to the seat next to him a sadness overwhelmed her, tears formed in her eyes with the reminder of past times spent with her brother at home. She wiped her eyes with the cuff of her sleeve and sat close so she could feel his body touching hers. He looked at her, a recognition spark shone in his eyes which prompted a flash of hope, short lived when he spoke out loud.

"Hello, it's you, the teacher".
"Yes Bron it's me".
"You gave me a name".
"I did Bron, how are you, what are you up to"?
"I finished all my classes".
"That's good where do you work now"?
"In the gardens".
"Do you like the work"?
"It is what I am good for".
"What do you do there"?
"They tell me what to do".
"What of the others in our old class do you see them"?
"No".
"Where is your house"?
"Don't know".
"Bron listen to me, do you have a house"?
"They take me home, I get lost".

His lack of interest and monosyllabic response made Sala realise he had not redeveloped any social skills as well as losing everything else. They had indoctrinated him enough to do simple tasks and no more. The education and happy life promised by Metrin had not materialised. She expected to find Porta and Star had been treated in a similar fashion. She stood and said goodbye, no more tears just the rising anger which she would control; thoughts of revenge must be put aside if she was to achieve her ultimate aim. Her need to find Porta and Star were not as urgent as they were. If Porta and Stars response to her were going to be so underwhelming as it was with Bron it was not what she wished to experience right now. She would wait, certain she would come across them sometime during the next few days. Her idea was to bring them all together and make continuous conversation with them try and find if there was any underlying spark left of their once gifted minds. She was not expecting a return of the memory but to draw out any natural vestiges of the human spirit which might still be in there somewhere.

One thing she was more than interested at present was the situation with the offspring from their mixed cohabitation. Star and Jeska had at least one child each, with Horden, Bron and Porta several by the Lethe girls they'd had union with. Not being sure how to find out where they were or information on their progress she decided to start with Science Master Soma and the Body Science hall. One thing was likely the children would stand out out as being physically different, a dark bronze and yellow skin combination might show up in many ways, she had no idea what colour their eyes and hair would be. She didn't know if they were old enough yet to have acquired language skills but it would be interesting to find out, especially if there were signs of mind speaking in any of the children. The care of babies was with the birth mother initially but not for long, group care was the norm.

Artificial insemination had been practiced for so long the need for males was almost obsolete, replenishing the preserved stock of their seed was also thought unnecessary as they had enough for a thousand seasons. Sala considered this strategy may have contributed to the decline in male births. With a few exceptions females dominated every aspect of life here unlike the shared workload prompted by balanced gender numbers in the communes. She wondered if nature was somehow aware of the way it was here so allowed or indeed caused the fall in the male population. If the trend continued unabated there would come a time when extinction would be inevitable.

She entered the Body Science hall not knowing what she would find, a few people were moving through the large entrance making their way to the moving walkways or to the many side rooms. She called to Soma asking if she was in the hall and if so would she see or at least converse with her. She responded but did not come to meet Sala, so no face to face conversation.

"I am here Sala. I sense your question already but I am afraid the new breed children are not here. They were never permitted to be part of my study".

"I am surprised, I would have thought Body Science as being the most appropriate".

"They have been kept, since birth, as a special group away from all others by the Mind Science Overseers".

"You mean Metrin took them from you"?

"I am saying nothing, it was not my decision but one made by the Overseers consensus. The interest in this group of children lay in their telepathic abilities alone so Mind took precedence".

"Not Sense either, a strange decision, I would have expected most Science Masters to have been involved in some way".

"Indeed. What can I do for you otherwise"?

"Do you mean to say Mind Science has not given any information on progress with these children ever".

"It is their prerogative".

"You listened to what I said at my arrival, do you have any thought or questions"?

"Not at this time Sala, there is little trust in your words, although your proposals have merit in many respects, it is not what you say but what you intend that is my concern. No Sala, please do not continue with more of your persuasive arguments, I will wait and reflect".

"I withdraw with respect Soma, I have more to explain if you wish to hear, remember I am very much like you and as you all kept telling us season upon season, I am only here for the wellbeing of Lethe".

Her sarcastic closing words were lost on Soma, but the fact that she did not reject her proposal out of hand or indeed eject her from the hall was good enough for now.

She was apprehensive about going to the Mind Science hall to find answers concerning the children in case she came across Metrin; she did not want a confrontation yet, not until she had established some clear support. Instead she would seek out another who may be an ally in her attempts to make changes. Ouisa was the Science Master she had most dealings with; her mentor in the science of Substance, which had been another subject of study. An ambiguous choice as a candidate for conversion to her ideas; she never trusted Ouisa as she was the one who extracted the memory destroying toxin from the Pinson tree fruit; she wasn't sure if it was her who instigated giving it to her family and friends or was she just following instructions from Metrin; now would not be a good time to find out. Ouisa was another Lethean with little compassion for others so wold not confront her this time, she moved on. Her chance of convincing any of them to consider her plan seemed more remote as she went through the list of those she knew would need to be persuaded. Franil was an obvious choice although not as influential as the Science Masters she had a more sympathetic nature but Sala had no idea where she was, having blocked out all attempts to be contacted; she would have known Sala was calling but refused to respond. The only male of rank was Science Master Peto, her next obvious quarry. She would go back to the building over which he presided and take it from there.

    She was tired and hungry so first went to the food hall near where she used to live, as she came near realised it would be some time before the food would be served so walked the short distance to stand in front of the door to her old house. One step closer and the door swung open. Did they know she was coming back or maybe the house had been prepared as soon as she touched down. 'Was it a trap, were they going to lock her inside regardless of Metrin's promise? Stop this, it's stupid', most likely they had just forgotten so it had been left untouched all this time. She held her breath and stepped through the door, it closed behind her, the thin layer of dust on the shelves and table confirmed her most recent idea, they had just not been in to clean; she touched the green panel anyway just in case; it opened, she breathed.

    Waiting to appease her hunger turned out to be much longer than intended. She'd fallen asleep in the chair well beyond the time the eating hall would be open so was left no choice but to obtain a drink and the sweet snack she did not like very much, from the auto dispenser. A frivolous thought to change the menu of the dispenser to some other snack when all this business was over was dismissed. She drank eagerly and chewed on half the biscuit before laying fully dressed on the bed, again asleep in moments.

The following morning she awoke refreshed and very hungry so her immediate thought was to go straight to the eating hall making sure to arrive in good time. She sat and hungrily ate the food delivered surrounded by people she had often seen before even some who had attended classes with her, one or two acknowledged her but showed little interest it was if she had never been away, maybe because they didn't know of her escape thinking she had been studying and dining elsewhere, probably the Overseers had kept her departure to themselves. Every insight into the strange psyche of these people gave her pause, a reminder of how difficult integration was going to be. She changed her mind about tracking down Peto; Mind Science was what she had been studying so it now appeared she would not be out of place there, it did not need to be avoided like she first thought.

The building was as familiar to her as home; the closed areas, where sometimes dangerous experiments were carried out, were only kept that way as a protection to any who may wander in by mistake; passcodes were available to enter if you needed. She probed the minds of those working behind these closed doors as she progressed along the corridors deep inside the building. All was normal so far, picturing only tests and experiments which were to have been expected. The one space she had never been in at the far end revealed a different story, this is where the children of Porta and the others were being cared for. She did not want it known she had been here so had no intention of entering. Gently and covertly she tried to probe the minds of the carers inside, the only response was a vison of many children, babies with the attributes of all combinations of hair, skin, and eye colour, confirmed these were the offspring of the experiment. A scan of the babies minds showed they were quite normal in every respect; basic language concepts were normal in the older children and all were growing physically as expected. What was missing was the ability to exhibit emotion or transfer thoughts from one to another; there was no chance they would develop the gift if it was not there to begin with. Sala remembered her childhood communication with her brother Bron when he was much younger than these children, the whole reason for the cohabiting had failed. Whatever it was that gave one the gift it was not just in the seed of men or the ova of women, it rested just The Waters of Lethe had not only taken memory it had stolen man's very essence itself.

 She left the building not surprised by what she had found but a little disappointed, for success would have meant her family had not lost their memory needlessly. It would however support her argument for a natural process of procreation. Satisfied there was nothing more of value to be discovered here she could now move on to try and secure support from the Overseers and readers who showed positive thoughts towards her.

 Her upsetting visit with Bron was put to one side she would now seek out Porta and Star, even Horden and Jeska if possible.

Chapter Seventeen

Like a sponge Sala had absorbed all the power from her friends of the Outerworld; it had been flowing from them to her each day during her unexpected and extended visit. The mind sharing was something Kitta had found possible when experimenting with her friends. Sala soon learned the technique where a single powerful entity appeared from within; the combined minds of those with whom she shared empathy, had also passed her a portion of their energy. Even though now physically isolated she would retain the power given to her as long as the giver remained alive; she was as strong as she would ever be. The Overseers had the ability to join forces mentally but the energy remained with the individuals; they combined only when necessary or when ordered to do so; there was no empathy so the power from one was never freely given to another. Once the Overseers had seen the enormous strength in Sala's mind they had yielded, no feelings of loyalty to each other, the comparative weakness perceived in their own minds and the primitive instinct of self-preservation made them shrink from her.

Metrin abhorred the impotence in some of her sisters when calling them to join her to rid Lethe of this threat to their way of life. The response only came from those who still feared Metrin, some closed their minds to her demand, a few others remained faithful. With the backing of her followers Metrin's confidence remained high, certainly a force strong enough to deal with this seditious child from the communes she would soon be hers to command.

She called Sala to meet her away from the centre, a safe distance from the doubting Overseers prying eyes and minds. To Sala the location by the lake seemed odd as it was a place avoided by everyone, on second thoughts perhaps a good choice after all as they were unlikely to be interrupted; a neutral and isolated location for them to settle their differences in private; Sala was hopeful that Metrin would understand. The scene was pleasant, the silver lake with the leaf laden trees as a background belied its ominous content. She made note of the black warning signs along the water's edge so sat well away on the grass some distance from the raised bank. It was warm and tranquil so Sala lay back relaxed and considered what Metrin might have to say. Her attempts to win her over had so far met with resistance whereas the elders, some of the Overseers and Science masters had slowly edged towards accepting Salas ideas on cohabitation, maybe they had brought pressure to bear and Metrin was now ready to listen.

Sala was unaware of Metrin's approach, she'd padded silently along the lakeside banking, stopping to see Sala at rest on the grass in the hollow below; regretting the long ago decision to spare her from the fate which befell her companions. She was not concerned with the subject of Sala's thinking but contrived to invade and take control of her mind, regain her position of power which was being undermined by this primitive girl.

The shadow cast by Metrin's tall frame fell across Sala's face drawing attention to her arrival. She stood defiant her eyes boring into Sala's, the fervent energy brought on by fear of failure was driven further by the adrenaline fuelled heart pumping blood through her veins. A powerful force radiating directly attacking her mind; Sala's block stood firm.

Metrin had been deceived by Sala into believing she would bend to her will and breed. She had given her the freedom to study and roam the halls of Science, pleased with the promise she would soon become a person fit to breed with the best of the Lethe males. Instead she ran away skulking into the night, taking the Lethe flying machine, leaving Metrin to deal with the incensed elders. Gone for near two seasons, gathering strength of mind and support from the communes to oppose Lethe, to bring down the very people who had succoured her. She had returned full of wild ideas attempting to turn the Overseers against her. Metrin knew it would be easy to fall in line with her weaker sisters and listen but instead ignored Sala's false overtures of conciliation.

Her egotistic nature emerged in full taking over her normally logical brain, all too aware if she let Sala have her way Metrin's power over all things may no longer be the dominant force in Lethe. She grew more and more angry letting paranoiac chaotic thoughts take control. Sala tried in vain to radiate empathy and a willingness to combine their minds to find a common ground.

Metrin looked down on her perceived foe from a high position on the bank by the lake's edge, screaming mental defiance at Sala who by now had raised herself to stand on the grass area in the dip below avoiding the overhanging branches of the Pinson tree. Concentration at maximum, her body relaxed knowing she had great strength of her own plus all the extra energy passed to her from Kitta's friends in the Outerworld, there was no one on this earth who could come close to break her shield. She tried again to calm Metrin but was left with nothing in response but a vision of frenzied loathing.

The rage in Metrin's pounding heart made her shake from head to toe as her will to break down this girl's defences were almost spent. The rotting leaves beneath her feet lost adhesion to the damp soil through the quivering of her limbs, her feet slid to one side on the now unstable platform, her balance shifted, she stepped back, and back again trying to regain her balance her foot finding empty space, one step too many, her arms flailing as she pitched backwards into the waiting lake of Lethe.

Sala acted immediately, her first thought was to call for help but there was no response, ignoring the threat to her own safety she scrambled over the mound in seconds to see Metrin struggling below the surface trying to gain purchase on the slippery bank. She reached down into the water grabbed at the material of her purple robe which had floated to the top and dragged her adversary upwards clear of immediate danger. Her head and shoulders rose above the surface Metrin was able to breathe. Blinded by the water running down her face, choking and spewing liquid from her nose she grabbed at Sala's arms for support, the sudden downward motion threatening to pull her in.

Sala mounted a crushing thought directly at Metrin to *'stay still'*, to which her body immediately responded, letting go her grip on Sala, becoming limp and unmoving. Still holding onto the sodden robe and keeping Metrin's head above the surface, Sala pulled her through the water further along the edge of the lake to where it was less steep and dragged the almost lifeless form across the muddy shallows out of the lake onto the bank. Metrin lay prone on her back eyes closed, the only movement was the rapid rise and fall of her chest. Sala's thought asking if she was hurt was met with silence. She gently stroked her face; the normal warm yellow glow of her skin had faded to become almost white; there was no reaction. Sala spoke aloud to her this time.

"Metrin are you alright are you injured, is there anything I can do"?

Her eyes opened and looked directly into Salas; she too spoke aloud.

"I am fine Sala, just cold, why am I so wet, what happened"?

Sala tried again to connect to Metrin through the mind.

"You slipped and fell ending up in the water, I managed to pull you out,. I was afraid you might drown".

There was no response; Sala concluded Metrin must have swallowed some of the water, it seemed she could no longer mind speak but strangely she'd remembered her name; Sala reverted to speaking aloud.

"You had a fall, let me help you get up; see if you can walk. We must get you back to your house and have Overseer Soma check you for injuries".

"I think I can stand" She rose with a little help. "I don't remember what happened. Why are we here it is not safe by the lake".

"You asked to meet me here".

"Did I? I wonder why? Something is wrong; why are we talking aloud and why can't I can't hear what you are thinking"?

Sala struggled to move Metrin with any kind of urgency, their wet and muddy clothes clung to their bodies restricting their limbs. Struggling through the uneven overgrown path, with the weight of the much taller Metrin dragging her back, it took all the physical effort that Sala's small frame could muster to move them out into the open. Eventually the houses came into view, a welcome sight. Sala paused to catch her breath and mind called a second time to Science Master Soma for help. Almost at once several people came running along the path immediately taking Metrin from Sala's supporting shoulder and bore her away. Sala started to follow but Science Master Peto appeared as if from nowhere and stood before her barring the way. He looked deep into her mind to see what had transpired. Sala released her ever present block to reveal remembered images and the truth of the incident. He was set to wreak vengeance upon her so was totally unprepared for what he saw.

"I thought you had pushed her, instead you helped Metrin escape from the water, why"?

"She was in danger and may have drowned".

"But surely that is what you desired, isn't that why you were by the lake"?

"It was Metrin who called me to meet here, I don't know why. Look into my mind Peto this is not what I sought to happen or how I am in my heart. My desire is for harmony not conflict, I met Metrin here hoping to resolve our differences, her uncontrolled anger at me and careless fall were a complete surprise. Lethe and the commune people's needs are much the same, we differ only in how we think these can be achieved. What happened here is far from what I expected or desired; I wanted her to be a part of the plan".

"What plan, she never mentioned you two had a plan only that you had to be stopped".

"It was my plan to bring our two peoples together she refused to listen, her raging at me just before she fell showed her to be totally self-obsessed. When she was recovering on the bank she appeared to have succumbed in some degree to the toxic effect of the Waters; she was quite distressed even so knew who I was but failed to respond to my question of her condition, whether this is permanent or not we will have to wait and see".

"If indeed she swallowed the Water she will have a loss of memory and more, I have never known anyone regain what was taken in this way. If she is lost to us, we the Science Overseers will have to select a new Mind Science Master".

She should not have been surprised by his uncaring statement and annoyed tone dismissing Metrin as no longer an Overseer of consequence but couldn't believe there was no feeling at all for what had happened to his colleague of many years.

"Is this your only thought Peto, finding a replacement? Are you not sad for her; she was your leader for a very long time, there must be some feeling of loss"?

"A replacement is a minor problem for me I admit and yes I do have some feelings, annoyance mostly at her stupidity, irritation that we have to find someone to replace her. Am I sad for her? No, she will not be missed. She only ever took from us and never gave anyone credit for their contribution. She evoked fear amongst the people, in truth many of us will be glad she is gone".

Again Sala was shaken by the lack of empathy, speaking out against Metrin in such a way, at least he did show signs of passion albeit negative; it was going to be hard to infuse positive emotional changes here.

"I would like to go and see how she is if that's possible"?

"Of course we will go together, Soma will be there to check her for injuries from the fall but she will be unable to administer to her for anything brought on by ingesting the Pinson tree water. I still find it hard to believe you risked yourself to save her".

Apart from Metrin the house was deserted, no one in attendance, no one left to care for her. Soma alone was waiting for them by the door Metrin was sitting in a chair facing out through the same door, she had been washed and significantly wore a clean white robe; her eyes were open but with the vacant look Sala had seen before. Soma spoke briefly.

"She has no physical injuries but her mind has gone, no memory remains. She will need to be re-educated. I will make arrangements".

Soma departed along with Peto leaving a damp and dishevelled Sala alone and somewhat bemused. Through the open door she took one last look at the shell of the once powerful woman who had in part caused her so much pain by allowing the destruction of her friend's minds, at the same time saving Sala from the Waters and it's terrible ravaging effects. Allowing her the freedom to learn and grow, albeit for her own divisive purposes; it was one more action in their relationship to prove beneficial for Sala. Her hope was to persuade Metrin to take a different path and until the fateful incident by the lake, she was attempting to gain some rapport if not her trust.

She was reminded of a mournful song sung by the elders when someone died too young, too soon, thinking Metrin could have achieved so much if only………..

….only the black remains, the glow has gone, all sounds gone
Hands full of emptiness gripping the darkness, deaf, blind
A silent questioning fills the void; dead unexpected, wrong
Aware of things to remember, no memories left to find
Admit her failings be absolved to leave this place of sorrow
Transcend this infinite moment between life and are no more
Entreat it presents to her when there's no tomorrow
To join with us the myriad those lives now gone before

She walked slowly back to her room to wash the drying mud from her body and hair. As she changed into clean clothes, a new plan of action formed in her mind; during the upheaval Metrin's fate would generate, the opportunity to gain support should not be missed, she would work to persuade both Peto and Franil at the same time.

Chapter Eighteen

Metrin was no longer Sala's problem so set her mind on dealing with the rest of the doubting Overseers, if there was ever to be a harmony between the two peoples now was her chance. The first line of approach was to solicit the help of Franil who always had some affinity with her and the communes, but her conversation with Peto hinted that he may be a good one to continue with; he was more senior and may have some influence over the others. She had studied under him during her spell with the Air Science classes and as the only male Science Master he stood apart from his female colleagues, outwardly more tolerant and open minded. The Overseers were mostly female, in fact she had only come across two other Overseers who were males in all her time in Lethe. Peto could wait, Franil would be easier.

The loss of Metrin's control over the Lethe Overseers was far reaching, an atmosphere less strained appeared everywhere, more people appeared outside, the children playing in the open areas produced more joyful sounds. She sent a call to Franil who responded at once.

"I feel your presence Sala, what do you need from me"?

Sala wanted Franil near, a face to face meeting so she could look in her eyes as they spoke, her way of knowing if the spoken words or thoughts were the true intention of the speaker.

"Come to the food hall by the green park near my house we can eat together and see what the future holds for us".

"I know what happened to Metrin was not of your doing, even so I am apprehensive being in the presence of such power that could have resisted her will".

"Have no fear Franil, your familiarity with the communes places you in a unique position; I need your help to save them and Lethe too".

"Do we need saving"?

"You may not think so but unless we work together all mankind will slowly slide back into oblivion".

"You speak as if you have had a vision of a future I am not sure is real however I will meet as you wish".

Sala was seated already eating when Franil entered; the hall was quite full with workers and others enjoying their midday break. Some chatter from those speaking aloud and more mental interchange than had been heard in a long time. She closed her mind to the constant noise and concentrated on Franil; as she entered the room fell silent, not used to seeing Overseers in their food hall, many eyes followed the purple robed figure to her seat opposite Sala before continuing with their conversations. The volume of chatter rose during this interruption, settling back to the normal level soon after. The servers brought Franil her portion of the meal on offer which she ignored. Sala felt her tension and discomfort, she never did like being amongst so many people.

"Relax my friend this is not an inquisition, a simple meeting of like minds that's all. You should eat Franil it is very good".

"Tell me what you want that couldn't be asked without this...this...crowd around us".

"In the communes we eat together and discuss our problems over a meal, a social gathering more often than not will achieve more then any formal talks. Of course you know this *already, you have joined our elders in our communes this way many times".*

"I take your point but please get on with it".

"When we first met and on occasions after you said what was going to happen to me and my family was for the good of the commune. I know at the time you believed it to be true; the real intentions turned out to be very different, do you agree"?

"Yes I suppose but if the breeding had gone well it would have been a good thing eventually".

The destruction of minds, forced breeding like animals was never going to be good now was it"?

"No but I never knew they were going to do that".

"If you did would you have told us, would you have still brought us here"?

"I don't know. I may have done".

It was here that Franil averted her eyes, Sala knew she was evading the true answer in her mind.

"You would probably have followed your instructions from Metrin is that right"?

"I expect so, she was so powerful it was difficult to say or do anything against her wishes".

"I know, she was so dominant you had little choice, I don't blame you for any of this but you are the one Overseer I know who has some empathy for the commune people".

Franil knew what Sala was saying was true; what had happened was wrong and in her weakness had ignored how she really felt. The commune life had something she envied she had seen it up close. Now perhaps this girl with the mind of a Master could bring some of that harmony to Lethe. She decided to help.

"There are others too, some who didn't agree to what was happening here. Most Science Masters and Metrin ignored the *thoughts of the people if they were not in line with their plans. In the past those who spoke out were fed the lake Waters".*

"This is something I didn't know".

"It has not happened for a long time but the threat is still in our minds; it is why everyone followed what Metrin wanted".

"The Overseers intended forced breeding idea had its merits but failed because it destroyed the very thing they were trying to preserve; in the communes breeding is a natural process. Two people Bond as you know for life, they produce and care for children in a family group. Here in Lethe you have lost the family, the children are isolated from this intimacy when very young, they end up lacking passion and ambition.

Franil now for the real reason I asked you here; I want to bring young gifted people from the communes to live here with the people of Lethe and in exchange take some of your young people to live in the communes, to learn our songs to meet and Bond with us by the joining of like minds. I can only achieve this with your help and those who think like you".

"I can tell you Sala I was convinced by what you said when you first came back but was afraid to expose my feelings. I thought it brave of you to return and to have done so must have been for a good reason. You stimulated many minds that had been dormant and submissive for so long, including mine. Without Metrin's overpowering influence you now have my support".

"I'm convinced the insemination used here has distorted the natural process of evolution. Let us bring back the missing essence that must surely have been part of the Lethean spirit for you to have created such a place as this. Franil I know you have a good heart; spread the word amongst those you know who are sympathetic, be careful of the elders Franil they are more likely to be entrenched in the old ways; leave the more powerful Overseers and Science Masters to me. Until I feel safe I will maintain a

strong block to all minds but will remain sensitive to your call if you need me".

They both left the hall, Franil to the Pyramid gardens and Sala to the Air Machine Building.

To Sala's astonishment she saw Peto lying under the rear end of the very old flying machine with Lunn kneeling beside him holding an instrument of some kind; she hadn't expected to find a Science Master so involved. This huge machine was now located in the main building and could be seen from end to end unlike in its former confined resting place. It was a body length wider than the one Sala had flown but considerably longer more than twice its length. The surface had a silky finish instead of the shiny material she was used to. Only one large window at the front but a double sized wide hatch at the side now fully open.

Sala opened her block a little for them to be aware of her presence. Peto wriggled out from his lowly position as Lunn struggled to stand still holding the obviously precious and heavy technical box in both hands. Sala held out her hand to Peto as a gesture to help him rise; he took it gladly as his old bones did not react kindly to being in such an unnatural place.

"Thank you Sala, I haven't done anything like that in a long time. Lunn put the engyscope away I am finished with it for now".

Lunn trundled off gathering up the instrument's probes and the bundle of connecting wires from under the machine as he went.

"How is it coming along"?

"Not much longer and we will be ready".

"How did you get it here from the Science Centre it must have been there for ever".

"We flew it of course, no other way".

"I am surprised it still worked after such a long time".

"So was I, Lunn is pretty skilled he can fix anything, he eats and sleeps with these beauties. I sense you did not come here to see our old machine, what can I do for you".

"With Metrin gone I admit my task may be easier. You already know my intentions and believe you may agree at least with part of my plan. I want to take some of the young gifted Letheans out into the world of the communes and bring the commune's young men here. Joining of the two communities to live together in a natural way have children with shared blood in their veins. I am convinced it will revive the fading mind speaking here".

"This was already tried and failed".

"The minds of those chosen were destroyed by the Waters, even Metrin realised the whole idea was doomed from the start. This will be a joining of two people who will become devoted parents caring for each other and for their babies not the callous travesty instigated by the heartless Overseers".

Peto held up both hands as in surrender.

"Hey enough Sala! I don't need any more of your incensed speeches. I admit I was one of those who reluctantly went along with taking their memories; I am not heartless and knew it was not the perfect answer but thought we had no choice when your people refused to join our breeding plan because of your Bonding ritual".

"Sorry to be so aggressive Peto, I feel I am constantly having to press hard to gain any kind of positive response from anyone. Let me explain, Bonding is at the heart of commune culture and cannot be put aside Peto, it is an agreement between two people to join in all respects for their whole life, all who make this vow would rather die than break it. They are the ones who had no choice, you did".

"I did not realise how strong this Bonding is, or I may have acted differently even so my dissent would have made little or no difference, the majority were in agreement".

"You say majority were there others who were against this"?

"Oh yes, Metrin for one, she knew the waters would destroy the gift like you said, Soma and Enno were of the same opinion but apart from one or two other low order Overseers the consensus of the elders prevailed. You were lucky Metrin was allowed to exclude you from the plan; ironic wouldn't you say"?

"I have always considered my relationship with Metrin predestined, now even more so. To move on, will you support me in my endeavours to save Lethe and the communes. What I ask is not far removed from your original plan and can harm no one even if it proves unsuccessful".

"You realise if we go ahead it will be many seasons beyond my existence and probably yours too before anyone can know if it has worked".

"If the gift is saved or not, the merging of our people into one can only enhance the welfare of us all".

"I do agree in that respect so I will help where I can. Remember I'm a man in a woman's society; I have only kept my position as Science Master because of my specialist knowledge; the influence I have with the hard line Overseers is questionable".

"You mentioned Soma and Enno earlier maybe a pair who would likely respond to you".

"I will see what can be done".

"Thank you Peto, my mind will remain open to you anytime".

And so it began, the word spread, Peto and Franil moved cautiously amongst their colleagues discussing the ideas put forward by Sala, carefully sounding out how they were disposed. Nurturing those in favour, planting seeds of doubt in the minds of the neutrals and backing away from those opposed. At first everyone was being cautious, even though Metrin had gone suspicions remained of retribution if you had a thought differing from the established ways. This biased mindset slowly relaxed as more and more fell in with embracing these new ideas.

For many seasons suppression had squashed the ambitions of those with some small degree of spirit, the hidden pressures now released enabled a freedom of thought not seen for a very long time. The ever present mind blocks began to disappear, group mind discussions openly took place. Sometimes groups of Overseers along with the ordinary people asked to mind speak with Sala to ask questions which she gladly did. The hard line Overseers and the powerful ancient elders saw the trend and as so many in Lethe were now in favour of the exchange of youngsters, they quickly set about protecting their positions by professing to have been in favour all along.

A closed meeting of the Science Masters and the elder Overseers was called, followed soon after by a universal announcement of their decision.

Exchanges of the gifted children would be allowed but it would be a group from the communes to come to Lethe first, how they were treated and what plans would be made for their education would be decided later. Sala accepted the inevitable control being exhibited by the Overseers, a change in their nature was never going to happen for a long time, let them have their moment; once the boys were here she Franil, Soma, Peto and their true followers would make sure the integration was a real and natural process.

The transfer of Lethean's to the communes was a different story, they had made no decision as to when this would take place, some wanted it to be as soon as possible others to wait till they saw if the visitors integrated. The end result was to wait. No decision would be made until the first group of boys had been here for long enough to assess the situation before they would make another announcement. The usual non decisive attitude of the Overseers, but a step forward, they could go ahead with the first phase of the plan.

Franil was to be the one to fly the machine to collect the boys from the communes, many didn't want Sala to accompany her but she was allowed to go as a non-participating observer; it was worded that way to appease the doubters but really they had no choice. Franil had no idea where the Outerworld lay or even that it was where the first arrivals would come from, she was expecting to go one of the communes already well known to her.

With the changes taking place Lethe was probably no longer a danger to the Outerworld but considering the skittishness of the Lethean Overseers it could all go wrong at the last minute; keeping the Outerworld location from the Letheans was a promise made to Rinn and one she would not break even though the reasons for doing so no longer applied. Sala would wait until they were on their way before telling Franil their true destination. If she had spoken of a commune no one knew anything about they may not have agreed to the exchange.

The debate went on and on even after the initial decision; how many boys would be permitted to come for starters and 'why no females' kept being asked when Sala had already pointed out, more than once, there was no point in worsening the huge imbalance already existing in Lethe. Who would pick the girls to cohabit with these boys was a question she ignored as it missed the whole point of allowing freedom for the boys and girls to integrate as nature intended. All this posturing made no difference, once the boys were here she knew what was going to happen and none of the Overseer's petty controlling attempts would be allowed to interfere.

Now she was accepted by most of the Lethean Overseers, Sala was able to move freely without the threat once imposed by Metrin and her elders; the prospect of change seemed to excite the population, not a reaction Sala expected to see. She visited all the Science facilities, spoke with the Masters at a personal level, the effect of which was an unexpected almost friendly response even from Ouisa. Her interest in them as individuals and discussing their needs and ambitions seemed to inspire them somehow. The collapse of Metrin and her totally restrictive practices released a flood of repressed ideas which had lain dormant for so long. In a very short time Sala's proposal had gained such momentum it had every chance of success, at least the first phase of bringing the young men from the Outerworld to Lethe was now unstoppable.

Her thoughts shifted from the impending project to her Bond Porta, the last torpid meeting with Bron still fresh in her mind did not stop her from seeking Porta's whereabouts; her improved mood would give her the strength to face the inevitable. From Lunns enquiries he told Sala he could be found working in the food preparation area close to the Science Agriculture building, another example of Metrin's failed promise. Porta was standing by a table chopping vegetables and placing them in a large pot.

"Hello Porta, let us go outside and sit a while".

Obediently he followed and they sat on the low wall next to a green area in front of the hall.

"Do you know who I am"?

"You are the teacher with stories and the one who gave me my name".

"Do you remember the stories".

"I think so, well some of them. I like the one with the dog and the ball. I have never seen a dog are they real"?

"Oh yes but they don't live here in Lethe".

"My friend had a dog once".

Sala couldn't believe what Porta had just said, did he just recall their childhood when Sala had a pet dog, or was it just some recollection from one of her stories.

"Where was that Porta"?

"Not sure, before we came here I think".

Salas heart rate jumped; this was significant, he is seeing the past and not one given to him during her story telling. She wasn't sure what to say next, urgently wanting to keep him on this tack. Prompting him about his former home seemed the best option, try to get him to recall something she had not previously spoken about.

"Was my Papa Regol there Porta"?

"He might have been. I don't think he liked the dog".

That clinched it, Porta remembered for sure. Sala had never mentioned her grandfather Papa Regol not once and it was true he never liked her dog because he would bark and jump up at him whenever he came to the house.

"No he didn't love dogs much, but I did and I loved Papa Regol".

"He was nice but he died, it made me cry".

"Me too Porta, me too".

Sala throat closed she couldn't speak, tears on her cheeks, not just recalling the death of Papa Regol but with the unpredicted change in Porta. After some time allowing herself to settle to a less emotional state, she continued her conversation with Porta feeding him information about Five and his family, eliciting fragments of memory from some deep recess of his mind. He became agitated when an Overseer came close and looked at him for a few seconds, nothing was said but he stood up and moved away.

"Thank you teacher, I must go back to work now".

He went inside before she could do or say anything more. She let him go, more than satisfied with what had occurred she would return tomorrow. She sent a mind speak directly to him.

"Porta, My name is Sala I am your Bond".

There was no response, she didn't expect one but there was a chance the message might get through.

Her memory of Papa Regol made her smile. Visions of him in his old chair, her as a young child sitting cross legged on the floor opposite with her brother so caught up in his stories they stopped talking and didn't move for ages. She didn't realise it at the time but her Ma would send them to see him when she needed a bit of peace from their boisterous playing and shouting. They went willingly for he was fun to be with and never failed to amaze. The stories were told as if they were all his own experiences, recounting his travels around the world meeting all sorts of strange creatures and exotic people. She believed every word; her childlike gullibility made her smile again.

She too remembered when he died and the tears she though would never stop. When they carried him to the fields with the elder singing the song of 'reunion' to be returned to the ground which had sustained him all his life. Her tears did dry as her Ma explained how dying was part of who we are and that he was part of me and Bron and everyone who knew him. He would nourish the soil and become part of the forest which covered our world.

To the soil you are returned
Your spirit will stay with us for a while
We feel your presence and will remember you well
And use your kind ways as our guide
Go now to a place which gives us life
For we rejoice in your reunion

The song of 'reunion' she heard on other occasions when others of the commune died, she felt sad then too but did not cry.

She would go back to Bron this time with more positivity in her approach. The path of the conversation with Porta had produced unbelievable results she would attempt the same approach with Bron.

When she found him it was if he had never moved.

"Hello Bron, it's me again, do you know who I am"?

"The one who came the other day".

"Yes but what about before do you remember me from then"?

"Are you the strange teacher"?

"Yes that's me. What's my name"?

"I don't know".

"Think hard, I did tell you, try and remember".

"Is it Metrin"?

"No it definitely is not. What's your name"?

"You're the one who told me, so you should know".

"I forget, remind me".

"You are strange, you used my name a minute ago so you can't have forgotten already."

Here it was the awkward streak she had come up against in her brother all too often. Not memories yet but a sign his inner character was intact.

"Who gave you the name"?

"You know already, it was you, Silly Sala".

Sala didn't know if she had told him her name since the memory loss, in all likelihood she had at some point, but 'Silly Sala' was a childhood taunt he used to use. Progress; like with Porta glimpses of what might be. She tried the Papa Regol name but he did not remember him so she decided to stop there but sent another hopeful mind speak message to him.

"My name is Sala Your name is Bron, you are my brother and I love you".

He did say goodbye and would be expecting her tomorrow; much more communicative than last time.

All enquiries by Lunn to find Jeska failed so she concentrated on seeking out Star, with no immediate location uncovered Sala went to the Mind Science building. She was greeted warmly by the staff who had been her long time teachers, even the two Overseers who had been very aloof during the reign of Metrin came to say hello. No one mentioned the proposals, the subject had been decided upon and was now the exclusive province of the elders. 'Old ways will not change overnight' her thought. She hoped to find Science Master Peto here as he should be looking to select a replacement for Metrin from the personnel on site. Peto had been here earlier along with Soma and had spoken to all possible supporters and candidates but they had left already. Sala stayed a while moving through the laboratories asking about new experiments and commenting on ones she was familiar with. The visit did little to show her any real advances in the science but cemented the relationships she had built during her time as a student.

Everyone she thought might help was questioned concerning the whereabouts of Star, Horden and Jeska. Horden was found quickly enough, he had been spotted out by the gardens by several people here; he was distinctly different physically so stood out when seen in public. Like Bron he worked in the pyramid gardens and ate in the hall nearby. The two girls seemed never to go out, so whatever their place in this society it involved being inside and perhaps never eating in the regular halls or they would have been noticed by someone for sure.

Horden unlike her brother and Porta showed no signs of recovery she feared his and Jeska's ingestion of the Pinson tree extract had been significantly more potent. She had yet to find Jeska and Star.

Her visits with Porta and Bron became more frequent now, there were good signs of the return of some memory, she began to enjoy being with them. She ate with them visited their houses and tried to re-establish a lost friendship. When she joked or teased them they responded with some emotion, a laugh or a smile showing her that something of their original personality existed deep down. Horden was included in her visits but he showed no sign of memory recovery but did respond favourably to being in the group. Perhaps it was part of their whole being, something different from the Lethe personality in their brains which could not be destroyed. She made a point of sitting close to Porta touching his face, stroking his hand, deliberately holding on to an arm for support when walking. He never objected and on occasions he responded with similar gestures of familiarity. She wondered if she could build a relationship with this shadow of her former Bond; it would be a hope, a dream; a hope with some small chance to succeed, a dream maybe never to be fulfilled; she let it go.

Her earlier attempts to jog their memories with direct questions about their past lives had caused confusion, instead she told them stories of where she and they were born, of her Ma and Pa and about life in the commune. Although they still believed they were from Lethe she showed them how they were different physically and were more like her. Although they listened and enjoyed the tales they seldom asked questions, the Lethean elders indoctrination and re-education techniques had been thorough, it would take patience and time for Sala to change the way they thought, she had neither the psychological skills nor the time at the moment. The Waters had taken their toll and were not about to give them back to her easily.

Her search eventually led to the two girls, she should have thought about it before, but hadn't felt their presence on her previous brief visit. They had been placed to look after the special babies in the hidden area of the Mind Science complex. The children had a mix of physical characteristics similar to them so the elders thought it may help to have carers who looked like them. They never left the building eating and sleeping there, constant and willing guardians. Several of these youngsters were the offspring of Porta and Bron, so Sala felt a pang of remorse knowing she was related to all of them in some way. Jeska and Star were probably the birth mothers of two of these children but did not know which they were from the fourteen youngsters under their care. Star was much more aware than Jeska and told Sala their babies had been removed at birth and they had only been assigned here several weeks later. Sala had to put the whole episode out of her mind, none of it seem real anyway, she would concentrate on dealing with the future and not dwell on things she could do nothing about.

Jeska did not remember anything of their previous meeting and like Horden was probably beyond help. Star was different, she knew of the original times when Sala's stories were first told, she also knew Salas name and that she had given her the name of Star. Early conversations uprooted some deeper memories of her childhood but Sala was unsure if they were false or not, maybe gleaned from the stories she had been told. The most rewarding reaction was how physical star like to be, she hugged whenever they met and was always attempting to hold Sala by the hand or arm wanting to be as close as possible. Time with her was limited as her caring tasks were something she took seriously and she would not leave the hall or the children for one moment.

Attempted mind contact with all three had not yielded a response but there was a definite reaction causing them all to stop what they were doing and look around when Sala sent a strong message. She would persist.

The time passed all too soon, her efforts with her family would have to wait a while for preparations to leave were well under way. Peto had instructed Lunn to recharge the power source, fit seats for eight passengers finally install the source with same living crystal which had become almost part of Sala during her distant travels. Soma, Enno and Sala had agreed that in order to ensure the boys would have a varied education and exposure to as many different girls as possible accommodation for the six boys was important; two to be located near the Pyramid gardens, two close to the Body Science hall and the final two adjacent to the Mind Science Hall; which boys would go where did not matter they would be given a briefing on arrival and they could choose who they paired up with.

Sala thought six young men was a good start but once established there would be more as she recruited from communes Three and Five. The next task will be to persuade some of the Lethean youth to go to the communes, more of a challenge than the reverse. In the back of her mind was the possibility to seek out other communes from the codes, locations still waiting to be deciphered, all laying hidden in the ancient sheets held by Rinn the Outerworld elder. She was wasting time thinking too far ahead, no more musing she was impatient to leave.

Franil entered the flying machine first with Sala close behind, there was no farewell ceremony just Peto and a handful of Overseers silently watching as the hatch door closed. Franil at the controls and Sala seated behind, the machine rose clear of the ground and slowly left the building, once clear of any obstruction the skilled hands of Franil set the machine on its course to commune Three. Sala waited until the ship was well under way before she intervened.

"Franil, we are not going to Three or even Five to pick up anyone, well not this time. Just think what would be their response if we tried to take their young ones away. The last time I saw them was when I informed them of what had happened with the waters and their children's lost minds; I warned them against any future advances from Lethe. Remember, it was before the end of Metrin's rule and the great move towards cooperation, they have no idea of what has happened since. I need to speak to their elders first explain how things have changed. We can come again later when they will be ready".

Immediate panic shot through Franil's mind.

"No Sala no, what are you doing, it is all planned; why did you not tell us they were not ready if we don't bring back anyone this trip is a waste of time"?

"Hey, calm down Franil, we are going to collect six boys and bring them back, just not from Three or from Five. There is another commune who have already agreed to provide some amazingly gifted children. I have spoken to them about the plan and what to expect, they are well prepared and wait patiently for the day I return to bring them to Lethe. I did not tell anyone for fear they may have rejected my plan. I am sorry I did not tell you before but promised to keep the existence and location of this commune to myself. They had children abducted in the past by Lethe and were fearful it would happen again".

"Why didn't you just tell me, I would have kept your secret".

"A promise, that's all. If I had told you and Metrin had seen into your mind, well you know what the consequences would have been. It doesn't matter now I will guide us there".

"This is not what the Overseers said, I was to be the controller and you the observer".

"We'll simply swap places for a while, give you a rest, they won't know".

Sala chuckled, Franil looked bemused but did not give up her place at the controller.

"Where is this commune what is its number".

"It doesn't have a number now although I think it was number four maybe, it doesn't matter it became known as the Outerworld a long time ago, a good name, you will see. I am not sure where it is but have set its location as an image in the memory of the crystal, I will only have to think of it and the source will take us there."

Sala stepped forward to take over but Franil continued to resist.

"It is my Overseers will that I command the machine on this journey but I trust your intentions were not to deceive me for your own ends but I should go back to Lethe for new instructions".

"No you cannot do that Franil, I only want what you know is right. Look let us do it this way you take the ship to Five first and Three so I can explain to them what has happened, that way you are following your orders, then let me instruct the source to make course for the Outerworld to pick up the boys; you will remain in command the whole time and no one will know where they came from. Once we have collected our cargo from there you can take back your position at the control for the journey back to Lethe".

"I do trust you Sala this plan will work for me, I will set course for Five".

The machine made a gradual move towards Five its new course only noticed by the angle of the light entering the window casting a different shadow across the cabin. They were on their way Sala was content, this change of plan would work out well, allowing her to explain the new situation in Lethe; give Five and Three time to prepare acceptance of Lethe's girls in exchange for their boys. Franil was less than pleased with Sala's lack of trust by keeping her uninformed, she hoped she wouldn't spring another surprise, one was enough.

The time dragged on as Five was the furthest away, Sala slept Franil stayed awake but silent and restful till the approaching destination grew near. No hiding out of sight this time she guided the ship towards the central square.

Once landed Sala alone entered the great barn where Ezekiel always greeted anyone who wanted to see him. She made the formal address before approaching and taking his hand.

"We are close old friend the time has come to prepare. Lethe is no longer master of our destiny no longer are we and their people under the ruler of repression. Soon I will bring young boys and girls to live amongst you and I will take our young people to Lethe in exchange".

"Sala, slow down your feverous words, what has happened; are you not deceived again, remember what has happened to your Bond and to you brother, is this not just another way to abduct our children"?

"Oh no Ezekiel if only I could enter your mind you will see the great change that has taken place in Lethe. The oppressor Metrin is gone and the once subjugated Masters have come to accept they were wrong, without all the peoples of the world coming together none of us will survive".

"You seem very sure; how can I know what you say is true. You may believe, but must I also trust your words when the past has proved us wrong too"?

"You will see my friend. Prepare six boys, volunteers for a journey to Lethe those who have mind speaking ability will be best. I will bring both boys and girls from Lethe as I said; speak with them face to face, judge them for yourself; let those among you who have the gift look deep into their minds, they will find no deception. Only then when you are sure allow the chosen ones to travel".

"It seems fair. I accept but will follow my heart when making any decision".

"I ask no more Ezekiel. I have worked ceaselessly for these days of change, ever since you sang to me the song of light".

The song of light had slipped the mind of Ezekiel, he indeed had thought Sala might be the one, it appeared he may have been right, if not the consequences for his charges would be dire.

"Go Sala, we will prepare as asked; when you return with your recruits, we will decide".

Sala left the barn content Ezekiel would be persuaded when the time came. She made straight for her house; her Ma was waiting by the door the air machine was visible to all so she knew Sala was coming.

"Alone again Sala, no Bron"?

"Not this time Ma but sometime he will come with me I promise. I can't stay, work to do, things are changing Ma you will see, it will all come right in the end".

"Don't leave it too long Sala none of us are here for ever".

She gave her Ma a hug hiding tears by burying her head in her mother's shoulder.

"It will be soon; we will come together Ma, I promise. Take care".

Franil sensed the mix of joy and sadness in Sala, emotions she knew little of, she did not think she would like either very much as they both made Sala cry, she had never cried.

"Okay Franil take us to Three".

Arrival at Three was at night so Franil held the craft aloft some distance away with nowhere to land safely. Sala was asleep so Franil passed the time looking out of the window at the views of the forest as daylight emerged above the hills surrounding the commune. She had seen it all before in passing but had never really studied what she was looking at. Patches of green in twenty different shades, areas of rocks where trees could not root supported yellow and blue flowers which grew in the crevices. A small dark snake shaped ribbon where the path of a stream meandered dividing the canopy in two. It was beautiful, the feeling of joy she decried in Sala enfolded Franil for a brief moment, she wanted more but was interrupted by Sala's noisy stretching and yawning as awareness dawned along with the day.

Again the machine landed in the centre of the commune, soon surrounded by all those awake. Franil remained inside as Sala stepped out. Recognition evoked greetings of welcome from some and more hostile thoughts about what she was here for from others. She moved to where the elder Brugan would be in the great barn. It was unusually early for the elders to be awake so Sala was prepared for a long wait. The news of her arrival had filtered through the commune in no time, Brugan appeared well before Sala had time to find a place to sit.

"Greetings Brugan I am sorry to have woken you so early".

"You are welcome anytime Sala, we old folk sleep lightly and do not mind an occasional early start to the day. Shall we sit".

They moved to the rear where old bales of hay used as seating were spread.

"It was not so long since you were here last, do you have some good news about our children"?

"I am afraid things are unchanged there however I do have good news. Lethe is no longer controlled by Metrin, she has gone from her position of power and Lethe is now struggling to come to terms with its possible collapse. I have reached an agreement with the senior Overseers and their Science Masters to help with their recovery".

Brugan's voice was harsh at Salas apparent nerve.

"Are you really expecting us to join in this recovery, is that why you are here"?

"I understand your anxiety Brugan, especially after what has happened to Horden and Jeska but please listen to what I have to say before you refuse my request".

"Lethe is no longer under the rule of repression. Metrin has gone and the opinion of those who are left has come to the fore, they truly seek cooperation and not the subjugation forced on them by fear. I want to bring young boys and girls to live amongst you and I would like to take your young people to Lethe in exchange".

"This is what happened before, I will not allow it".

"It is not the same Brugan, a great change has taken place in Lethe for oppressor Metrin is no longer in control. I have persuaded the Science Masters to accept that our coming together is essential, without your cooperation none of us will survive. This is to be an exchange where you have so much to gain".

"We were wrong last time how can I trust your word. How do you know you are not being deceived yet again"?

"I understand your caution and agree you must be satisfied that what I say is true before you commit to what I ask".

"How can I be sure when last time you told me to be aware and not be taken in by any overtures from Lethe, yet here you are just a short time later telling me to ignore your warnings".

"That was true then but not now. I may have a solution but it will require at least a little cooperation on your part; just choose six gifted boys willing to travel and wait for my return; I'll be back as soon as I can with six girls from Lethe. When they are here test them, check they speak the truth with your gifted ones, they will see no harm intended. When you are satisfied and only then allow the chosen ones to return with me".

"I have grave doubts and do not trust the Overseers. I will do as you ask but if I have any qualms I will not send my boys or welcome Lethe's children here".

"Agreed but please put aside prejudices because they look different, inside we are all the same. I wish I could enter your mind you would then see the good in this".

"Perhaps it is good that you can't, my decision will be through trust and the wisdom of age not some mental manipulation".

"You are a hard man to convince Brugan but I will honour your decision. One more thing for you to think on, we are about to transport six boys from another commune to Lethe and have the agreement from commune Five on similar terms to your own. You are not alone, no one in this world is or ever will be. Goodbye Brugan I'll be back soon".

She didn't linger to visit the family of Horden but returned to the machine eager to be on her way. Franil's refusal to go straight to the Outerworld had served Sala well, the visits to Five and Three had paved the way for the eventual transfer of girls from Lethe.

"Right I'm all finished here, let's go Franil next stop the Outerworld".

"You'd better take over I have no idea where this Outerworld is".

"No Franil do as the Overseers requested, stay where you are, I will pass my vision of the Outerworld to you and you in turn to the source. The crystal will know the way.

Three and the Outerworld were quite close, as soon as Sala sent Franil the symbols for its location the vessel left the ground and was immediately on course. The wide fields of Three were quickly left behind, replaced by tall trees and dense vegetation; a forest of green which covered most of this area of their world. A short while later the craft slowed as arrival at the Outerworld commune drew near. Earlier mind contact with Kitta warned of their immediate arrival and to make sure the space was clear for them to land safely. As soon as the vessel settled gently on the soft ground they were surrounded. It was like they were under siege with bodies pressing all around the machine, the whole commune seemed to have turned out to greet them.

"Is it safe Sala, all these people"?

"Of course Franil, they are just a bit over excited. They will move away when we exit".

"I hope so, you'd better go first".

Sure enough as soon as the hatch door started to open those close by moved back. Kitta was waiting a step away and as Sala moved out she came face to face with a beaming smile and the hand of her friend who gripped it so tight it almost hurt. Kitta wanted to wrap her arms around her but resisted the temptation with everyone looking on.

"Steady on Kitta can I have my hand back".

"Sorry, I'm so glad you came I wondered if everything was going well I had not heard until your message telling me you were about to land".

"I tried to mind contact from Lethe but there is a limit to my range, after all you are half a world away. Anyway all is good the decision is for six boys to return with us as soon as they are ready. I will need to brief them first, a day or two should be enough, have there been any changes"?

"No the same as before as far as I know, you can decide when you meet them. But we must go to Rinn he is waiting inside".

All the while Sala and Kitta were mind speaking, Franil nervously stayed inside, the throng of people all touching each other was not what she was used to. Sala turned expecting to see her standing to the side or behind.

"Hey Franil, don't be afraid come out, these people here want to meet you."

Franil came to the door and stepped through. Long black hair framing her golden yellow face on her tall frame in its purple cloak cast a magical spell on the crowd craning to get a peek at the new arrival; they fell silent for a fraction and then started clapping and cheering in delight at the vision before them. Sala had been living with the Letheans for so long she hardly noticed the difference but to the Outworlders this was a new experience.

"Don't worry Franil they have never seen an Overseer before, it will quieten down soon, just smile and give them a wave".

Franil did what Sala suggested which brought on even more cheering and louder clapping, which made Franil cringe and Sala to laugh out loud. The three edged towards the great hall where Rinn would be waiting, as they did so the crowd shuffled back to make room. Once inside and out of sight the mass noise dropped to a gentle hum as their rapture reverted to debate and speculation. The space was darker than outside but Sala's vision adjusted as her eyes met Rinn's smiling face; seated in his usual spot, he rose as she approached to addressed him in the expected manner.

"It is good to see you Elder Rinn I hope I find you in good spirits. I come with good news and a message from the people of Lethe. This is our friend Franil an Overseer of Lethe who is to transport your young men to her land as we arranged".

"Greetings Sala and Franil both, please be seated and join me in a welcome drink and food after your journey".

The formalities over they sat together, drank the juanda and ate the pastries as they talked about what had been happening in Lethe and the Outerworld since they last met. Kitta, who knew she was too young to be included without invitation, was obliged to stand just inside the door listened intently. Franil understood the formal courtesies at the initial meeting but was fascinated by the frank and open conversation being conducted by these two different peoples. All she saw were the differences, ones they either never noticed or, as she was beginning to understand, more likely didn't care about. She relaxed as the juanda made its way through her veins to quell her doubts and confusion. This integration was to be full of surprises.

The meeting over they re-joined Kitta and walked together through the much depleted crowd towards the house of Sheff. Some young children followed behind right up to Sheff's door, the adults left them in peace their initial interest satisfied. Being away from Lethe even for a few days caused Sala concern; although she was well supported and her plan accepted, there were some remnants of the still powerful elders, with minds fixed in the old ways, who did not like such drastic changes. If she stayed away too long the dissenters among them may gain momentum and take control; what they were faced with when they arrived back in Lethe could be less than friendly.

"Kitta, I need the visit here to be a short as possible, returning to Lethe before there is any kind of change in their

intentions. Please assemble the young men in the clearing I wish to brief them before we leave".

"Couldn't you do that on the journey"?

"I need to be sure they won't change their minds when they get to Lethe, any with doubts now will not be coming with us".

"Shall I include those who are in reserve"?

"Good idea, but don't give them hope that they may travel today, they will have their chance later".

"You are really leaving today"?

"Yes".

"Oh"!

Sala entered the house but Franil declined and waited outside with Kitta. She found Sheff and Frag waiting patiently as usual. Sala had to see them even briefly, they were as close in her heart as her own family.

"Sala, it is good to see you again".

"Thank you Ma Sheff and Pa Frag you are well"?

"We are. Please sit, will you be with us a while"?

"Not this time I'm afraid I must return with the boys as soon as possible. I just wanted to see you for a few moments, when all is done I will come back and stay much longer. I am sorry Sheff but I have so little time I must not even sit with you now"?

"I understand Sala, go do what is needed; come back when you can".

Sala left with Kitta and Franil to go to the clearing, she needed to see the boys in person when she told them what to expect, they may hide things in the recesses of their minds, things they don't want her to know; they couldn't keep secrets from her, the eyes would give them away every time. Every one who goes must be fully committed.

At the clearing nine boys were waiting, Sala opened her mind to all including Kitta and Franil.

"Well the time is here; we will be leaving very soon before dark I hope. I know you have been anticipating this day and are ready to leave but before we go a few things you will need to know. The Letheans are hard work when it comes to making friendships, the effort will be all yours don't expect them to seek you out, it will be you who will make first and continued contact. Their physical appearance is different, Franil here is an example of what to expect, although she is just a little older. Like Franil most girls are as tall as you or even taller. As you can see, colouration in skin hair and eyes are different but none the less beautiful. If you are put off by that you can step down now.

Remember you too will appear very different to them. The men and boys are tall also but almost never do manual labour so are smaller in physic than yourselves. Apart from some females who have been forced to cohabit out of fear, there is no Merging or Bonding but you already know that from my previous visit. They may not accept physical contact with the opposite sex as easily as you, touching each other is not normal for them so it will take some patience on your part so respect their ways.

Your task is to live your lives with them, to mingle, learn from the Science halls, make friendships and endeavour to bring about a social change eventually joining with a Lethean female of your choice. Whether you Merge or Bond in a traditional manner or not is your choice, we want babies of the future to be born there who will have minds as one, conceived out of love and nurtured by you and your chosen partner as a family".

Sala studied the faces and minds of all and could detect no disquiet. These original chosen six would be the ones to go. The three who were not chosen were already resigned to staying behind as they were in the knowledge their turn would come later. Sensing their colleagues unflinching desire to depart they shook hands and said goodbye wishing them well.

"Go home collect your belongings and prepare to leave now, say your farewells and meet me at the machine a soon as you are ready".

Sala Franil and Kitta went to wait by the flying machine where Rinn was standing, he knew their departure was imminent.

The boys had gathered together out of sight so as to arrive all at the same time, a disciplined column marched through the waiting crowd to stand by their elder Rinn.

"If all goes well Rinn I'll return with six girls from Lethe; I don't know when but in the meantime prepare places for them with the families who have sent boys. Explain they are just ordinary people, although they are tall and look like Franil emphasise they are not Overseers just young girls basically the same as our own. The physical differences are unimportant they should be treated the same as they would their own children".

"We wait in hope for you to come back soon; we will be ready. My age is great and my time left is short so will not see the outcome of this melding of our peoples. My heart says it will be special so continue your work Sala, your endeavours have my blessing".

"Thankyou Rinn without your help I would still be wandering this world lost or more likely have been pulled back to Lethe by the power of the Overseers and been fed the Waters. Life would have remained unchanged here but for the communes and Lethe the future was bleak indeed. I'll be back as soon as I can, goodbye old friend".

The farewells over Sala walked slowly towards the waiting young boys and her companion Kitta. Six eager volunteers along with Kitta and Sala were ushered aboard the flying machine by Franil. The families surrounding the craft with its precious cargo, their apprehensive minds full of doubt, sorrow in their hearts to see the boys leave; some cried, others smiled brave faced and waved as their sons stepped through the door into the unknown. Sala felt the sadness but also the euphoria emanating from her human cargo. These were the first; she hoped there would be many more who would make the journey.

Chapter Nineteen

Her chance encounter and subsequent astonishing union with the Outerworld had brought great change in the life of Sala. Her role as mediator amongst very different peoples and the driving force behind these exchanges were only possible through the intervention of the living crystal and that fateful second landing by the river.

During their time in the Outerworld Kitta constantly demanded to go to Lethe with Sala, who in reply constantly refused.

"You are too young Kitta it will be at least another season or two before you can merge. The whole point is to have these boys find partners amongst the Letheans. You will only be in the way; girls there are not like you, full of life; they are aloof and look very different so the boys will have to put aside any qualms when forming friendships. You are a beautiful girl Kitta, any boy would be proud to Bond with; you would be a constant reminder of what they had left behind which is the last thing we want".

"I am not going there to Bond or Merge with anyone, I just want to be part of this.... whatever it is; after all you wouldn't have had the power to win them over without me. Another thing you are just as much a reminder as me, even though you are getting old and a bit different the boys will find you quite good to look at too".

This counter argument made her smile she was even slightly flattered by it being possible. The reasons why she should go went on and on till in the end Sala gave in. Kitta's mind was as powerful as any so would be an asset if there were any difficulties, an ally she could trust implicitly would not go amiss. She didn't see any real problem as she was still too young to Bond so the boys would not be looking at her in that way. Once landed there would be little the Overseers could do when Kitta appeared as a visitor along with the boys, Sala would say she came as her assistant; the Overseers always expected others to wait on them so it would seem quite normal to them for Sala to have a servant.

The flight took off with plenty of light left in the day; the boys first experience of travel should not be at night, the views of their home amongst the forest of trees was not to be missed. Once all were seated Franil took the control, the vessel rose slowly at first, moved away from the centre then rapidly climbed to a height where the vison below of the houses forest and river shrunk to blend into one green blanket. The boys strained to see, eyes wide in amazement; a combined sigh from all as the ship accelerated away towards Lethe and the vision became a blur when white cloud vapour engulfed them.

Sala woke with the change in motion as the ship slowed, 'We can't be there already' she thought. She left her seat at the rear and moved forward next to Franil looking out the window ahead as she went. She spoke aloud but in whispers directly to Franil not wanting to disturb the boys.

"What is it Franil"?

"It's only the Badlands, we have to change course and go round".

"We never passed it on the way here".

"I know, there are other areas laid waste on all the routes, I don't know exactly where the Outerworld is and as the crystal is used to me coming from Five or the other communes it follows the path I am familiar with".

"I have been here before or one just like it, I didn't realise there was more than one; when I tried to go through it wouldn't let me".

"Just as well, if you had gone in too far you would never come out".

"Both times I came across it the machine stopped and waited for me to tell it to go round, why is that"?

"I have no idea it's the same for me; it just does that's all".

"How did the land get like that, forest and green all around and complete desolation beyond the rim".

"Science Master Ouisa came with me once with an instrument of some kind. When we came near it made a whistling noise and the numbers on its screen began to count higher and higher the closer we came. She told me to turn round quickly and get out, I didn't hesitate she seemed very afraid. She said later the place was dead and would kill anything that entered. She never explained the instrument and I never asked".

Sala's curiosity was roused, she tucked away a mental note to herself to speak to Ouisa later. The boys who were not asleep woke the others to look. Their view was restricted but could see enough to wonder what was going on. The unasked question she answered anyway, explaining the Badlands were an unsafe area where nothing grew or lived. The other questions of how, why, what and who, she confirmed was an unknown. Kitta left her seat and moved to get a better look; her eyes widened in astonishment; her thoughts tumbled out for all to know.

"Look at all that destruction! What happened here? looks like someone set fire to the forest and it has burned for ever, look

there, smoke is still leaking from the ground, there's nothing left. Who would do such a thing"?

It had never occurred to Sala that people could have caused this terrible destruction, she assumed it was a natural phenomenon. What happened long ago is recorded in the songs, there are none she remembered relating to such a catastrophic event. When she returned home she would ask Ezekiel if he knew of the Badlands and were there any songs telling of their creation.

Once the vessel had skirted the outer edge and was again on track everyone settled back in their seats with the boys speculating on what or who had caused such devastation. The conversation soon died down as no one could come up with any feasible explanation, some dozed others slept more deeply; the flight continued.

No more views or events to interrupt the journey, they would arrive later than planned, now continuing in silence till the hills surrounding Lethe's valley could be seen in the distance silhouetted against the darkening sky. Franil's mind reached out to Peto to warn him of their pending arrival. She then invited her passengers to prepare for landing. The sounds of yawning and of exhaled breath from bodies stretching their limbs stiff from being motionless for too long, were the only response to her call. Gradually as their sleep shrouded senses roused, a buzz of excitement filled the air; six necks craned forward to see a first glimpse of their new home.

With her usual dexterity Franil brought the machine calmly to ground. Sala moved to the door her hand held up palm facing the boys. She wanted to make sure nothing had changed before she exposed them to anything unexpected.

"Please stay seated I will call you when it's time to come out".

Franil moved to the rear and removed the source, Kitta remained where she was alongside the boys. They opened the door Franil went out first followed by Sala. The reception was very modest, Peto, Kalli and an Overseer named Vee whom Sala knew from her classes at Mind Science. An open minded greeting from Peto started the proceedings

"Welcome back I trust all is well".

"Thank you Master Peto, we had a fine journey and achieved our intended mission. I have eight passengers, Sala and her assistant Kitta along with six young men from the communes as agreed".

To safeguard her position Franil never mentioned the Outerworld or that Sala had changed the plan diverting from the communes to this unscheduled stop; she also agreed with her to introduce Kitta as her assistant a lowly servant and of no consequence in the eyes of one so senior. Sala followed behind Franil who moved away to hand over the source to engineer Lunn discreetly out of sight at the rear of the machine. Sala pleased to know there had been no change of position within the hierarchy of the Overseers called to Kitta and the boys to step outside. The boys moved in line passing by Sala to stand smiling in front of the small group assembled to meet them. Kitta stood to the side and one step behind Sala as she had been instructed. There was no indication from the reception party there was a problem even though the boy's and Kitta's blue skin with silver hair had probably never been seen before.

"I am Science Master Peto; these are Science Master Kalli, Science Master Soma and Overseer Vee. They will be your mentors during your first period here. Accommodation has been arranged in three areas one close to The Agriculture Science Hall which is adjacent to the pyramid gardens and the province of Science Master Kalli, next near The Body Science Hall under

Science Master Soma and last rooms next to the Mind Science Hall; there is no Master for this centre of learning at the moment so the Overseer Vee here will be your instructor and guide. Two young men to each area you decide who goes where. You will not miss out by choosing one or the other at this time as all the sciences will be studied at some point. You are free to go almost anywhere in Lethe but some areas in the Science halls are unsafe without protective clothing so look out for the warning notices. We will take you to your houses shortly where you will be given a brief introduction to Lethe's layout and daily routines".

Franil now stepped forward, It had been agreed with Peto she would be the one to show them to their houses and the food hall. Tomorrow Sala would introduce them to the Science Centres, give them a guided tour and brief them on what they would need to do during the initial period.

"You must have noticed from the mass of mental noise almost everyone here uses mind speaking all the time, voice communication is generally saved for those who do not have the gift or on formal occasions like meeting someone for the first time. You will soon get used to the constant interchanges and learn to block them out, you are probably doing so already; it will come naturally to you in no time. Don't be apprehensive about us splitting you up, the three sets of houses are within walking distance of each other and to start with you will all eat together. The plan is to mix with us Letheans as much as possible, so three pairs at different locations will help here. As you know there are far more females than males so you will be spread pretty thin but soon there will be plenty more boys following from the other communes".

Franil looked to Sala for her to continue.

"The Lethean girls you meet will be shy and unresponsive so it will be up to you to make the first move. You will go to

lessons at the three Science halls so will soon meet the others in your class probably all female so don't waste too much time, use your youthful charisma to full effect before the other young men arrive and take your place".

The boys looked at each other and smirked at Sala's last remark.

"They have been forewarned of your coming here to live, study and integrate. They are aware of the long term purpose of your arrival and that they are expected to mix and form friendships the idea of cohabiting and raising children in a family group however is a way of living very new to them, they will not have a full concept of what it really means. You are used to social contact and family life they are not, so be very tolerant of any reluctance. Remember you are free to go anywhere so explore your new home, seek out different places to eat ask questions of everyone you meet; don't restrict mixing to just those in your class. Peto said you can go anywhere but failed to mention one restricted place, probably because it is instilled in them from birth and assumed you already knew. The river and lake are to be avoided, disregard this warning at your peril, the water is contaminated and extremely dangerous, the unsafe area is clearly marked with black signs, stay well clear. Right grab your bags and follow us".

Darkness in the Outerworld made it impossible to move anywhere when away from the house so the boys were fascinated by the hidden lights guiding them along the paved walkways; one of many technical encounters they would meet in their new home. Franil in the lead, Sala next with Kitta and the six boys following set off towards the accommodation blocks stopping a short while later.

"Lye and Phin, come here, your homes are next to each other; each of you stand in front of one of the doors, note and

remember the symbol shown there, all the homes look the same, it is very easy to become lost, use the mind picture of this symbol to ask anyone they will guide you. In a few moments your image will be scanned and the room programmed to open to your faces alone, when it does please step inside. To leave just touch the green panel inside and it will open. Come out straight away you will have time to explore your homes later".

The doors opened and the two boys went in, each door closing behind them. A few moments later the doors opened again and they stepped out. The column move on and some while later arrived at a new block.

"Right, Grel and Han your turn, these are your homes, the same as for the others".

The boys entered their rooms and came out as instructed. A further march to the final block where Fon, and Wu like the others were given their new homes.

"As you can see all accommodation for study is in the central area of Lethe except the Air Science hall which is next to the building where you landed in the flying machine. This will not be a place of study at this time. We will now go to the dining hall, the one nearest to all your homes. You can use any hall to eat ask around you will soon get to know where they are. There are several to choose from most are close to each of the Science Halls. We will eat together now, after you will go to your rooms on your own".

The column of nine headed back the way they came till Franil stopped outside a large arched door, she stepped forward it opened automatically. They entered a large room through the now open archway the doors of which closed behind them once they were all inside. It was well lit and the air had a sweet smell of some kind, three round tables with ten chairs around each were empty, Franil motioned for the six to be seated at one of the tables and joined them sitting opposite. Sala and Kitta remained standing.

"I am sorry I was unaware of how late it is but the time for eating has passed however you will find refreshment in your rooms. I can feel you want to ask questions please wait till the morning. Tomorrow when you are called you will come here to eat; after your meal Sala will be here and will take you on a tour of Lethe and introduce you to your Science Masters. You will need to explore your rooms, I'm not sure why but Sala told me to say no more she said it would spoil the experience. You can leave whenever you wish, I am sure you can find your houses from here they are not too far".

Franil Sala and Kitta left them seated a little bemused with a dozen or more questions jumping from one to the other. Franil walked away mind speaking a goodnight to Sala as she went but ignored Kitta. Sala returned the thought as she and Kitta walked in the opposite direction. Their minds closed to the boys queries.

"Will the boys be alright on their own? Where are we going Sala, I thought we were going to eat I'm starving"?

"They'll be fine Kitta don't fret; I'm going to my home now, you have the one next to mine, we can get a snack and something to drink there. I know you are hungry Kitta, me too; it is different here no one prepares food in their houses all the meals are made in the food halls. The work is shared everyone has to do their time preparing and serving you'll find out soon enough. The food halls are open at specific times, unfortunately we missed the last serving; we'll have to wait till morning for a decent meal".

"You mean I'll have to serve and cook"?

"Maybe not, but you will spend time in the kitchens and the gardens whilst you are here, you can't expect to eat and not contribute in some way".

"Did you?"

"Oh yes I did my share; every one except the Overseers work in the kitchens and gardens some time or other, even they did in their youth".

Sala showed Kitta the automatic facilities in her room, left her nibbling on the sweet cakes and changing the images on the screen.

"I know It's not much but it will have to do. Goodnight Kitta I'll wake you".

"By the way can I get another of those cakes"?

"Of course as many as you like, just ask, they are always the same though you'll soon get bored".

"Not me, this is great. Sleep well Sala".

Sala did not sleep; not straight away that is. Her vision of the future was finally underway in the form of six young men from the Outerworld, a place she never knew existed until the living crystal took her there. Her thoughts of the crystal immediately drew her to feel its presence; all she knew, it knew and more besides. Hidden in its gas filled chamber forever waiting; her past and her future were interwoven with the lives of those it had touched over seasons uncounted. She slept soundly and dreamed of Porta as he once was. The night passed all too soon a tapping on the door invaded her slumber, bringing her slowly awake, desperately trying to hang on to the fading experience, the memory of happier times slipping out of reach.

Chapter Twenty

Kitta was bubbling with excitement, discovering the automatic functions in her room had set her imagination alight, wildly picturing what she might find the next day. Sleeping little, restless and awake before first light she showered twice, the second time using the sweet smelling soaps she had missed seeing the first time. She put on the white outfit and sandals found by her bed, now standing outside Sala's room eager to explore debating what to do next. Succumbing to impatience she tapped gently on Sala's door regretting her action even before she'd finished knocking, stepped away intending to return to her own room when too late the door opened.

"I knew it must have been you Kitta couldn't you sleep"?

"I'm sorry Sala I didn't want to mind speak if you were asleep so I thought if you were awake you would hear me, if not it wasn't so loud it would wake you".

Fully awake now the threads of her pleasing dream finally severed. She opened the door wide inviting Kitta inside.

"It's fine Kitta, I was about get up anyway, we have a busy time ahead. I see you found the whites, good, you looked odd in your old skins. The food hall will open as soon as it is light; gives me time to get a shower and dress; you can be the one to call the boys and tell them to meet us there, after all you are supposed to be my assistant so it's time you did something useful".

"Yes Mistress Sala, at once Mistress Sala"!

Kitta spoke out loud, did several deep bows with a full blown smile across her face. Sala smiled too at her joking words and subservient acting, but inside she had a sudden thought, this is just how the ordinary people of Lethe defer to the Overseers, the smile dissolved into a frown.

The hall was packed, nowhere for the eight to sit together so Sala told the boys to find a free space and stay seated after they had finished eating to wait for the congestion to clear. The mental hubbub doubled when they moved amongst the Letheans searching for a vacant seat; anyone who wanted to be close to the commune boys made space wherever possible so one of them would sit with them. The news of their imminent arrival had been rumoured for days, now those nearby just ignored their food staring at the strangers, the ones further away stood to try and get a better view, even the servers stopped mid-stride, full plates and empty dishes held precariously in unsteady hands. The moment passed, disturbed food delivery and consumption restarted and the lookers turned their attention back to their meals and original conversations. Not Sala's intention to mix the boys with the locals like this but pleased to see the reaction. Each boy without exception turned to those seated either side offered his hand introducing themselves. The hands were largely ignored, simply because the Letheans did not know what to do, two did take the hand offered instinctively but withdrew as soon as contact was made. The mental connections the boys attempted were automatically blocked, but the words of introduction, spoken aloud, were heard by all.

The food arrived; the boys hunger prevailed, ignoring their initial reluctance to try something new when faced with strange unknown fare; they ate all that was offered. Sala had become used to the largely green and root based diet, with different beans, fruits and the sweet bread that were being served most days. Fried ground beans had a flavour not unlike ox, however meat from mammals were never eaten here, protein from eggs and bird meat being most common and on rare occasions river fish were available, not something seen in their commune.

Sala noticed one on one conversations were occurring between the boys and those next to them. Their curiosity overcoming the Lethean's natural reserve, she even noticed smiles on the faces of the girls as the boys teased them with quite personal questions. She knew Letheans seldom smiled, this was good. The physical differences which she thought may be a problem were proving to be the opposite there was a definite and obvious attraction pulling both ways.

"Hello, My name is Phin".
"I am called Mase, why is your skin blue"?
"I didn't notice it was, it's just skin. I guess it came from my Ma and Pa, probably why yours is yellow and Sala's is golden brown. Can we mind speak it will be so much easier, will you unblock for me"?

Mase unblocked but limited their mind conversation to themselves.

"Phin, did you know your Ma and Pa"?
"Yes I was with them every day; I know it was different for you here in Lethe they told us. Are you not curious to know who your parents are"?
"No, we are all one here all of us come from our ancestors, it matters not who they are".
"I never thought of it like that, I suppose we do too but are raised as individuals instead of in groups. What do you study"?
"I am studying Air Science now; I have finished my time with Substance last season. Will you be studying whilst you are here"?

"Oh yes Mase, it's one of the main reasons for coming here we do not have the Sciences in the Outerworld, I will start tomorrow in Agriculture".

"What are the other reasons you came to Lethe"?

"We are here to integrate to find a partner and Merge to make a Bond".

"What is a Bond"?

"It is when two people join together for their lives, to cohabit have children and raise them".

"That is not the Lethe way, why would we want to do that"?

"It is the natural way, the minds of the children from Bonding will be strong".

"I don't know if I could do that; would you want to Bond with me"?

"I have no idea Mase, we have only just met I would need to spend time with you to find if we like each other enough to commit for a life together. You are a beautiful girl so if not me you will find someone you will want to Bond with".

"I have to go to class now Phin will you mind call later"?

"I may well do that, thank you for talking with me".

Mase left the table and the food hall thinking how strange these commune people are, when he said 'hello' he held out his hand, I think he expected me to do the same; if I see him again I will take his hand. I never looked at his face close up either I don't even know the colour of his eyes. His clothes were strange too thick and dark, she had no idea what they were made of. If what Phin was saying was right they will not find many girls who will want to do this Bond thing. Still she had enjoyed his company and would like to see him again. What few boys that were here were weak and all they ever talked about were their studies, some of them couldn't even mind speak. She forgot to ask Phin what was this Outerworld he spoke about, she thought they had come from commune Three at least that is what they were told by the Overseers.

Some of the girls had been selected to go to the communes as part of the exchange plan and were being prepared in the Mind Science hall, she was glad she had missed being picked, she liked it here in Lethe. This boy Phin was interesting and he had a nice strong looking body, she liked that too. When she saw his skin had a pale blue tinge she wanted to touch his arm, it looked like it would feel cold. She'd resisted taking his hand when offered and held back from her urge to make contact; now feeling a regret for her restraint, she promised herself she'd not hold back next time. She would take more notice too, look at his face and into his eyes; physical and visual contact certainly not something she was used to doing, it would require her to change old habits.

Once the meal had finished, the room slowly emptied with the odd exception of an inquisitive girl or two hanging back to see what was going on. The boys moved from their dispersed places to sit together at one table waiting for the room to finally clear and for Sala to guide their next move.

"We are going to take a tour of the central areas of Lethe and visit the Pyramid gardens. The Science Halls except for that of Air are in this area. "Lye, Phin, will attend classes at Agriculture Science, Grel and Han at Mind Science, finally Fon and Wu Body Science. Make a note of their locations as we pass by, you will go there to start your classes after eating tomorrow morning".

"How will we know when to go"?

"There is a universal wake call each morning Han, enough time to dress and eat before class, you will leave the food hall with the others there will be plenty of time".

"Do we go there every day"?

"No, you will be given a schedule to follow, it will include duties of food preparation in the kitchens and work in the gardens, there are other maintenance tasks requiring special skills which you may learn later but for now just these two. It is not compulsory to attend all the classes, you can go to the other science halls too, sit in their classes and observe if you wish, as I said before you are allowed to go almost anywhere, you are free to do what you want. Take notice, it is important barring sickness, for you to never miss your work duties. No more questions for now we have a lot to see so I will explain about the different places as we pass so let's go".

One advantage the Outerworld had over the communes was their ability to read, write and understand symbols, most things to remember here were written down; this will be a problem when bringing the commune's young men here having never had these skills. The brief instructions given to the commune elders by Sala were poor but hoped at least the concept had been passed on to the young during their lessons. She would speak to Franil to arrange training outside the science classes when the next groups from Three and Five arrived.

They left the food hall to find the streets empty except for some children and their carers; almost everyone else had gone to classes or to attend to their duties. Sala led the way with Kitta by her side the boys followed. The sky was cloudless but a mist hung over the damp grass areas, the sun just showing above the distant hills still lit the pathways and buildings with the promise of a warm day. Accommodation blocks and recreation areas were passed with little comment the first major building being the Substance Science building the first point at which they stopped.

"This is the hall of Substance the Master here is Ouisa she is also the leader of The Physical Sciences our next stop".

Ever curious about everything it was Kitta who asked the question.

"Why is Ouisa a Master of two Sciences"?

"The previous Master of Physical died and has not been replaced as yet, her position there is temporary. The process to replace a Master is slow, the Instructor Overseer Pares is under training to take over when they consider her ready, it could take a season or more before she takes over".

The mention of Ouisa reminded her of her conversation with Franil; she must seek her out and ask about the tests she did in the Badlands and what it had to do with the living crystals. They moved on passing by the hall of Sense and arrived at Body Science Hall where they stopped.

"Fon, Wu this is Body Science Hall the head here is Science Master Soma. You will learn much about yourselves here and be able to deal with health problems in a practical way, the herbs and medicines of home may work in a small way but here is whole new approach in helping those who are sick".

The march continued till they reached the hall of Mind Science.

"Gren, Han, this is where you will spend the next season, there is no Master here at the moment but Overseer Vee will be here tomorrow to take you to your class. She is the one you saw when we first arrived".

Han asked the question this time.

"Why no Science Master here, did she die too".

"No, Science Master Metrin recently had an accident and is unlikely to recover fully so can no longer remain a Master. Vee is very competent; you will learn much from her and the others here".

"Is Overseer Vee being trained to become the Master".

"It is too soon since the accident for the elders to decide who will be temporary Master or who will be trained to replace Metrin".

"What happened to Metrin"?

Sala was at a loss to answer, she couldn't tell the truth and did not want to lie either. She decided to evade the question.

"It is not for me to say at this time, it is being reviewed and will probably be made public later".

Han nodded accepting her reply, a relief for Sala as she did not want to explain what had happened. The party moved on to their next stop outside the Hall of Agriculture.

"Lye, Phin, the Agriculture Hall here is the province of Science Master Kalli, you will report to her here tomorrow. Much of what happens here extends to the large pyramid garden behind, the four smaller ones which can be clearly seen from here down in the valley, will be included in your study. Apart from any work duties you will probably spend as much time in the gardens as in this Hall. Make the most of this period of study it will help, if and when you return home. I know you are hunters and do not grow crops but this technology could enable you to do both".

Sala decided she would give no more guidance for now; the time has come to set them free to explore and make their own way in this new world. The seeds are sown, her vision of the future ready to germinate.

"This completes the tour of the Halls; it just leaves the Science of Air Master Peto's place of study. There is no need for us to go there again now as you already know where it is, right next to where we arrived yesterday, the building adjacent to where they keep the flying machines. I will leave you now, I suggest you go back to your allocated Science Hall go inside look around if you like, ask questions of anyone you meet there they won't mind. Seek out the food halls nearby explore a little, get your bearings. Oh one more thing there will be clothes in your room like the ones you have seen the Letheans wearing, use them from now on it will help you to fit in. I won't be far away you can call me or Kitta anytime".

Sala and Kitta walked away leaving the six boys outside the Agriculture Hall.

"Where are we going".

"Go back to your room Kitta, I'm going to see Ouisa about something, I won't be long, we can both go eat together then meet up with Peto and Soma after to see if they have selected the girls; we will soon have another journey before us. Put your used clothes in the green box you'll find a fresh set of whites in your room every day, we can meet in the eating hall later".

"What about my old Outworld clothes".

"They will have been disposed of I should think".

"They really have thought of everything. Why do you need to meet Peto and Soma when you can mind talk with them"?

"I still am not sure who to trust, I can only tell if they are being straight with me by seeing the facial expressions, the eyes and body movements whilst talking; I don't know how but it gives me some assurance we are working together. Some of the Overseers are not happy with what is going on so I want to detect any changes in case those I believe are allies are really what they say they are".

"Do you want me to come with you"?

"Not to see Ouisa that's not necessary but after is fine; you will be ignored by them as they would any servant but you have a sense that can quietly judge the mood, a precaution against my missing something when we are in deep discussion. Get some rest I'll call when it's time to eat".

Ouisa was at her usual place in the laboratory, she didn't mind call her first she wanted to see her reaction when asked about the Badlands, Sala had a feeling there were secrets around the subject and didn't want Ouisa to close her mind, not an easy thing for her to do when mind speaking face to face.

"Hello Ouisa, I'm not disturbing something important am I, if so I'll come back later"?

"No its okay what can I do for you Sala"?

"Somethings been worrying me Ouisa it's about the Badlands".

"How can I help"?

"I'm not sure if you can, except Franil was telling me about a trip you made with her there, she said you used an instrument of some kind which made some weird noises, what were you trying to find"?

"That was a long time ago Sala why are you interested"?

"Curiosity really, every trip I have made the machine takes us right up to the edge between the forest and the barren area full of red rocks then stops. The way forward is barred and you cannot move much closer no matter how hard you try; I had to instruct the controller to go around each time; I was just wondering if you knew why".

"Franil reported the same problem so I went to investigate with a couple of devices, an optical magnifier and a frequency monitor. The frequency measuring instrument showed the presence of ultra-high energy radiating from the surface way beyond the range of the monitor's range; when I pointed it towards the centre it was of sufficient strength to melt the flesh from your bones if you came too close. We left as soon as I saw those readings I didn't get a chance to use the magnifier".

"So you never went back"?

"I didn't see any point it was far too dangerous".

"So you don't know why it stops every time waiting for me to instruct it to move on".

"Not from the trip no, however I did delve a little deeper though and looked into the digital history records".

"What did you find out"?

"Not a lot from those records, very sparse; the Badlands were hardly mentioned except to say they were to be avoided. There were references back to items in the old tomes, so I managed to dig out the relevant sections from the archives to see what was there. The writings were handwritten and difficult to decipher and whoever wrote them used words I never knew so I gave up".

"How old are the tomes"?

"Hundreds of seasons I believe; when they began to show signs of decay the ancients sealed them in a controlled cabinet, it's never been opened since as far as I know. What I looked at were copies they made before they were sealed away. I don't even know if the copies are complete".

"Is that it you just stopped looking"?

"Not entirely I discussed it with Peto so he had a look and came up with some pretty wild ideas. According to him before we came to this world there were other advanced but destructive humans who evoked storms and fires that raged for many seasons killing all in their path. Eventually the forests returned but the Badlands remained as a reminder of the first people's stupidity in allowing such a thing to happen. He said the ancient tomes hint that the essence of the many millions who died in the fires remained after their bodies were turned to dust. Eventually after a thousand seasons they evolved into a new crystal life form. Seems more like myth than truth don't you think; just made up stories to explain our crystal power sources"?

"Probably Ouisa but the last time I was near some unseen force urged me to move closer, it was only the machine's crystal control halting and refusing to go further which stopped me".

"Just an inbuilt safety feature of the flying machine more like. I know Peto did say he thought the Badlands are where the living crystals come from; I don't believe it Sala, nothing alive can come from there".

"What was the magnifier for"?

"I never had the chance to use it".

"I know you said but what were you hoping to see"?

"Nothing special, I just wanted a closer look".

Sala had her doubts thinking Ouisa was holding back about why she took an optical magnifier, what did she really expect to find, crystal maybe. Where did the tag 'Living' added to the word Crystal come from, she was sure the one she had been using since her first flight had some benevolent influence over her. Where it really came from may never be known and not important at this time, it worked it's magic for her enabling the machines to fly taking her wherever she wished to go.

"Thanks anyway Ouisa I guess I will stay well away in future".

"There are many unknowns in our world, secrets we should seek to uncover but must recognise those it is best left undisturbed".

She left with Ouisa's hint to desist hanging in the air. On her way back to her room she mind called Peto and Soma to request they meet by the old Air machine being renovated by Lunn. They said it was unnecessary to meet but Sala insisted saying she wanted to look at the machine and discuss the possibility of using it to transport the young boys and girls between the communes and Lethe; they would need to be there to do that. The time was set for later that day after classes and the mealtime had ended. Sala was glad of a brief rest and some food; it would refresh her body and mind after the constant effort of the last few days.

The eating hall was busy as usual, she and Kitta sat together and noticed the boy Han was sitting on another table with two girls one either side. One was holding his arm as they chatted aloud the other looking intently at him and smiling. Sala couldn't hear what they were saying but their actions showed a familiarity that was encouraging; she wondered why they were not mind speaking, early days, she should not be concerned mind blocking strangers was quite normal here , she hoped all the boys were settling in as well as Han appeared to be. The food arrived, they ate without real enjoyment a different version of the same vegetable mixture, it satisfied the hunger and provided all the nutrition needed but lacked the flavour and protein in the form of the meat both Sala and Kitta were brought up with. Next time she was at home she would collect a few herbs, peppers and spice plants, give them to the pyramid gardeners to see if they could be grown here. A sudden idea to bring back Menga tree seed pods she put to one side as being over-indulgent.

Sala arrived early for the meeting at Air Science, she made straight for the air machine building. The craft she had flown and was familiar with was located at the rear with the much larger and older machine occupying most of the area right up to the entrance. She moved towards the door sensing Lunn's presence somewhere near so called his name.

"Hello Lunn".

He was working inside the machine, the most likely place he would be found. He came out the already open hatch and took her hand the look of joy on his eyes.

"I wondered when you would come; we couldn't speak when you arrived the other day, not with all those Overseers about; how was the trip"?

"It's good to see you Lunn, the trip was fine; can I have my hand back please".

He quickly released his grip unaware he had been holding on so tightly.

"Sorry I wasn't thinking it's good to see you too".

"This is Kitta my friend from the Outerworld".

"Kitta? Outerworld"?

"Don't look so puzzled it is the name of a commune that does not use a number".

"Oh. Okay. Hello Kitta, I was thinking you were from Three".

"No and the boys are not from Three either. I'll explain later".

Lunn still looked perplexed so Sala changed the subject by commenting on the new location of the machine.

"I see you must have taken this big beast outside to have swapped them over"?

"More than that Sala we took it for a considerable test run, full height and near maximum speed, it's a bit slower and the turns are wider compared to the smaller one but it is a great machine to fly: it is almost ready to go".

"What have you left to do"?

"Not much technically, a few changes with the crystal interface of the power source, the connections were different so I am installing a completely new unit the same as the other machine, that way I can use any of the crystals".

"Is that all"?

"Not quite, I've been told to fit it out with new seats, only more comfortable than the old ones. There are some stored away too big to fit the smaller machine but I can install at least twenty in this one with room to spare. They can be fully laid back like a bed, much better for long journeys".

"Was it Peto who told you to do this"?

"Not exactly; he came with Soma, Ouisa and five or six Overseers to watch the test. Soma came along with me during the flight and after the successful trial it was she who gave the instruction to fit the seats".

"Did you hear anything or sense their reasoning".

"No nothing. There was a complete block when they were talking together, is there a problem"?

"I'm not sure, I don't think so. Did she give you a time for the ship to be ready"?

"No, the request was almost casual, she even thanked me as she left, no one ever thanked me before, let alone a Master".

"A good sign I would say, a relaxing of tension since the demise of Metrin. Peto will be here soon so I suggest you go somewhere out of sight. I'll come and find you later".

Sala entered the open door of the aircraft with Kitta not far behind; the inside was similar to the other vessel but much larger of course and Lunn's estimate of twenty seats seems conservative even if they were able to be laid flat. The rear was like the other ship with toilet, some storage and a galley. The front however had a little less frontal window area and the control position had no seat at the moment. The body was under a cover so she could not judge the size and number of side windows. There was a strange smell too, one she couldn't place, familiar, not unpleasant, probably the aftermath of cleaning. Kitta went over to where the power source would normally have been to find a void and a multitude of unattached connections.

"Hey Sala, come and look at this".

One glance was enough, Sala knew she could never be an engineer.

"Aren't you glad you don't have to sort that lot out".

Kitta looked again and nodded in agreement. The respect for Lunn's technical skill rose considerably at the sight of such complexity. Not much to be gained further here so they left and sat on a low wall by the building side entrance to wait for her co-opted partners to arrive.

Having been lenient with the true source of the six boys already here she decided to come clean when they discussed the next phase. Peto and the others obviously had something in mind with the renovation of the large air machine, she would listen and adapt her ides to fall in with their plan especially if it was to use it for future journeys to the communes.

Peto appeared alone which was not unusual, the need for Soma to be there was unnecessary when images and conversation could be shared wherever she was.

"Your boys seem to be settling in, are we ready for the next step"

"I believe so Peto, however I have to confess to the change I mentioned earlier. There is another commune not numbered called Outerworld and this is where the boys this time came from. I visited Three and Five but they were not willing to give us their youngsters at that time without preparation. I knew the Outerworld commune was ready so went there instead; their telepathic abilities are more developed too; they also have a written language which Three and Five do not so I thought they would be better suited as our first candidates for integration".

"It matters not to me where they came from you know better than I which are the most suitable people however if we are to succeed we need more than a few to come here, communes

Three and Five will give us just twelve at best, we need more we must mix as many as possible".

Was this was their plan for the large flying machine, she hoped the intention was not to raid the other communes and bring in unwilling and unsuitable prospects.

"I agree we must tread carefully though Peto, I hope Three and Five will be ready this time. I will investigate the other communes for the right ones later".

"No problem we have prepared the large ship so we can take our girls out to the commune, we will be ready anytime now. I thought twenty or so girls enables us to make one round trip take them to commune Five leave maybe ten girls there picking up your six boys, the same for commune Three or maybe even save some of the girls for this Outerworld commune on your way back".

This acceleration of the schedule was not what she expected but it was ideal in terms of journey time and she was certainly not expecting to be taking girls from Lethe so soon.

"I like the plan but what of the girls where can we find so many to be available in such a short time".

"It is not a problem we have over fifty girls already undergoing training and more eagerly waiting, I couldn't believe the response created by the arrival of these first six".

"Tell me Peto how did you manage to persuade the Elder Overseers to agree to such rapid and dramatic changes".

"It wasn't me it was Soma; she did a detailed analysis of the birth rates and decline in males as well as loss of the telepathic gift. The results were clear and indisputable. Lethe would have no male babies in two generations, the continued use of the male seed bank would mean those born from now on would have no telepathic ability. The fact which clinched their acceptance was when she told them fertility would cease soon after. Lethe would no longer exist when the last of us now alive

died. One possible way to save Lethe was to use our few males to cohabit and breed naturally but that would be too little too late. What she said to the elders may have been exaggerated but the fear it generated ensured us of their complete cooperation especially when a solution was offered by the introduction of gifted fertile males from the communes".

"I can now see why you have been able to move forward so rapidly and why you have been preparing the large Air Machine. Soma did all this research on her own in such a short time"?

"No, it has taken many seasons; it was a study instigated long ago but the data had been put to one side when we decided to bring you and your family here. Soma sensed a resistance building with the aged elders so she worked for several days to analyse the information and produce the report; when it was distributed all resistance crumbled".

Peto went inside and entered the machine calling to Lunn as he went. Sala and Kitta followed with Lunn appearing on cue as always from a hidden vantage point.

"How many seats can be fitted in here Lunn; it will be a long trip taking in three and later more communes so they need to be for sleeping".

"Twelve one side and eleven the other, that makes twenty three filling all the floor space with enough room to move freely down the centre, another one if we squeeze them closer and block part of the doorway".

"Good do it but leave the doorway clear. Have you finished the new interface"?

" Yes it is working fine all I have to do is wire it in".

"How long to finish and run a test flight, I'll send over a couple of girls to help".

"These chairs are really unwieldy and in a store the other side of the compound, four helpers will speed up installation by a day at least. Three days plus a day to test, if that works out I can be ready on day five".

"Good Lunn, four helpers it is. Now Sala you and I need to see which girls you should take".

Phin found himself unsure how to proceed, he had met several girls at the Agriculture classes who were nice enough but were so engrossed in their studies they paid little attention to his advances and never unblocked when asked. He made several attempts to contact Mase but with no response. He had even gone to the eating hall where they first met but she was nowhere to be seen. The classes weren't going too well either, he followed the lessons if he concentrated really hard, made notes where he could but their written words for the various plants were too difficult for him to remember. His mind often drifted to Mase during which time he learnt nothing. He knew she studied at Air but that was on the far side of Lethe, he wouldn't have enough time to get there during his break from the pyramid gardens where he was assigned to work for the next few days.

Mase ignored the calls from Phin; didn't he know you never called anyone during class. She realised he was probably unaware of the rules when it came to contacting others; they weren't exactly rules but had become the normal way so as not to interrupt anyone during important and personal moments. It was expected to restrict calling to pre-arranged times as much as possible, this time she would accept his next attempt at contact regardless of when. Sure enough the following morning he called in the middle of her assembling an altitude metering system with the instructor watching her every move. She did not respond as she had promised herself but continued with the task fumbling over the final connections. Annoyed at herself for being distracted she decided to break form and call him at the first opportunity. She slipped to the back of the classroom whilst the next pupil went through the same assembly procedure she had just bungled and made the call.

"Mase its you, at last, I've been calling and calling".

"I know Phin, you must not call during class it is forbidden".

"Sorry I didn't know".

"I will meet you this evening at the same food hall as before, I must go".

She cut off and turned her attention back to the lesson before the tutor noticed she was not where she should be.

Phin continued his thought transfer confirming he would be there before realising the connection was broken and she was gone. He felt elated and light-headed even his hands shook; he left his seat and walked in small circles to calm his nerves he could hardly wait. The others of his group turned to watch curious as to why this boy from the communes carried out such a strange parade.

He sat on the hard food hall seat uncomfortable, impatient, his meal untouched, now cold and unappetising. He had come far too early waited by the door of the hall before it opened. The building had filled quickly with most everyone now served; many having finished already and were leaving. Still he sat, his mind no longer paying heed to the comings and goings. She stood behind him without him realising she was there. She opened her mind.

"Hello Phin, sorry I'm late, I had to stay after class".

She didn't tell him why; she had to go through the whole procedure again, the one she had messed up when he called her earlier.

"That's okay Mase, I am so glad you are here, come sit beside me".

She deliberately sat very close so the whole of her left side pressed against his right. She reached out and touched his arm.

"Oh, It's warm"!

"What did you expect"?

"I don't know really being blue like that I thought it might be cold".

"That's silly, the skin colour has nothing to do with body temperature it's something in the structure and the way it reflects the light".

"I know I just wanted to touch you and was surprised how warm you felt. Are you not eating".

"I'm not hungry; what about you"?

I'm fine Phin, can we get out of this place go somewhere quiet".

They left the hall arm in arm which caused a stir amongst those left who noticed such unusual intimacy.

Peto led the way, Sala and Kitta followed.

"Where are we going"?

"To the Mind Science Hall, its where we are training the girls who are going to leave us".

"What does the training involve, I had no idea you were preparing them whilst we were away; how close are they to being ready"?

"You can judge for yourself. We have been instructing them on the way different families are joined by Bonding or Merging and how the resulting children are nurtured within the family for their whole lives. How insemination is no longer to be used so they must put aside any reservation about physical contact if they want to have children. This concept has been difficult for many so we have excluded those with serious doubts although they may change when the project shows positive results. Strangely we have found some girls who show an enthusiasm for the prospect of cohabiting. We think this is a deep rooted innate function of the human psyche coming naturally to the surface".

"I can tell you Peto the need to Bond and mate with their partner is in the mind of every commune youngster well before they are really old enough, so your girls will have no problem finding partners, my only reservation is we cannot send too many at once as this will unbalance the natural order which exists".

"Do you mean I am preparing the large flying machine for no reason".

"Of course not, reducing the time of travelling is important too and say six or seven girls to each commune will not upset the stability; we will then need to see how many Bond before we exchange any more. Our next target will be to seek out other communes not considered before. New blood is what you want and new communes will provide that".

"The other communes visited in the past showed little sign of telepathic children do we really need to include them"?

"I believe the children with the gift exist everywhere; it is the fear of those who do not have it which is holding back those that do; we will find many gifted young people hidden away somewhere in all the communes".

"I hope you are right. Let's go and see these girls and pick the first twenty three".

The room was large so the fifty or so persons present did not seem so many. They were seated in a semicircle with two Overseers in front. Sala reached out to listen to what was being said. The Overseers were working in tandem firing questions at each girl in turn. The questions and exchanges were rapid, surprising Sala as they were quite personal and involved the girls answering about explicit physical and sexual contact, also finding their response to living in a strange commune with little of the comforts of Lethe. The question of bearing children and having to look after them without help was an important factor in their selection. The reaction to physical differences of the various people was a target question where the Overseers looked for any prejudicial thoughts. Every now and then the proceedings halted and a girl would get up and leave the room.

"As you can see Sala we are selecting only those who are mentally and physically suited. We will soon have the best twenty and probably more if needed".

"You don't need me here the selection process is excellent. One more thing, I think we should take a few boys too, it will redress the small imbalance in the communes a little and it would do them no harm to work on the land for a while and maybe find a girl who will wish to Bond with them. The more diversity we can introduce the better; we must ensure some of the Lethe male characteristics are included if we are to have any chance of reviving what has been lost here. Success and the gift will come to all in good time".

"You are right Sala we should not exclude our males just because we have a surplus of females. I'll ask Soma to select three or four who still retain the gift, we need to check they are fertile too, so many are not".

"Not enough, let's set a target of six boys and fifteen girls. Two boys and five girls at each commune, don't forget me, Kitta, too as well as Franil. She won't be able to fly all the time so I will share the control position and seat for sleeping with her".

"What are your plans for bringing males back from the communes".

"Nothing fixed at the moment, the Outerworld already has made their contribution, we could maybe bring a couple of girls from there, Three and Five I will judge what is best when we get there for now say six boys from each is a good number".

"You know what Sala I feel excited, inside my stomach there's a tenseness I haven't had for many seasons".

"I knew you had a soft streak Peto, you Letheans are not really so different from us as you profess to be. I'm excited too, only a few days to go".

They walked side by side away from the Mind Science hall a smile on their faces sharing a warm feeling of contentment.

"Mase who do we need to ask"?

"I don't know Phin, what about your elder Sala or the Overseer Franil".

"Shouldn't it be one of your elders first, its what we do in the communes, the girl asks her parent first and then the elders for permission to Merge. You don't have parents so ….. I'm not sure. I'll ask Kitta she will know".

And so it began the first signs of two diverse peoples wanting to Bond.

Sala hadn't seen Kitta for some time, two days at least, even when she called she was met by a strong block. She knew she had taken an interest in Air Science and was currently attending some classes, her and Sala had discussed the living crystal conundrum which stimulated her to take up study at the Air Science classes. Even mealtimes had been missed or maybe she was eating elsewhere, this seemed strange as Kitta had been following Sala's every move since they had come to Lethe. She had been back to her room to sleep but Sala was loathe to wake her and by the time she awoke in the morning Kitta was already up and gone.

"Where are you Kitta"?

A strong demand this time, even though the block was still in place Sala knew Kitta would not be able to ignore her this time.

"I'm at the Air Science building, do you need me"?

"Why have you blocked my calls"?

"Sorry Sala not intended for you, it's just I've been having extra lessons and did not want to be interrupted".

"Who is giving you extra lessons"?

Kitta couldn't hide the fact she was spending time with Lunn; the thought was already at the forefront of her mind when Sala posed her question.

"You sly young lady, what's going on with you two"?

"I knew I couldn't keep anything from you for too long, he has been explaining about the forces of gravity inversion".

"And you understand it do you"?

"Some off it, the maths is new so it is taking some time".

Sala sensed her evading what she was really interested in so teased her a little.

"I bet it is! What else are you two investigating that takes all day and half the night, missing meals and creeping home after everyone else is asleep"?

"Are you keeping tabs on me"?

"No just looking out for you, he's a real nice man you could do much worse".

Kitta couldn't keep it to herself any longer.

"I know I'm a bit young Sala but I would really like to Merge with him but do they do that here or would I have to wait and go home first"?

"I thought there was more to your absence from the food hall than extra lessons. Bonding is not something I've discussed with Lunn even though we have worked together for ages. It's been mentioned to the Science Masters, they have little comprehension of what it really means hence their earlier treatment of Bonded couples but they now agree it is one of the main reasons why we brought the boys here; we hope they will take to it, maybe you could lead the way, the first Bonding in Lethe. Kitta and Lunn".

"You're teasing me again".

"Not really my young friend, explain what Bonding means, see Lunn's reaction, there are others close to making the commitment too, you are not alone so you never know. Speak to him and make sure you are back for the meal tonight I want to know what he said".

When she realised there were several couples wishing to Bond including Kitta and Lunn, she knew she might be expected to conduct the ceremony. Bonding was normally presided over by the elder of the commune, here there was no one who understood what would be needed and how serious it is. She must think; she had no idea who else who could do it.

They would have to wait a while for she and Kitta had a journey to make first and when she returned the Overseers would have to agree and a set aside a time for the ritual. Kitta by convention should ask permission from her parents first, maybe she could do that on the impending trip. Recalling the process was easy it was one of her treasured memories. The song was engraved on her heart, the day she Bonded with Porta would stay with her always. Porta was lying asleep on the chair in front of the screen, whatever he was watching had passed and the screen was blank. She sang quietly to herself not wanting to disturb him......*The land and rain sustain our need*........halfway through the song he opened his eyes and joined in with her, at first he hummed the tune and then with the words of the final phrase......*To nurture those whom we enfold till to air and land expire.*

He was in her mind singing together as they did on that wonderful day long ago.

"I remember that song Sala, you and me, that was our special day wasn't it"?

At first she couldn't speak, her pulse raced, her throat closed, tears formed in her eyes, she swallowed several times reached out to hold his hand.

"Yes my love a very special day, just like now".

At last a real sign of recovery. The memory was still there, her Porta was still there somewhere deep inside, even the Waters of Lethe could not destroy their Bond.

Lunn stood proud next to the craft he had been busily working on making it airworthy, the cover removed, its sleek body looking like new; fully fitted with new seats and charged ready to go. The test flight he undertook with the Overseer Soma at the control had shown no faults, but to be sure Lunn took it out for a second run later by himself where he reached extreme speeds, height and manoeuvres not carried out in the earlier test. He was satisfied all was well.

Seventeen girls went through the door and selected their seats as they wished. Only four boys were found to be suitable, they also entered the craft; it was not a problem the original plan would be modified slightly, six girls and two boys at communes Three and Five, with the remaining five girls to the Outerworld. Sala spoke to the girls and asked them to decide who goes where, the same with the boys; she wanted it sorted before they arrived avoiding problems by her making any unpopular selection. Franil entered next followed by Kitta. Sala stood by Peto and Soma who were surrounded by all the Science Masters and many elder Overseers all realising their very existence depended upon the outcome of this journey. Peto took her hand and squeezed as he spoke loud and clear for all to hear.

"Thank you Sala, our salvation is in the hands of these young people deliver them safely and come home soon".

Sala said nothing, squeezed his hand in return looked into his eyes and smiled, released her grip and stepped through the doorway closing it behind her.

Chapter Twenty One

None of the young on board had done more than imagine what it was like to fly in the famous machine, the same one they had often seen as an obsolete exhibition piece and even studied sometimes during their short lives. For a people who hardly ever showed emotion, the mood of excitement was strangely tangible. Franil held the machine at a low height above Lethe moving slowly across the landscape so they could take in the spectacular views of their home. She did two full circles before gaining height and setting the course for Five. Sala was pleased with Franil in showing signs of kindness, she had made the manoeuvre without any prompt from her. Five was the furthest away so the journey would take much more than a day; she had a few words to say but no hurry, she would give them a chance to settle first for conversations about the machine, the scenery and the unknown future facing them were bouncing from one restless mind to another. Daylight faded, the windows were blanked and everyone slept. Sala took her turn at the control whilst Franil rested. Kitta left her seat and stood by Sala wondering why she had been carried along taking the seat away from one of the Lethe girls.

"I hear your thought Kitta, did you not want to join me in this enterprise"?

"Of course but it seems unfair of me to take up a valuable space".

"I value you Kitta, without your help none of this would have happened. I must confess I have an idea you may or may not like which will make your reason for being here more than justified".

"Sounds interesting what do you want me to do"?

"Its not why you are here that was an indulgence on my part a reward of sorts for your loyalty and help but if you want another reason how do you feel about staying at Five with the Lethe girls"?

"I didn't see that coming, you do surprise me sometimes. I'll have to think; do I have a choice and when do you want an answer"?

"Of course you have a choice, an idea that's all. It only just came to me when you asked why you were here."

"How long would I have to stay and what about Lunn"?

"I don't know it wasn't in the plan, Lunn wasn't in my mind either when I suggested it, I hadn't thought it though, sorry, go back to sleep Kitta; let's forget it eh"?

"Hm"!

Kitta really wanted to get back to Lunn but would also liked to have stayed in Five for a while; then there was her Ma and Pa, if she stayed at Five she would miss visiting them this trip and asking permission to merge with Lunn. She wished Sala hadn't mentioned it.

The day came quickly as the craft sped towards the rising sun; it breached the horizon uninterrupted by the hills beneath the ship at full height. Stirring amongst the passengers initiated by Sala unblanking the windows. Franil left her seat and took control from Sala who made her way to the rear of the compartment, took a sweet cake and water back to her seat.

"Listen everyone, the facilities here are limited, food and drinks are ready, order what you want it's quite basic though you'll soon find out what is available. Come back two at a time starting at the front".

The meal and toilet took quite some time with such a small area, Sala wondered if there was another way to improve the layout, she'd ask Lunn later. Once they were settled Sala began.

"A few things you should know that didn't come up in your induction. Most adults in Five and Three do not have the gift, you will always speak aloud in their presence; mind speaking is not forbidden but to use it amongst those who cannot is highly disrespectful. You have been told already the communes live as families, one house shared by all relatives; what you didn't know is you will each join a family, probably with one where one of their boys will be returning with us. The elder will select your new home. Life is different here, harder for sure; you will be expected to work alongside the others. The family is headed by a Ma and Pa, there may be brothers and sisters of differing ages, babies even; older members too who work if they are able; they command respect, you will do as your seniors ask without question".

Anxiety emanated from each mind mainly concerning the work they will be required to do.

"If a boy has gone from a family as part of this exchange you will replace him as a source of labour, you may therefore be asked to work in the fields; the people from Five and Three are not hard or demanding they will not expect you to do anything you cannot master. I worked in the fields when I lived there; I was much younger and smaller than any of you so don't worry you'll manage. There will be times for learning too a very different experience you will enjoy I know".

Again another flood of questions, ones she never intended to answer.

"Look this place and its people will be a new and special experience, if I tried to answer all your questions we would be here for ever. You will find your answers soon enough, don't be afraid of making mistakes these people are free of animosity,

embrace their ways and hope to find a boy or girl to become your friend and partner. Life there is good, be happy".

The old air machine continued on at a good pace, Lunn's confidence in the ancient science and his preparation was well proven. A quiet settled over the band of travellers and their guides, the evening approached as did the first stop on this fateful journey. The familiar hills made Sala's heart beat faster, almost there. Too large to land in the centre of the commune Franil guided the vessel along the ridge behind the fields looking for a suitable place to stop as close as she could. A field where the crop had already been harvested seemed ideal it was the best available so the she slowly brought the machine to rest. All were fidgeting in their seats straining to see through the windows but the landing site was not close enough for a view of anything worthwhile.

"Right, as you can see we have arrived at commune Five, the six girls and two boys who are to live here will follow me, the rest will stay with Franil and Kitta for the time being. Take it easy you will be allowed to come outside as soon as we have completed the formalities with the elders. It hope it won't be long, I'll call when you can leave. Remember everyone speak aloud from now on reserve you mind speaking to when you are alone with others that can".

Whilst Sala was giving her instructions Franil moved to the rear compartment to disconnect and stow away the power source. She watched as the chosen seven young people hustled towards the hatch door. She shuddered as a cold breeze entered when the door opened, her skin bristled, a feeling of excitement swept over her, it was really happening; the knot in her stomach urged her to stretch her arms above her head and relax, it was going to work, it had to.

Kitta remained in her seat curbing her impatience to see commune Five as Sala led their small group out the door to trek along the edge of the field and join the path leading down towards the commune. It was cooler here than in Lethe their lightweight clothing would afford little protection in the cold to come, it would need to be changed before the winter weather arrived. She could see a few people who were working nearby, stop and hurry to converge with them at the road. By the time they reached the centre many more had joined the march. She stopped outside the great barn and set her group to line up behind her facing the entrance.

Ezekiel stood in front waiting for the crowd to settle and quieten down.

Sala stepped forward with her usual formal greeting and response from the old man. They moved closer together each taking the others hands as a sign of their friendship. She quickly explained about the two boys. They stood side by side facing the gathered families. Ezekiel addressed his commune.

"Here we have five fine young girls and two strong boys who have come from Lethe to live and work amongst you for many seasons to come. They may look a little different but they are clever willing and well educated; you must put physical differences to one side for they will make a great contribution to our commune, please make them welcome".

A cheer and clapping of hands erupted from the crowd even before he had finished speaking. He had to wait a good while before it abated enough for Sala to add to Ezekiel's introduction.

"These seven have come today as part of an exchange; six boys will return with me to Lethe where they will integrate as others from another commune have recently done. They will be educated in the sciences and many will return with their new skills and possibly new families to help improve the life here".

Again another cheer and the loud murmur from a multitude of conversations. Sala had almost finished her speech anyway so did not attempt to stifle the obvious happy mood by continuing further. She turned to Ezekiel.

"That went well, are the boys chosen"?

"Yes ready and waiting we have far more volunteers than you requested but have the chosen six".

"Six is a good number. I have a much larger flying machine than before with twelve other Letheans who will be going to other communes, may I invite them down to meet everyone for a short visit or will it upset any plans you may have".

"I was only expecting six but no problem; five of the families who are sending boys to Lethe will each take one of the girls; the two boys can stay together for now at the other; let us get them settled before we add to the excitement by bringing the others down".

Ezekiel called to the heads of the chosen families to come forward to take the girls and boys to their new homes. A hush fell as the throng parted and six men, the fathers of their households, moved to the barn entrance. Smiles and offered hands calmed the seven apprehensive looking Letheans who were led away in silence.

"Okay Sala now call the others to come down, I presume you still mind speak".

"Oh yes, and so will everyone one day".

"Kitta, follow the path at the end of the field you'll see the road bring everyone down including Franil she knows the way".

"I'm listening, do I have to? It feels so strange I have been here before under such different circumstances".

"Franil you can't refuse Ezekiel; he wants to see you besides you are a large part of what we are doing here. Kitta don't take no for an answer".

Any excuse for the people of Five to eat plenty and drink menga was always sought out. The exchange was no exception. The Lethean visitors stood mesmerised at first but soon joined in the party when a cup or two of menga had passed their lips. The young elder sang all the usual songs to mark such an occasion, everyone joined in the singing with the more familiar ones. Sala watched with joy alongside her Ma, Pa and Kitta.

Later in the day before darkness threatened the visitors returned to the ship. Sala said yet another goodbye to her parents, having given them hope that Bron may be able to come home some time later. She collected the six boys and led them to join the others already waiting. When she arrived at the ship she realised Kitta was missing.

"Kitta where are you"?

"I'm with the elders"?

"Well hurry up and get here we will be leaving soon".

"Okay I'm coming. By the way I've been thinking about what we discussed earlier, I have had a long talk with Ezekiel he thinks I could help a lot here with the writing lessons so I've decided to come back with Lunn next trip; your Ma said we could stay with them".

"I like that Kitta you will love being here and my Ma and Pa will treat you and Lunn like a daughter and son".

The craft eased into the sky turned towards the setting sun as Franil instructed the crystal to set a course for Three. Sala wasn't sure what to expect but knew it would not be one big happy family day.

Not quite as exuberant as the welcome at home the exchange at Three was much more formal; no welcome speeches and no celebration party. Franil, Kitta, the boys from Five and the girls intended for the Outerworld stretched their legs around the outside of the craft but were not invited to the commune centre. Sala understood the reasons and agreed, for there was still a measure of mistrust in the mind of Brugan. Sala came towards Three with the selected girls and two boys, moving as she had at Five, along the pathway by the fields. The crowd that followed as they entered the commune and approached the square were inquisitive but strangely quiet. Brugan waited by the barn and after a short formal greeting invited them all inside but leaving Sala at the door. He came out later with the youngsters as well as six other boys which Sala sensed were the ones chosen to leave.

"I have spoken with these children of Lethe they are somewhat afraid I think. Our boys and girls who are mind speakers tell me they are no different from them and just want to live a normal life, they shared visions with them of Lethe and the transformations taking place were as you said on your last visit. I will follow my instincts and hope I am not being deluded. Our chosen ones are very keen to go, so I will allow it this time, if it does not work out I trust we can return your Letheans and bring home our boys with their minds still their own".

"If that is what you want I accept but have little doubt this exchange will be a success".

"I have made space with selected families for six girls I believe that is what was agreed I don't know what to do with these two boys".

"It will be unfair to split them; how would it be to ask one family to accept them both".

"I will ask or find another family. They will be cared for".

"These are clever people Brugan your commune will benefit greatly. The changes in Lethe have already begun with the promise of Bonding between the two groups. I know you will do well by these boys and girls and I will take every care with your young children; they too are part of our future".

"You have grown wise Sala since our first meeting, I trust you are not deceived this time. I still have my doubts but hope the old ways of the Lethe Overseers are gone for good".

Sala left rather deflated; she had hoped for a more enthusiastic welcome; at least Brugan had not turned them away which seemed a possibility when they first arrived. He was more positive when she left so felt satisfied.

Six boys followed her to the waiting machine, she had only spoken to them briefly asking them to follow her and about the seating arrangements in the craft, the briefing planned to ensure the boys had no concerns before boarding did not happen, she hoped they would all be fine. She would check later not feeling much like conversing now, she just wanted to sleep.

The trip to the Outerworld was interesting, boys from Three and Five had moved seats so we're conversing with the Lethean girls some speaking aloud and one or two mind speaking. It was mainly the boys asking questions about Lethe, the girls were quite reticent at first, but soon became used to the pushy inquisitive nature of those from Five, the boys from Three were less demanding. It was good to see, even Franil glanced back to Sala with a knowing nod, acknowledging the unusual event. Eventually they fell asleep, the seats reclining one by one until all was quiet. Franil remained at the control till Sala took over a few hours later. As usual, the unblanking of the windows letting the light of a new day triggered movement and the rustling from those raising their seats to an upright position, some stretching to see outside; they were too high and surrounded by cloud so they settled back to wait for any information which may be forthcoming.

Unlike on other trips the Badlands had not been seen, no stopping or skirting round the forbidden rim. Perhaps the crystal had shown Sala what it wanted her to see so did not need to take her there again; maybe her investigations were somehow known. After her talk with Ouisa she had put it to one side not intending to delve deeper, perhaps when the migration journeys were less demanding she would look again.

A problem to find a place in the forest close to the Outerworld where the large Machine could safely land was solved by a clearing appearing as they cruised over the central area. Franil heard from the mind speakers who were watching the ship from below of how it had been kept clear of trees after Sala's last visit. They had no idea of the size of this new machine so had cleared the area with the known smaller vessel in mind. Franil's skill in manoeuvring this much larger ship enabled her to push its nose into the forest between two trees whilst settling the rear at the extreme edge of the clearing. Sala held her breath as protruding leaves and small branches brushed the side windows during the descent.

"That was close Franil I'm glad you were at the control".

"We were lucky they had cleared what they did or we would have had to find somewhere else, somewhere on the river a very long way from the centre. I think I'll ask them to clear a little more before we leave".

The seven remaining girls were assembled by the door. The boys were told to remain seated for the time being. Franil remained on board and moved to the power source to remove and stow it whilst they were here. Kitta was keen to exit so was at the front waiting for Sala to open the hatch. They stepped out under the canopy of trees which seemed to have moulded themselves around the craft after it had landed. Rinn was standing close by surrounded by families all eager for news of their sons. Kitta ran forward into the crowds ignoring the protocols of welcome searching for her Ma and Pa. Sala followed more slowly, the seven girls gingerly stepping behind scanning the busy scene. The earlier mixing on board with the boys from Five would surely make this transition easier.

Rinn habitually followed the traditional formal greeting, Sala responded accordingly.

"Welcome Sala I hope your journey was satisfactory".

"I thank you; it is good to see you Elder Rinn I hope I find you in good spirits".

"All is well with me I see you have brought our guests please bring them to the barn where we can introduce them to their new families".

"I have seven girls not the six I believe you were expecting, also the boys from communes Three and Five are on board who are going to Lethe, may they come outside whilst we deal with the families".

"I see you have Kitta with you, she can show these boys around while we conduct our business. An extra guest is not a problem we have many families who wish to be involved. He turned and spoke to an elder at his side whom Sala assumed was being sent to find an additional family.

"Kitta where are you"?

"At my home with my Ma. What do you want Sala"?

"Of course, sorry Kitta, come back to the ship and fetch the boys outside; show them around a bit will you. We'll be here a while you can see your family later".

She didn't wait for a reply but turned her attention back to the seven girls by following Rinn into the barn. The introduction was very simple; each girl stepped forward and spoke their name aloud at the same time as the Ma of a family did the same. They then left to go to their new home.

"That went smoothly enough Rinn".

"We have been waiting for this day and for news of our sons, how is it working out".

"Early days but they are enjoying their new experience, some have made friends already and I anticipate a Bond or should I say a Merge or two soon".

"We understand the word Bond well enough now, you have used it often enough".

"The girls we brought today know of your sons and will report their progress to the families. Thanks for the landing area too or we would have been forced to the river and lake for a place to land ".

"This new ship is much bigger I think we can extend the clearing before you leave".

"That will please Franil".

"Franil is staying on board".

"Her choice, she feels out of place, old ways are difficult to change, from being a powerful Overseer to becoming a servant of the people takes time to accept. She is a good person at heart she will come round".

"We will have a celebration tonight make sure she is there; go say your hellos to Sheff and everyone, I will see you later".

Rinn and the elders departed leaving Sala to make her way first towards the old clearing where she first achieved the mind transfers from the young telepaths of the Outerworld. She sat on one of the logs laid out in a circle, opened her mind to find she was not alone.

The party of welcome was an affair to remember with fine food and plenty of Juanda juice as always, it continued on till the sun rose the following day. Sala slept at the house of Sheff with Kitta by her side. Franil was curled up unmoving on the couch far to small for her long frame.

The next day came and went in recovery and sleep, for the visitors had not understood the true effects of Juanda. That evening three young men and two girls were instructed to prepare for departure the following day. The second wave from the Outerworld was ready and about to descend upon Lethe. It was not part of the original plan but a welcome addition. The departure was delayed a day as no one had been in a fit state to extend the clearing and Franil would not attempt to move the craft as she insisted the forest had grown overnight trapping her inside its canopy. Sala said Franil enjoyed being here so much she was just looking for an excuse to stay longer. She denied it of course but during the extra day she secured a large flask of Juanda to take back to Lethe.

Finally the way was clear the vessel climbed majestically with the crowd below clapping and shouting their goodbyes as they always did in this Outerworld.

Chapter Twenty Two

The Bonding ceremony was to take place on the largest green area of Lethe, it was close to the front of the main pyramid garden which would make a wonderful backdrop for this special occasion. There were no buildings or places where the Lethean elders met or addressed the people, it had never been needed, so this open air venue was a natural choice.

Although it was assumed by the Lethe elders that Sala would conduct the ceremony she felt she was not of sufficient standing or age to do so. She approached Peto as one of the respected Masters to perform the ritual explaining what was involved in Bonding and what it meant for those taking the vows. He consulted with Sala and Kitta how the Bonding and Merging ceremonies differed, it was much the same but instead of Five's special song, Three made a spoken promise, including a gift to the couple of an animal skin sheet with the promise words written by the elder. Peto decided he'd only take it on if Lethe had its own version which would reflect the new beginning. He went away to work on the way it would be.

Kitta and Lunn, Phin and Mase were to be the first couples to be joined. Large numbers of people along with those from the communes assembled to see the first ever joining and significant event to take place here in Lethe.

The four to be united stood on a platform erected so the gathered people could see clearly. Peto arrived with Sala and the other Science Masters who stood in front of the platform. Peto ascended the steps to stand next to Lunn. He spoke aloud as well as open mind speaking.

"Lethe today has come to a point in its journey where you the people have decided to embrace the world and all who live in it. Our past, where our selfish desire to seek out and take from others what we already have hidden within ourselves, is gone.

Today will be the first of many joinings of a man and woman, witnessed by you the people before me. In the communes they have traditional ways to make this joining but today I will make for Lethe a new custom using both the Bond from Five and the Script from Three. This will be our ceremony for Bonding with a necklace of fine wire tipped with a single gem given to each as a seal of their union. These black tokens have been cut from a long dead but once living crystal and by the acceptance and wearing of this symbol these couples will be joined for life".

He called Phin and Mase to step forward gave them each the text his own version extracted from the song sung by Ezekiel written by hand on a scroll of fine paper.

> We come together side by side
> The crystals seal the promise made
> Preserve for each the life untold
> We now are one, one Bond entire
> To nurture those whom we enfold
> Till to air and land expire

They read the words together as Peto placed the necklaces around their necks. He repeated the process with Lunn and Kitta and then spoke the final words; words Sala had been waiting to hear for so long.

"You are now Bonded for life I wish you well".

The four stood holding hands smiling in front of the gathered throng. It was the boys from the Outerworld who started the clapping, the other commune boys joined in and soon all the people were clapping and shouting. Sala's tears of joy ran down her cheeks she made no attempt to hide or wipe them away as she clapped and cheered too.

More Seasons had passed more than Sala could remember; the number of Bondings since were too many to recall. The land of Lethe was now on the way to recovery; her task complete she was ready to go home. The new children of commune and Lethe were growing strong their minds restored to former vigour.

The Outerworld, communes Three, and Five were now inextricably joined by Bonds with girls and boys from Lethe. Programmes of education with songs and writings were becoming a normal part of everyday life, small versions of the pyramid gardens had been constructed to provide more food when the cold descended on the commune fields.

All commune children who wished could now come and study the Sciences, in exchange the young of Lethe would learn to work in the fields or hunt in the forest alongside their kin in all parts of the earth.

Plans to make exchanges with other newly rediscovered communities were in place; a new more natural way of life had finally been established.

Sala had travelled back and forth many times and announced to Peto and the Science Masters she was finally ready to go home to stay and live in Five.

It had never crossed her mind; when the offer came it was a shock; Mind Science Master; what was their thinking, keep her here maybe, no, that was not their way they were very methodical; they would have looked at all the students and helpers of the Mind Science facility and by consensus had selected her as the most suitable candidate.

She certainly had a very good academic standard but far from the best. Her telepathic ability was certainly superior to anyone in Lethe and her insights and the experiments she had started during her spell as a student and more recently as a teacher were new and innovative. Perhaps she was the best choice but she could not accept, it was ludicrous, she would be committed to a task that would take over her whole life, especially with one or even two seasons of training before she would take up duties. Her aim here was to bring harmony between Lethe and the Communes so she could finally return home, that task was now complete; would acceptance of the position help with her final true objective? it may well do but is unnecessary as 'True Man' would come about one day without further help from her. Even so she would have to think long and hard before making this decision.

Porta and she were now living as one, certain parts of his memory had recovered and what was missing she had replaced with her recalling stories of their home and earlier life in the commune; he now understood what had happened and although he had only recovered part of his telepathic ability he and Sala could now enjoy intimate moments with images and shared thoughts; the Bond was secure. Bron had eventually fared better, he began to recall their childhood together without too much prompting and Star absorbed the stories told by Sala to the point where she accepted them as her own memories, maybe some of them were. Bron and Star had restored a little telepathic ability and the signs of further recovery were promising. Sala and Kitta mind exercised with them daily, it had worked with Porta so they would never stop trying to improve the gift.

Sadly Horden and Jeska remained unchanged and wanted to stay in Lethe; they had been moved from domestic and garden duties to join study groups, it was the best that could be done, for their minds had been subjected to the Psion tree essence far stronger than was given to Sala's family. They were now too entrenched in Lethe with no memory of their origins at all, returning them to their commune home was considered to be unfair on them. Their family once made a brief visit to Lethe; they spent a few days with their loved ones, saw they were comfortable and happy so accepted the situation. They came home, finally able to move on knowing they would be able to visit later if they wished.

The position of Mind Science Master had been open for so long now another season would make little difference, it was well taken care of by Overseer Vee, Sala didn't understand why Vee was not given the post, it must be they just want Sala to stay in Lethe and thought the offer might keep her here. When she spoke to Peto he told her it was the elders way of saying thank you; she was not expected to stay in Lethe it could be an honorary title.

She would return to Five with her family first before telling them of her decision, in her heart already knowing she would not accept even an honorary title; it was her wish it be offered to Vee, she was far better equipped and ready to start without further training. An idea to perhaps start a Mind Science school in Five came to mind; *'I'm too tired'* she put it to one side.

Lunn had finally relinquished his position as engineer for the Flying Machines having trained two young men to take over. Their Bonding had produced twin boys, soon Kitta would finally achieve her wish and with Lunn come to live in Five. She would be there to continue with Sala during her family's mind exercises.

Travel all over this world had occupied Sala's life more than enough; she vowed to return home and rest for a very long time. Her presence was no longer needed; the next generation will take care of the land of Lethe or anywhere else newly discovered, they would manage quite well on their own.

Chapter Twenty Three

Sala stepped down at last, the transition would continue without her; she was looking forward to returning home with her family by her side. Kitta and Lunn with their two boys were ready and impatient to leave. Eleven seasons had passed since the Lethe girls first came to the communes and the first Bonding in Lethe; the birth rate of children which followed from the great fusion had grown, all retaining the telepathic gift, finally a common people at one with their World. Young adults riding the wave of a new beginning, children and new babies recently born, others growing in their mothers' wombs and future children to be conceived were awaiting their time to come. Every generation one step nearer to perfection. Sala sang the song seen in the mind of Ezekiel, remembered from when as a girl her gift had first blossomed.

The day will come when word will shine
All around this land of thine
Upon the children whose minds do speak
With never pause or moment weak
Light up the life for now to stride
With never thought to step aside
From fateful journey undertaken
Whilst bearing hopes that never weaken
The one True Man will then embrace
Eternal life and light and grace

She now believed the live crystals held the spirits of those who had passed centuries before and were the force which guided her along her chosen path. The true man she dreamed of was not here yet and may not come to fruition for many seasons but she had faith, now the old ways were gone 'Homo Veritas' was sure to emerge in this world.

In the days before she left Sala visited the Masters in turn to thank them and bid them farewell; lastly she said goodbye to Peto with a kiss, leaving him knowing she would probably never return. Peto felt a pang of sadness as he had grown fond of this remarkable woman who had save him and the people of Lethe from inevitable decline and eventual collapse. She made one more visit to Horden and Jeska who had changed little despite her efforts, they were just two of the casualties cruelly stricken by a struggle that was finally over; she would have no regrets for having Bonded anew, they now shared a home and new real memories.

Franil insisted she pilot her friends to their home with the assurance she would visit regularly, after all she was still an important Overseer with a duty to check on the wellbeing of commune Five as often as she liked.

The small vessel landed in the square by the great barn; Sala's brother Bron walked through the open door, he looked at the woman standing before him held out his arms and spoke.

"Hello Ma".

Postscript

Of possible interest to the reader, these notes were made by the author during his investigation into the Mandarin Paradox.

Mind of man has remained unchanged since he evolved from "Homo Erectus" (Upright Man) to "Homo Sapiens" (Thinking Man) a rational being who is able to reason and make intelligence based decisions still retaining the instinctive reactions of his forebears. Although "Homo Sapiens" is the name we have given ourselves at the current stage in our evolution, we do not always think clearly before we act; to be totally a "Thinking Man" we are still some way off. The choices anyone makes in their life are not always within their ability to control. Some are instinctive, innate, such as 'self-preservation' however many are nurtured, instilled in us from birth by interaction with our environment and the influence of our parents and those around us. Man's conditioned experiences decide his moral decisions, almost always survival or advantage for him or his offspring will motivate his decision and his subsequent actions. He will endeavour to follow the codes of behaviour accepted by the community in which he lives with but will ultimately break the code if it is detrimental to him and his family's wellbeing or in some instances if it gave him an advantage over others. The paradox modern man often faces today is a watered down version of what lies in this long ago proposed question.

*Would you with a **wish** kill a wealthy man in China to inherit his wealth if you knew for certain you would never be found out?*

When this paradox was first expounded China was as far away as one could imagine and a wealthy Mandarin a mysterious entity. A means used by the questioner to mentally isolate the person under question from the event under discussion. The '**wish**' meant non-contact and the remoteness enabled one to disengage from the physical act of the death and a knowledge of its consequences to the friends and family of the dead Mandarin. Acquiring his great wealth, without anyone but yourself knowing how you came by it is a temptation indeed. Almost everyone would accept wealth if it did no harm to another but if they had to kill someone first would they do the same?

In most societies it is normal that inbuilt self-control, anticipated retribution or punishment will motivate man to make the accepted moral choices. In its simplest form retribution might be just the disapproval of another, or through the societies laws a range of possibilities like a fine or more seriously in some societies a flogging, mutilation, incarceration, even death.

If there is a lack of consequence will he still do the 'right thing'? Herein lies the conflict; when questioned none I have asked say they would make *the* **wish**; although I suspect there are a few who might do so but will not admit it. Most say they could not, others that they would not; it depends upon how deep the initial moral conditioning is entrenched or how seriously they take the question. The difference between would and could, in the response, is significant as in this instance the question was hypothetical. The real answer underlying the question is, when faced with a difficult decision are you one who will never waiver from their beliefs no matter how detrimental the personal result; you only have to look through history for large numbers of religious martyrs dying for their beliefs and those during conflicts who have sacrificed their lives to save others. On the other hand when faced with danger there are those who will always 'save' themselves, although the choice is probably instinctive and involuntary at the time. No one can know how they will react unless faced with a real problem and having to make that choice.

Once an amoral decision of this kind has been made self-recrimination is a kind of punishment which allows one to accept the transgression; at least to some degree; (*I'm sorry I did that, but it's too late now but I promise I won't do anything like it again*); also self-justification (*I can now do some good things with all this wealth, I will become a better person from now on*). Both can give the transgressor the ability to move on, to disengage from his wrongful actions for a while, before moving back on the moral path. It is said '*There is none so righteous as the reformed criminal*'. I am not so sure, I'm more inclined towards '*Once a crook always a crook*'.

Most moral men who cross the line, in a weak moment, and decide to make *the* **wish** would find it impossible to self-justify their decision to kill another person, leading to insoluble self-recrimination, regret and misery. However the few amoral self-seeking humans who's drive to acquire wealth and power will nearly always succumb to the temptation without qualms. History documents many such men and women. Even now the powerful and rich, so corrupted by their greed, are blindly and lemming-like, leading us all towards the near destruction of their fellow man and this fragile World.

When men first walked upon this Earth every day they beheld the abundance about them, it should have lasted for ever. Now daily man continues to strip the earth of life giving trees and pump the air and seas full of toxic waste; we are rapidly approaching the abyss. I wonder whether man will become true to himself and through his ingenuity pull us back from the brink; it seems we are leaving it to the last moment; maybe we have crossed the point of no return already and soon man will no longer exist on this earth.

If there is a God perhaps we should pray or is this part of his plan; is this our 'Great Flood'? If so where is the 'Ark' and who will be our 'Noah'?

If not, the descendants of those who survive, if indeed there are any, may yet become *"Homo Verum"* or will the self-seeking nature of *'Homo Sapiens'* remain unchanged and come again to wreak more havoc.

Our seeming inability to deal with massive population growth and the constant demand for energy is right now having quite dire unstoppable consequences. This with the hope envisioned in a Greek mythological tale about the River Lethe. *'When man has drunk from the waters of the Lethe the past will be forgotten'* enabling a new untroubled human being to emerge.

Like so many unanswered questions it seems we have to have faith in what we are told by others or die in order to find out the truth if indeed there is one……..

If you believe in God may he bless you, if not, I wish you good luck, either way you are going to need it. PWL

Other Books by Philip W Lawrence

The Eight	The Life of an English boy
Time and Emotion	Short Stories and Verse
Looking on Darkness	Book 1 Detective Toni Webb
The Blind do See	Book 2 Detective Toni Webb
Then Begins a Journey	Book 3 Detective Toni Webb
No Quiet Find	Book 4 Detective Toni Webb
A Silent Goodnight	Book 5 Detective Toni Webb

About the Author

Philip Walter Lawrence was a wartime baby living in London during his early years. He studied electronics at technical college and started work as a marine electronic engineer travelling the World for more than twenty years installing and repairing Radar equipment.

Whilst still at school he met Margaret; they married in 1960 and had three children. The family moved to Africa in 1970 where he worked for four years.

They returned to England to live in the County of Hampshire where he retrained as a teacher and became a college lecturer in marine electronics. As an expert in the subject of Electronic Warfare he wrote many diverse technical papers on the subject as well as training the military.

He retired in the year 2000 and took up writing detective stories as a hobby. Having lived and worked in Africa, the Middle East, South America, Canada and most of Europe as well as the UK he was exposed to a wide variety of peoples and places; a varied source of humanity from which to draw his characters.

Printed in Great Britain
by Amazon